Spin Cycle

Also by Nick Duerden

Sidewalking

Spin Cycle
Nick Duerden

FLAME
Hodder & Stoughton

NORTHAMPTONSHIRE LIBRARIES	
80002280197	
H J	22/06/2001
F	£10.99

Copyright © 2001 by Nick Duerden

First published in Great Britain in 2001 by Hodder and Stoughton
A division of Hodder Headline

The right of Nick Duerden to be identified as the Author of the Work has been asserted by him in accordance with the Copyright, Designs and Patents Act 1988.

10 9 8 7 6 5 4 3 2 1

All rights reserved. No part of this publication may be reproduced, stored in a retrieval system, or transmitted, in any form or by any means without the prior written permission of the publisher, nor be otherwise circulated in any form of binding or cover other than that in which it is published and without a similar condition being imposed on the subsequent purchaser.

All characters in this publication are fictitious and any resemblance to real persons, living or dead, is purely coincidental.

A CIP catalogue record for this book
is available from the British Library

ISBN 0 340 76621 2

Typeset by Palimpsest Book Production Limited,
Polmont, Stirlingshire

Printed and bound in Great Britain by
Clays Ltd, St Ives plc

Hodder and Stoughton
A division of Hodder Headline
338 Euston Road
London NW1 3BH

For Elena

ACKNOWLEDGEMENTS

Hats off, without whom, etc: Gilbert McCarragher, Danny Scott, Ria Higgins, Matt Whyman, Judith Murdoch, Philippa Pride, Jodi Shields, Alison Fletcher, Julie Clark – even Richard Fallon. Music by Tracer.

One

Establishing Shots

Excerpts from a diary

'It is a truth universally acknowledged,' she writes, sucking the end of her pen for inspiration, 'that a single woman in possession of a lot of money must be in want of a husband.' She puts down the pen and admires the oddly familiar sentence. Maybe she's written it before. Or maybe it's just the handwriting that rings bells. Resting her chin in her upturned palms, she gazes through the living-room window across Hollywood's rolling hills. It is the middle of the day, and the sun is blazing in a blue, cloudless sky.

'I am a woman in the prime of my life,' she says to herself. 'I've not been to a casting in four months now, and I've no boyfriend to speak of.' Her bottom lip trembles, as it does so frequently these days. 'What's happened to me?'

She gets up from her desk, picks up the telephone, puts it down again, and walks into the bathroom. She opens the mirrored cabinet, watching her reflection rush towards her, contort and disappear, then reaches on to the top shelf for the bottle marked Prozac. She takes two tablets with water, then shuffles back into the sprawling living room where she clicks on the television, presses PLAY on the remote, and sees the screen burst into life. Familiar music swamps the room – the irritating theme song that went on to reach number fourteen on *Billboard*'s Hot 100 a few years back. Then the show's title comes up, *Central Park Six*, and the names of its six stars: Tiffany Charles, Malory Cinnamon, Gina del

Marco, David Grossman, Anthony Paul, Trey Soprano. Episode One: Café Oley.

She watches the half-hour pilot episode, tears spilling down her cheeks. She laughs in all the right places, and wishes with all her heart that she were back there again, on that Manhattan lot, younger and in the first flush of fame, when the whole world knew her name, when every door lay wide open. The show finishes, the screen turns to snow, and she presses REWIND, ready to watch it all over again.

The Prozac kicks in during the second viewing, and her laughter is a little quieter now, but Malory Cinnamon enjoys the episode just as much as she always did, and always will. She's in that Saturday-afternoon rut where misery can give way to melancholy, a sensation she revels in. Later, as she finds the energy, she struggles up from the vast leather couch, and makes her way to the hi-fi where she cues up Barbra Streisand, Liza Minnelli and Celine Dion, singing along to the show tunes and crying to the love songs until sundown and beyond.

When the Prozac wears off, she roots around her chaotic bedside cabinet and finds a few loose Valium. Bingo. It's going to be a soft-chocolate, slow-motion night. Sunday morning is a forever away.

Oops

It took me unawares, as most things do these days. Hit from behind, I spun, flailed, and fell forward. I landed awkwardly, sprawled across metal tracks, face up, staring into the night sky. The wind had been knocked clean out of me and I fought for breath. But as the death rattle approached, increasing the waves of electricity with it, I lay back and waited, blinking slowly, my eyelids suddenly heavy.

It was late, close to midnight, the tubes arriving with less frequency as the service was winding down for the night. There had been few commuters about, some, as usual, drunk and disorderly. I had been ambling along the above-ground platform as inconspicuously as someone who hadn't bathed in months could, waiting for the lingering crowd to disperse, so that I could take up residence in the small cubicle on the above-ground platform with the words Wa ting Ro m *above the door. I'd called it home for almost a week.*

A few minutes earlier, an argument had broken out behind me — two young men, friends until then, now with fresh anger in their eyes. Along with the raised voices came a horrible sense of déjà vu, *and I walked away, my head ablaze. I reached for my cider bottle, deep in my coat pocket, drank, then paced the platform back and forth, a nightwatchman guarding nothing but his privacy, lips moving imperceptibly beneath a thick bush of matted facial hair.*

Gradually, the argument behind me increased in volume. I grew dizzy with memories but, determined to steady myself, I tipped my head back, and poured some more cider down my throat.

But the argument was now no longer harmless. People were looking my way, at the commotion beyond. Suddenly, there was an exclamation, the sound of someone running my way. A harsh, raised voice followed it.

And then I was hit from behind and fell forward. From the corner of my eye, I was aware that the young man who had collided with me was not stopping, and neither was his companion. If anything, their speed increased, and they ran off, fast, towards the exit. Surely they should apologise, at the very least, I thought.

I landed with a crack, my head hitting wood and metal. My bottle of cider smashed beneath me, and a shoe flew off. Above me, the North Star was winking calmly, but below that, on the platform, there was nervous excitement and screaming hysteria. People rushed to the edge and peered over, waving at the train that was racing towards me. I screwed up my eyes, and my muscles tightened as I prepared to feel the steel wheels cut through me as easily as a kitchen knife through soft cheese. Five seconds, four, three. I was about to be disconnected from life.

I held my breath.

Game over.

Then, nothing but an all-encompassing silence, a velvet darkness.

A vast stretch of time passed. Then, 'You all right?'

The voice — female, concerned, hesitant — floated down from somewhere above. 'Excuse me, hello? You, down there, are you all right?'

I opened my right eye. A group of people stood above me, shock on their faces. Then my left eye opened, and I saw — inches from me — a Piccadilly Line train, the driver pressed up against the glass window. When he saw me lift my head and shake it slowly up and down, he burst into tears.

I opened my mouth to speak. 'Am I . . . am I alive?' I asked.

The woman smiled with what I took to be relief. 'You tell us,' she replied. 'Are you?'

I staggered to my feet, and began to frisk myself, checking that I was intact. 'I . . . I think so.'

Another voice — male, gruff — cut in. 'Why didn't he get electrocuted? He fell on to the tracks! He should have fried!'

'Well, sorry to disappoint you,' I said, starting to enjoy the audience I now commanded, 'but I seem to have been rather lucky.'

'It's a miracle,' said one. 'Christ Almighty! A miracle!'

People started to clap and cheer. I gave a theatrical bow, but amid the laughter, I was interrupted by another male voice. 'Look, mate,' it said, 'if you're all right, can you get up out of there? No offence, but this is my train. I want to go home.'

A couple of hands reached down and pulled me back on to the platform, and — perhaps due to my dishevelled state, the unholy smell I gave off, or reverence for the miracle — I was afforded a lot of space.

I stopped. 'What about my drink?' I asked.

'Sorry, love,' said a nearby woman. 'It didn't make it. Smashed to pieces.'

'Oh.'

She fished around in her handbag, brought out a couple of pound coins and offered them to me. I took them, thanked her, then turned, and made slow progress towards the Wa ting Ro m. *I opened the door and went in. Nobody followed. Gradually, the train pulled into the platform.*

Some people alighted, others got on, and it pulled out again. The station emptied of people, and things grew quiet.

I sat down on the bench, and looked at my hands, which were still shaking slightly. One contained the two pound coins. I was missing a shoe. I was without drink, I had a bump the size of an onion on the back of my head. I felt confused, and a little dazed. I should have died but I didn't. Somehow, I'm alive. A miracle, surely. And I had witnesses, too.

All except those two young men guilty for my fall. They never looked back, just kept on running.

They must think I'm dead.

They must think they're murderers.

Meanwhile, the two young men were scrambling haphazardly to the top of the stairs, both frantic, both riding on adrenaline. Faced with the ticket barriers, one leapfrogged them, snagging his foot, and crashed to the floor. Only his nose broke his fall. The other sailed over with the ease and grace of a hurdler.

Once out of the station, they split up. The first ran down the high street, which would lead him back to Shepherd's Bush. Tears, caused by wind, streamed from his eyes, blood from his nose, and his heart bounced like a basketball against his ribcage. The other slowed to a casual jog, and nipped around the corner, wove through a few smaller streets, and soon arrived at a decrepit kebab shop. He doubled over to regain breath and composure, then straightened and looked at the perplexed owner, who was watching him, with a finger hovering over the alarm button. Breathless, he ordered a large doner kebab, with extra chilli sauce. He thrust a hand into his pocket and found a balled-up five-pound note, which he flattened on the vinegar-smeared counter.

'A Coke as well, please, cocker,' he said, grinning, and wiped his forehead.

With the change, he fed twenty-pence coins into the fruit machine until he'd run out of money. Then he sat on one of the plastic chairs, both elbows up on a table pockmarked with cigarette burns, and ate, sweat prickling his brow with every gulp of chilli. Afterwards, he stood up, loosened his belt a notch and decided to walk home.

His friend was sitting in the kitchen they shared, his head in his hands, toilet tissue inserted into his nostrils. A neighbour, Sanjay, had seen him arrive and had joined him. Sanjay was wearing his usual silk pyjamas, with a big plaster under one eye. They were at the table, each sipping a double shot of whisky, which Sanjay had felt the situation required. Intermittently, he fiddled with the small wire glasses that perched on the bridge of his fine nose, a sure sign of anxiety.

'I can't believe it,' he repeated once more. 'Are you absolutely sure?'

Danny looked across at his neighbour, his friend, and nodded slowly. Although it was hardly compensation, he felt every bit as bad as he looked. The blood, still flowing, had worked its way down the toilet paper which needed replacing. His eyes were pink-rimmed and swimming in tears that were no longer caused by the wind. His pulse beat far too fast.

'Of course I'm sure,' he said. 'What happens when

someone falls on to live train tracks?' The question was rhetorical. 'He's dead, all right. I heard screaming as we ran away. Sanjay, I just killed a man.' He snorted. 'And it's all that bastard's fault. If Flox hadn't gone on and on, we wouldn't have got into the argument in the first place. And, Sanjay, you wouldn't believe what he's suggesting now.' He buried his head in his hands. 'If we hadn't had the argument, I wouldn't have run off. And I wouldn't have . . . killed someone.'

The front door opened, then slammed. A belch preceded Flox's appearance in the kitchen. He ran a hand through his long brown hair and grinned. 'Look, Dan, no hard feelings, eh? Maybe I went a little overboard back there. Let's forget about it for now, all right? Just pretend I didn't say anything.' He noticed the empty whisky bottle on the table. 'Any more where that came from?'

Danny looked at Flox, then at Sanjay, who returned his incredulous gaze.

As ever, it was colder in the kitchen than it was outside. The walls retained the sub-zero temperature without any possibility of a thaw. Small icicles hung from the windows and the perennially leaking tap. As the three friends spoke, their breath steamed.

'It's late,' said Sanjay, eyeing his watch and rubbing himself for warmth. 'I've got work in the morning. Goodnight, Danny.' He stood up and walked towards the door, passing Flox, who nodded agreeably enough at him.

Flox located another bottle of whisky, unscrewed it, and retrieved a mug from the sink. He rinsed it out, poured himself a large measure and knocked it back in one. When he turned back to the table, he saw that Danny, too, had retired for the night.

Some hours later, as dawn approached, Danny awoke with the thin duvet wrapped around his chest and neck. His feet were poking out at the other end, quite numb, almost blue. His heart was pounding, and his naked body was soaked in sweat. He sat up. For the next seven seconds, he convinced himself that it had been nothing more than a vivid nightmare. He sank back into the lumpy mattress, and breathed a sigh of relief. Then he realised that he had not dreamed it, that for some time things had been leading up to an event like this, and that last night would come back to haunt him.

Outside, a cold sun rose and the day began.

Pause

Rewind

One

Danny

Morning, and blazing sunshine streamed in through the windows. His head felt as if it was filled with cotton wool and his eyes only opened after much methodical rubbing. He sat up, yawned, pulled back the covers, and peered down at her sleeping form and felt a fist plunge into his stomach, so strong was his continued love for her, despite everything.

She lay on her back, her arms curled carelessly above her head, her strawberry blonde hair fanned out on the pillow. She was wearing his old Harvard T-shirt, red with faded white lettering, and during the night it had ridden up to settle around her taut midriff, leaving her lower half exposed. She was slender and perfect, her legs smooth and firm. On the third toe of her left foot, she still wore the tiny silver ring they'd bought together years earlier, and the nails were painted bright red. Her eyes, however, were noticeably pink and puffy, a reminder that the night before had been unpleasant and, once again, tearful. Danny leaned down, kissed her forehead, then slipped out of bed. He put on an old blue T-shirt, and went downstairs to fetch her some breakfast: perhaps tea and toast would act as the white flag of truce and they could start afresh. He and Amy were worth another go.

The cold light of day also told him that she was all he had.

One week earlier, Danny Fallon and Amy Allen had finally split up. They'd been together for four years, but the last eighteen months had seen their relationship change: from lovers they had become acquaintances, then virtual strangers who happened to share the same living space. Arguing was their only form of communication now. Yet splitting up had proved near impossible: they had a past together, a rich history of shared memory and intimacy. Walking away was never going to be easy.

Danny and Amy were born on the same day of the same year, and met over two decades later in a noisy Soho restaurant when they were both celebrating their twenty-fifth birthday with respective friends. The constant flow of alcohol promoted rapid familiarity between the groups, and the tables were pushed together. With the arrival of two birthday cakes, Danny and Amy, strangers until fifteen minutes before, were summoned to their feet for a toast, which they followed with a brief kiss that soon developed into a duel of wandering hands.

Their courtship began in earnest.

The first six months reeled by in a honeymoon glow. Danny moved out of his flatshare in Shepherd's Bush and in with Amy, who had bought her own one-bedroom flat in Hammersmith with money left to her by her grandfather. He was working in a small record shop on the concourse at Victoria station, for which he was poorly paid. His long-term prospects were minimal. Nevertheless, he enjoyed it: the pace of his life was easy, uncomplicated, and ambition had never troubled him.

Amy's career path was more constructively established. Within a year of their meeting, she had left nannying, joined an advertising firm in west London, and begun to climb the rungs of the ladder to success. She started working on the kind of flyers that tumble out of magazines to remain unread, but quickly progressed to billboard, radio and television campaigns. Her salary grew, and indications from upstairs suggested that a glittering future lay ahead, as long as she was willing to put in the groundwork.

She was.

And it was here that the differences between them became increasingly evident. While Danny enjoyed the benefits of his girlfriend's labours without the twinges of resentment men are supposed to feel when women out-perform them, he wasn't prepared to fulfil the role of Amy's dutiful companion at innumerable *soirées*. Imperceptibly at first, their lives split into two separate paths, heading in opposite directions.

Amy only acknowledged how little she needed him when Danny went away for two weeks to visit an ailing grandparent. In his absence she felt nothing but relief. She applied herself aggressively to her work, putting in overtime eagerly, and produced a campaign for television that made an already fast and sexy car appear faster and sexier. She and her colleague, Julian, celebrated the campaign's success with a bottle of champagne, and sex on the photocopying machine late on the final night in the office. It was only when she returned home later, alone, that she gave her absent boyfriend a thought. She switched on the bathroom light, rinsed her face with cold water and peered at her reflection in the mirror. Suddenly, an image of Danny hit her right between the eyes. Christ, she'd almost forgotten he existed.

When he returned home the following weekend, she had planned to end it there and then, but found she couldn't. Danny was a habit, she realised, a hard one to break. When, eventually, she did summon the courage, many months later, she did so for one overriding reason: sheer exhaustion.

His response? Blind panic. 'Please,' he begged, 'let's work it out. We can, I know we can.'

Amy breathed hard. 'No, really, Danny, it's too late for that. This just isn't working any more. *We*'re not working any more. We hardly ever speak to each other, these days, and when we do we just argue. We don't even really *like* each other, much less love. And sex? We haven't done that for ages.' This was true. Amy was secretly embarrassed that now she was more reliant on the mild pleasures elicited by her right hand these days than at any time since her teenage years. 'Come on, you know this as well as I do. There's nothing left between us.'

Danny dreaded being single, dreaded what it would bring – loneliness, the absence of sex or, worse, sex with strangers, without love. 'I'll quit my job,' he pleaded. 'I'll become more of a go-getter, like all those . . . all those ponytailed friends of yours.' As soon as the jibe left his mouth, he knew he'd made yet another mistake. He tried to backtrack. 'Sorry, I didn't mean it to come out like that. I just want to make things better between us. We still love each other, Amy, you know we do.'

'No, we don't, Danny. It's over.'

The sting of defeat was sharp. He grabbed his jacket from the back of the chair that stood between them, and left, closing the door behind him very quietly.

Alone at last, Amy felt enormous relief and mounting regret. Suddenly, she felt devastatingly alone, and terribly cruel. What would Danny do now? She imagined him walking through the rain, alone and confused, with nowhere to go. She sank into the sofa, and cried.

The following morning, after Amy had left for work, Danny returned to the flat and packed his things – clothes, a few CDs, some books. Everything else belonged to her. He placed the key on the table, fought the urge to leave a note, and left the flat for the last time. He moved back in with his old friend Flox who, conveniently, had never got round to renting out Danny's old room.

The house had been a rare find: a large three-bedroom semi, rent-controlled at eighty-five pounds a week, and effectively theirs for ever. The council planned to tear it down for redevelopment at some time in the future, but the time for action never quite arrived. The houses on either side had long since been renovated, with a large family on one side and a bunch of converted bedsits on the other. Their house, however, was the scourge of the neighbourhood. It was afflicted with subsidence, and only a wooden scaffolding construction kept it from collapsing on top of them. Inside, it suffered from rot, damp, a leaking roof, electrical problems, woodworm, and a permanent draught. Were it human, it would have had advanced Aids, chronic cancer, and a severe case of Parkinson's. Regardless of the temperature outside, it was always freezing inside, but its inhabitants beat hypothermia by wearing several layers of clothes, and drinking whisky. Also, at such a modest rent, and with all that space, it was a stellar bargain from which Flox could never imagine walking away. He often had people to stay for anything from a night to several months, but as he currently lived there alone, he had welcomed the return of his old friend with the kind of smile that suggested many late nights to come.

Danny wasn't quite so enthusiastic.

He arrived mid-morning at an empty house, and made slow progress up the unsafe stairs in a fug of depression. He swung open the door of his room to discover that it hadn't changed, which was rather unfortunate. The floorboards were still bare, and the gaps between them just as wide. He crouched down and peered between the rubbish that collected there, and saw the kitchen below. A sharp breeze whistled around his ears. He walked over to the window and looked down on the garden, which was magnificently overgrown, the weeds thriving. He shivered, then went over to the bed and collapsed on it. His breath clouded around him, and silently he berated Amy for splitting up with him at the end of January instead of in June or July.

The rest of the week passed by uneventfully. Danny returned to work as usual, finding a smile when necessary, but inside he was nursing a broken heart. Evenings would find him wrapped up in his room, steadfastly avoiding endless offers from Flox to accompany him to the pub or to a new lap-dancing venue that had opened on the other side of the Green. He tried not to think of Amy; he thought of nothing else.

It was past midnight on the following Thursday when he caved in. Flox was already snoring in bed as Danny tiptoed down the creaking stairs. He picked up the telephone, unravelling its cord until it stretched into the icy living room. Over the chattering of his teeth, he dialled his old number, now the sole property of Amy. She picked up after the third ring. Her sleepy voice was a bolt of electricity to his very core.

He cleared his throat. 'Hello, stranger.' He asked her how she'd been. Fine, she said. You? Oh, so-so. And back and forth it went, the familiarity of each voice comforting not only Danny but Amy too. One last meal, Danny suggested, with a tragic inflection of hope in his voice. There are things we have to sort out, put to rest. Please? Amy allowed her pause to become pregnant, then made the only response she felt strong enough to offer: yes. When? Saturday night.

One last meal.

To Amy's distress, Danny had made considerable efforts with the food. With the aid of a cookery book she'd never seen, he had prepared *confit* of duck, something he would never have attempted when they were still together. He preceded this with avocado halves filled with a delicate mixture of extra-virgin olive oil, balsamic vinegar and a handful of tiny brown shrimps, and followed the duck with what he insisted was homemade tiramisu.

She couldn't hide her surprise. 'Makes a change from spaghetti Bolognese, I must say,' she said, with genuine tenderness.

Danny blushed. 'I thought I'd make an effort.' He swallowed. 'You look lovely, by the way.'

She thanked him demurely, then concentrated on her food, which tasted wonderful, while Danny stole endless glances, hoping she'd start talking. She didn't, so he did.

'What have you been up to?' he asked, feeling foolish – they'd only been apart a few days.

'Well, I've been really busy on this new account, so I've not been getting home much before midnight, really.'

'Midnight? Wow, that's late.'

'Yes, well, you know, commitment and all that.'

'Yes,' he said, tasting poison on his tongue. 'What did you do for food? You mustn't neglect yourself.' He sounded like an idiot, but he couldn't help it: he was so nervous.

'Oh, we either ordered something in or went out afterwards.'

We.

'Oh, that's all right, then. Great.' He shut his mouth and attempted, inwardly, to zip it. But jagged-edged words forced themselves out regardless. 'We, did you say?'

'Yes. Mostly me and Julian, but occasionally Hannah, Mark and Gemma came along too.'

Danny's face remained blank.

'You know them,' she said. 'I introduced them to you loads of times.' She frowned. 'But you never seemed particularly interested.'

'I remember. At least, I remember Julian. How could I forget him? You were always talking about him.'

'Well, he is my art director, and we work as a team, so why shouldn't I mention him? You talked about people at the record shop all the time.'

'That's different.'

'How, exactly?' Amy put down her spoon and pushed away her tiramisu.

'For starters, I don't know any flash fuck who drives an Audi and dresses like a ponce.' He tossed aside his spoon, which bounced oddly and ended up in Amy's lap.

'Right, that's it.' She threw down her napkin, and stood up to leave.

Gripped with a horribly familiar sensation of panic, Danny rushed to her and threw both arms around her, squeezing tight. He apologised repeatedly, and once again begged her forgiveness.

They took a gas heater into the living room and perched awkwardly on the sofa – to talk it through, Danny said. Amy felt a heavy tiredness settle on her.

Shortly after midnight, her mobile trilled into life. She lunged for it, and spoke noncommittally into the tiny mouthpiece, her cheeks flushing under Danny's gaze. Within seconds, she had hung up, but the damage was done.

'Who was that?' snapped Danny.

'Just work.'

'Work? At midnight? On Saturday?'

'I did tell you it was a big account.' But the deception was there in her eyes.

'Bullshit.'

And so it started again, slurs and accusations elevated into a form of sado-masochism. After an hour, they'd exhausted themselves, and an uneasy silence descended. The ultimate dead-end. Then something strange happened. They looked at each other and hugged, so tightly it hurt.

'Do you have a heater upstairs?' Amy asked.

Danny nodded.

'Then let's go to bed. We're both really tired. We need sleep.'

Without ceremony, they changed into their nightwear – Amy borrowed a T-shirt, Danny braved it in boxers – and got under the covers. Before he switched off the lamp, Danny wished her a goodnight and whispered another apology. In seconds sleep stole them away.

Back at the morning after the protracted night before, Danny put toast, tea and cereal on a small tray. As he walked out of the kitchen and down the carpetless hall, feet bare, he heard her coming down the stairs above him. They met at the foot of the staircase, just a few feet from the front door.

'Breakfast?' he asked, attempting to inject optimism, no matter how futile, into his voice.

'No, thank you, Danny. I really must go now, you know?'

And finally he did know. He nodded slowly. She leaned over the tray and kissed his cheek gently. As she pulled away, their eyes met and focused despite the build-up of tears. For a second, the scene froze. Neither moved. They continued to stare at one another, taking one last mental snapshot as a keepsake.

''Bye, then.'
'Yes,' he said. ''Bye.'

As she closed the door behind her, Danny walked back to the kitchen and put the tray on the table. He went out into the garden where he stood stock still and felt the cold winter's air whip around his bare arms and legs. Then he hugged himself, because he was trembling.

Two

Flox

Inevitably, they all call him Flox. His full name is Quentin Flox, but as Quentin is such an irredeemably idiotic name – regardless of its recent rescue out in Hollywood – he is known largely by his surname. It suits him, too, lending him a vague air of mystery, which he plays upon whenever possible. He is twenty-nine years old. In a little under eight months, he will turn thirty, a transition, so the media informs him, that is a significant landmark. Works of fiction are published celebrating or, rather, bemoaning it; magazines are full of articles about what people should have achieved by the time they reach the big *three-oh*. He must, for example, be a regular in a restaurant where the manager knows his name. He must earn his age in thousands. He should know what Viagra, Ecstasy, curry, malt whisky, and older women taste like. The list was as long as it was infuriating, for most points remained far out of his reach.

In another universe – the one that exists only in his imagination – everyone is familiar with the name Quentin

Flox. He is a maverick actor with the steely determination and unwavering vision of a borderline obsessive. His films are wired, on the edge, Dogma-inspired, and popular with people who favour carrot cake over popcorn, broadsheets over tabloids. He is the toast of alternative Hollywood, the talk of New York, this year's sensation at Sundance and Berlin: a young, hip, independent actor whose main motivation is quality of character, not quantity of cash. Treated with a mixture of fear and respect, he is one of the few originals in a world of toothpaste-bright teeth and hennaed hair. Style magazines crave interviews, think pieces, Q&As. Photographers want to shoot him in black-and-white, an example of heroin chic hanging off his arm in clothes that barely cling. Woody Allen has requested him for his next project. Julia Roberts sent him roses . . .

He is also a recording artist, trading under a mysterious pseudonym, making records that dazzle the dance-floors of underground clubs on both sides of the Atlantic before crossing over into the mainstream charts while retaining their previous cool. Bands are queuing up for him to remix and produce them. His initial decision to refuse all interviews – to maintain mystery, heighten allure – has gradually become impossible, because the demand for him to talk is now too strong to ignore. *The Face* calls him the Face, *Zeitguy* pronounces him the only zeitguy that matters. He has a TV-celebrity girlfriend, and the tabloids court them relentlessly . . .

And, of course, he writes books. Books about drugs, about football hooliganism and, occasionally, about drugs and hooliganism combined, attracting an across-the-board readership. People who normally don't read books read books by Flox — he is as popular in Peckham as he is in Primrose Hill. Suddenly, the Northern Line is full of intriguingly hairstyled young men in skate gear poring over Flox's pages, ingesting his words as if by osmosis, reading between the lines, and getting off either a stop too soon or a stop too late, having consequently found themselves a new direction in life. He recently scooped a Betty Trask, was nominated for the Whitbread, and went head-to-head with Zadie for the Booker. He has been on a tour of clubs after dark, revels in readings but refuses requests for autographs because signing books is shallow, ego-led, and, worse, expected — the norm. *Publishing News* calls him 'a major new talent', and the *Observer* concurs. Will Self thinks him prodigious, and Will Self would know . . .

Fingers in pies, talent oozing from every orifice, every extremity, the world a plump oyster. In this alternative universe, Flox is forever in demand, forever blinking in a dazzling spotlight.

Back on planet Earth, however, Flox was merely blinking. The neon light above him had burned out again, casting his green computer screen in shadow. The tiny print was now hard to discern, the screen protector smudged, and his fingers were aching from either premature arthritis or RSI. He inhaled deeply on the ninth illegal cigarette of the morning, drank some cold coffee, cracked each knuckle and carried on. The working day was inching slowly towards lunch, and the pub next door was beckoning.

Flox was music editor for a London listings magazine.

His fingertips typed in which bands were playing at which venue, what time they took the stage, how much the tickets were, and which was the nearest tube station. Each concert was star-rated out of five — most garnered two because Flox had grown to hate the music he was forced to write about week after week. It was methodical, exacting work, and tedious in a manner to which the word didn't afford full justice. His desk was situated in a corner of an office that hadn't received a lick of paint since 'Mull Of Kintyre' was at number one. The sole window was frosted like a bathroom's, so any sunlight that penetrated it was hazy. The computer was the colour of stale oatmeal, the desk a plastic brown, the carpet grey, stained and worn. Various potted plants were dotted around the room, all mottled like bruised bananas. The hi-fi emitted low sounds from one speaker only, and refused to play vinyl but had an insatiable hunger for cassettes, which it consumed with gusto.

The office was home to four other individuals. The magazine's editor, Imelda Cousins, was an unmarried, middle-aged wallflower in twinset and pearls, watching life pass her by behind a pair of thick-lensed glasses that rarely saw the benefit of a tissue. A stickler for rules and regulations, she could always be relied upon to impose on her colleagues the office's code of conduct. Swearing was punished with a fine of a pound deposited in a sealed box, the contents of which went to a children's charity once a year. Personal telephone calls were out of the question, cigarettes frowned upon. The eating of sandwiches in the vicinity of the elderly hardware was outlawed, and no one was allowed to claim more than five pounds in expenses each month. Every afternoon, about an hour after lunch, she would hiccup three times.

Nathan, the youngest at twenty-eight, presided over the theatre section. He still lived at home and his mother cut his hair. The only girlfriend he'd ever had was at the end of a www address. He wore non-brand jeans and tucked his shirts into his underpants. Occasionally, he would wear embroidered waistcoats. He read fantasy novels.

Neville, forty-four, was the cinema editor, with the deathly pallor of one who spent far too much of his life within the dark confines of Soho screening rooms. Long divorced, and now a confirmed bachelor living in a bedsit at the end of the Jubilee Line, he had a pronounced inability for happiness. In over two decades of reviewing films, he had yet to enjoy one. Since the death of Bergman, he'd say regularly, all films had become either too long, too pretentious or too inane. He wore corduroy jackets with vinyl elbow patches, and evidently didn't own an iron.

And there was Philomena, the magazine's own Queen of Arts, whose karma was dictated by the position of the planets. A bespectacled vegan purportedly allergic to leather, Philomena wore only hemp-based clothes and would eat nothing during the day but watercress on rye, supplemented by gallons of dandelion tea, which weighed heavily on her bladder: she was never out of the toilet. She was thirty-six, but could quite easily have passed for forty-plus. Office rumour had her marked down as a virgin.

While some listings magazines were rather good, acting as a bible for those city dwellers intent on spending their free time profitably, Flox's was handed out free at certain tube stations. It was impossible to make the journey home at night without either sitting or stepping on an abandoned copy. The magazine was only able to continue thanks to the regular advertising at the back, which consisted exclusively of the male-only saunas where it was not just the temperature of the steam that made you hot. Prostitutes also ran weekly ads, offering their services at a discount price to regular customers.

Flox had joined the magazine six months after finishing university, and only then to pay off the colossal debt from four years' study and a costly post-finals twenty-six-week holiday. It was to have been a temporary position, but eight years on he was still there, every long-harboured ambition now dead.

At first, his seeming inability to leave became a standing joke among friends. 'Next week,' he'd promise. But the debts never shrank. Instead, they mounted consistently: the longer he remained there, the more miserable he became, and the more he relied on drink and drugs – an expensive outlet for his frustration. Eight years later, he'd become as familiar an element of the office firmament as the withered receptionist who had answered the telephone in an identical manner, between puffs on her high-tar cigarettes, for close to a quarter of a century.

This prompted in Flox a severe depression, and an anger that consumed at least 70 per cent of him. Flox was now teetering on the edge of a precipice, at the bottom of which a permanently dark mood waited to swallow him. Institutional care, he feared, was not so unthinkable a possibility.

And away from the office?

Away from the office, Flox could be terrific company. He could wire himself up as his electrician father would a plug. By night, he transformed from someone hounded by suicidal thoughts into the life, the soul, the firework of any party. The dull melancholy of his work mask would disintegrate when he stepped into a crowded pub or throbbing club. Within seconds, he'd push himself to the front of the bar and get in the first of many drinks, money no obstacle. Then he'd seek out the nearest dealer, press a wad of notes into a greasy palm, and come away with a selection of pills, each of which, when mixed, would prompt in him a chemical reaction so euphoric he'd stick to the ceiling like Velcro. Throughout the evening, he would work the room meticulously, flirting with women and bonding with men, until everyone was on his side, everyone suddenly his trusted friend, confidant, or potential sleeping partner. His ability to reinvent himself from moribund daylight dweller into nocturnal man-about-town was what his friends and enemies alike envied in him most.

His dark mood, the point at which reality settled back in, returned the morning after, when the flesh under his eyes sagged and the colour drained from his face. He'd arrive at work looking in need of a blood transfusion or, at the very least, a guide to better living.

They say that everyone battles with their inner demons. Flox's were more pronounced than most.

A snapshot: Venice Beach, some years earlier.

Flox is wowing California, having done similar on his route from east to west over the previous weeks. He is stretched on the sand, sunning himself, a beautiful woman by his side. The tan is golden, the cold sore temporary. Later, he will meander along the boardwalk. He is as happy as he has ever been.

At the end of university, Flox slapped the price of a premium economy air ticket on to his overworked credit card and flew in style from London to New York. There, he partied like a fiend and made enough fleeting acquaintances to ensure that his holiday wouldn't be lonely. His intended week there lasted four, and by the end, he'd seen the inside of every Manhattan club, been initiated into a night-time diet of ketamine and Perrier, and had his left lobe pierced three times, his right nipple once. Like most white men, Flox was possessed of a rhythm at odds with much of the music he heard but, unlike most white men, he couldn't have cared less. Along with a chemical loosening of limbs, he became possessed by the frantic bpms and danced with Travolta vigour. He was often the first on the floor and girls would gravitate towards him like bees to nectar. He would often end a night at dawn, spreadeagled on a bed, thrusting like a Barcelona bull beneath a specimen of vixen proportions, and screaming for more narcotic fuel.

As a consequence of such nocturnal habits, Flox saw little of New York during daylight hours. Throughout his entire month's stay, sunlight to him was merely a rumour he'd heard people mention. The ketamine battered him senseless, leaving him largely unconscious until darkness descended, at which point he would resuscitate himself under a freezing shower, then hail a cab to another club. On one such evening, he was introduced to the novelist Jay McInerny who, after sharing a couple of tequila slammers, promised to one day make him a protagonist in a future book.

He emerged, thirty days later, pale, ravaged, and approximately two stone lighter. But somehow it suited him. Flox was not exactly handsome, but with his ponytailed hair, razor-sharp cheekbones, dancing eyes, and crafty cunning, he was as attractive to the opposite sex as a magnet is to a fridge. And the emaciated look worked wonders on his frame: he now had the air of a catwalk model. Women wanted to mother him.

When it came time to move on, he did so with mixed feelings – he had come to love New York. Throwing his backpack over his right shoulder, he hightailed it out of the apartment he'd briefly called home, and made his way over to the Lower East Side, where he had been told he could find a rent-a-wreck yard. An hour later, he pulled out of the lot behind the wheel of a low Oldsmobile that had been shoddily transformed into a convertible. It was the colour of burnt wood, and drank an awful lot of gas, but it was still a bargain. His drive across America was now under way.

The route was labyrinthine, and cost a fortune. From New York, he went south to Washington DC, then hung a sharp right and headed for Cincinnati, down to Nashville, left to Atlanta, a virtual three-point-turn back to Birmingham, Alabama, then south-west to New Orleans, where he parked the car, substituted ketamine for bourbon and insinuated himself into the fabric of the French Quarter for two sleepless days and nights. Then he drove up into Dallas, before a sharp down-turn took him via Houston, along past San Antonio, El Paso, through

Phoenix to Flagstaff where he peeked over the rim of the Grand Canyon and whistled through his teeth in amazement, then steered down to San Diego, where he was non-violently mugged of twenty-three dollars, and crossed the border to Tijuana — where he contracted a minor sexual disease but concluded later that she had been worth it. Finally, he crawled up along the Pacific coast and arrived in Los Angeles. He got out of the car and stretched his legs. Liking what he saw, he quickly found himself a small motel off La Cienega, checked in, and resolved to slay Hollywood.

Which, he still secretly maintains, he might well have done were it not for Malory Cinnamon, née Alicia Feldstein, who burst his bubble, permanently.

Three

Malory

Despite the exotica of her adopted name, Malory Cinnamon had grown up as Alicia Feldstein in north-east Philadelphia, the ordinary daughter of a lawyer and an orthodontist. Until puberty hit, she was a model Jewish schoolgirl. But a subsequent predilection for outrageous daytime talk shows, a need for rebellion exacerbated by the messy divorce of her parents, and a brief obsession with the singer Billy Idol made her teenage years stormy. Ostracising both parents and friends, she retreated into her airless bedroom, decorated in shades of purple and black, where she wrote blank verse, mused on suicide, and later fell in awe of an emergent Winona Ryder. And she kept a diary, religiously documenting the day-to-day nothingness of her meaningless existence:

Excerpts from a diary

Why oh why am I hear? I mean, is their a purpose or do I just exist for the entertainment of a god I don't even believe in? That's what I want to know! Oh Billy you are my Idol. I want you to come rescue me, to take me a-way from all this! Since Dad left, Mom has been like totally insufferable. She doesn't understand my needs, and when she's not shouting at me she's crying in her bed all day long instead of going out to work. Why is this happening to me??? I think I shall slash my wrists – or at least that is what I would do if it wasn't such a like total cliché. Oh Billy you are my only pleasure in life. Come to Philly, come find me!

By fifteen, she dreamed of Hollywood. She rid her delicate face of its Gothic makeup, went into denial over her brief obsession with Billy Idol, redecorated her room in pastel shades, and began to take her studies seriously. She begged her parents individually for an aeroplane ticket to Los Angeles where she might fulfil a technicoloured dream. Her father was initially devastated – he'd hoped she would follow him into law, although her mother had always harboured the idea that she would enter into the lucrative business of mouth maintenance. But Alicia's persistence did not abate, and on her eighteenth birthday her father finally relented – much to her mother's fury – and presented her with a return ticket to LAX. Five years later, Alicia had yet to return home – though not because she'd found success.

So far, she had succeeded only in failure, and facing either parent was not an option. In half a decade, she had landed nothing more promising than several hundred auditions and a succession of poorly paid waitressing jobs. Her resolve, though, remained steadfast, her ultimate ambition unwavering. As far as she was concerned, the silver screen beckoned, and she was helpless but to follow its call. While those around her fell by the wayside and returned to the familial home to 'ordinary jobs', Alicia held firm. She floundered only once, when she faced eviction because of unpaid rent. Then, reluctantly, on the recommendation of a flaky friend, she agreed to appear in a skin flick. It was a blemish on her CV, for sure, but no pink was shown, and the camera's lens was always soft focus. She had not seen the end results, nor did she want to, but she was assured that her performance was tasteful – and the pay check saved her life. But, as sure as her name was Alicia Feldstein, those days were behind her.

Of course, she floundered again, a year later, but by now she was Malory Cinnamon. Like so many around her, she was forced to take a job that paid well but did little for her self-esteem.

For the past week, she had been inexpertly lap-dancing in a grotty club on Sunset Boulevard between the night-time hours of ten and three thirty. She wrote entries in her diary in lipstick red, a metaphor for blood, pain and suffering, and thoughts of suicide were, once again, paramount in her mind as she bared her breasts for fat men sitting at small tables. The tips were often astronomical, but the taste in her mouth was sour, and she drove home at four each morning in a torrent of tears.

But salvation, of a kind, lay in store.

She met a man, an English man.

Flox was new in town, knew no one, and required undemanding female company. Driving down Sunset one night, he saw a club flashing its red neon sign across the road, and made haste to the adjoining parking lot. He paid the thirty-dollar entrance fee, positioned himself at a corner table near the stage and began to drink successive bottles of weak Mexican beer. It was midweek, and a slow night. The club was barely a quarter full, and Flox was easily the youngest there by twenty-five years. The sound-system dribbled out anodyne, percussive disco beats, and the women greasing themselves up and down the poles on stage managed to defy gravity only thanks to the surgeon's knife. One, however, caught his eye. Unlike the others, she was natural – Flox could always tell in an instant – and, also unlike the others, she didn't flash an equally siliconed smile. Instead, she looked positively wretched, as if she'd just learned of a death in the family. But she was exceptionally pretty, in a manner Flox considered *earthy*. She attached herself to her pole with little enthusiasm and staggered about the stage, gyrating her hips like a pepper grinder. He approached her, cash in hand, and requested a private show. Without looking at him, she shrugged and instructed him to follow.

Alone with her in a thickly carpeted, many-mirrored room, Flox took his seat and poured two glasses of champagne from a bottle he had been required to buy in exchange for the privacy. Malory hovered uneasily to one side, avoiding eye-contact, examining her hair for split ends. Presently, she approached, and as she neared him, Flox saw that she was about to cry. Her eyes were shiny, her lower lip trembling. He watched, fascinated, as she tried to pull herself together and made a concerted effort to look sexy – an undemanding task,

Flox thought, given that she was wearing only a white G-string and two frilly garter belts – swaying silkily to the music that poured in from the club. Now, standing mere inches from him, she tossed her hair carelessly from side to side, and Flox shifted in his seat. He focused his eyes on her breasts, which betrayed her youth and advertised her beauty with breathtaking emphasis. But, try as he might to concentrate on the act, it was impossible, for Malory was actually crying now, her black mascara spidering down her porcelain cheeks. He voiced concern, and she fell to the floor, her shoulders shaking as she wept.

Flox felt awkward and embarrassed. 'Would fifty dollars cheer you up?' he asked.

At this, Malory emitted a low wail, and Flox covered his reddening face with his hands. What on earth was happening here?

Through hot tears, Malory looked up at the young man with the English accent and immediately felt a tenderness for him. She also felt a strange connection with him: neither of them should be in a place like this. She took a breath, then took a chance. 'Do you have a car?' she asked, between sobs.

Flox looked down at her and nodded.

'Then meet me outside in ten minutes.'

He looked confused.

'Please,' she said, imploring.

Flox knocked back both glasses of champagne, grabbed the bottle by its neck, and went out to the hire car, which was due to be returned the following day. Twenty minutes later, a girl with cropped brown hair, wearing a plain white T-shirt and blue jeans, slipped into the passenger seat beside him. Flox's gaze was uncomprehending.

'Wig,' she explained, before glancing nervously towards the door of the club. 'Quick, let's get out of here.'

Inadvertently, Flox burned rubber as he pulled out into the road. He had to fight back the grin that was spreading across his face. 'Where to?' he asked, as they passed the Viper Room on their left.

'Just drive,' she said.

Three long days and sleepless nights later, Flox checked out of his motel room and moved across town – away from Beverly Hills and its cinematic connections – into Malory's tiny studio apartment. The two-room flat was situated above a seedy tattoo parlour where one day she convinced him to endure the inky application of a life-size snake, which still curls artfully down his back, the tongue flicking at his bony left shoulder, the trunk winding like a vine around his spine, the pointed tail ending at his coccyx.

Their relationship progressed rapidly, an emotional freefall in which Malory scaled the extreme highs and lows that seem to happen only to Americans on daytime television. On her good days, she loved Flox with almost suffocating enthusiasm. She had quit lap-dancing and was again a budding actress. The reason? Flox, Flox, Flox. Whenever they were in public, at a bar, say, or a restaurant, she would proclaim her love for him at the top of her voice, and always she would receive a round of applause from the other customers, and a free bottle of champagne from the manager, keen to promote this kind of atmosphere.

But when her mood changed – and it did so with schizophrenic irregularity – she turned into a complete wreck, practically certifiable, and bore down heavily on the Englishman's supply of sympathy. She made for an ungainly cryer, the contents of her nose rarely remaining the contents of her nose for very long when the water works flowed: no movie tears, these. Though Flox was never the reason for the mood-swings – they always came from within, propelled by self-hatred – he was, nevertheless, their focus. She would scream at him with satanic intensity, then hurl objects at his head – ashtrays, hot food, a chair, even the neighbour's cat. When she realised belatedly her unfounded cruelty, she'd turn the anger on herself and thrust a hand through a glass pane, or attack her arms with knives. Consequently, they made many nocturnal trips to the local ER where, over stitches, Flox insisted he wouldn't press charges.

Trying times, but also, for him, so very electric and traumatically erotic.

A month went by, then another, and the happy couple fell into a routine. Malory began to see a therapist, and got a job working in a kitsch fifties-style diner over on Sunset, which proved great for networking: studio employees would often stop for breakfast there or break for brunch, so she and the other fame-fuelled waitresses made many useful contacts. With Flox's help – and that of the saintly Prozac – Malory began to keep both calm and fit, eating only fruit and vegetables, cutting down on smoking, and managing to locate a positive outlook on life. The moods stopped swinging with such intensity, and temazepam helped her sleep soundlessly at night.

Flox, too, had begun to establish himself in his new town. He went to half a dozen auditions a week, and was busy working on a screenplay based on his experiences and those of the many Brits he met on Venice Beach – he had befriended a cluster during languorous evenings at shore bars. Many had long since abandoned their own dreams of celluloid glory but now worked happily in local gyms and restaurants, some even running their own business hiring out rollerblades on the beach. It was an easy trap to fall into: while downtown Los Angeles lived under a blanket of thick grey smog, Venice was a permanent ray of sunshine that produced in its inhabitants a soporific stupor. No one wanted to snap out of it – and why should they? They all tanned beautifully, sex was on tap, for accents like theirs were as readily accepted as a Visa card, and as long as they all made enough money to take to the bar at night, they remained happier there than they ever had been in suburban England. Returning home was not an option.

In no time at all, Flox regarded himself as an honorary Yank. He and Malory had become quite the young couple about town, their social life buzzing. While he'd yet to pass a single audition, he remained boundlessly optimistic and, anyway, his screenplay was progressing, the daily read-throughs with his friends adding ideas and twists to the story. Then Malory landed a small role in a long-running daytime soap. She was to play a nurse for six episodes, waiting hand and foot on the show's star, whose irreversible brain damage, sustained in a terrible car crash, would lead him out of the show and, the actor hoped, into major film parts. Malory was euphoric. To celebrate, she and Flox went out to Venus Envy, the latest media hangout, where they drank, mingled and enjoyed some illegal Cuban cigars with other young actors. On following evenings, under Flox's direction, they procured some ketamine and, for a brief time, all enjoyed some explosively good times, making quite a reputation for themselves.

By the time her six shows were up, Malory was officially hot property. It was universally agreed that the camera loved her. Like Sandra Bullock, she looked simultaneously wholesome and sexy, the archetypal girl-next-door who, in reality, never lived next door to anyone unless the neighbourhood happened to be Beverly Hills. Local magazines showed an interest; she was a guest on a cable talk show. Old schoolfriends somehow tracked her down and sent begging letters. Then came the big one: Malory was invited to fly to the East Coast to audition for a pilot comedy show called *Central Park Six*, which revolved around three New York couples juggling careers and babies. She read over the script with Flox a million times – it was tight, clever, funny, and destined for surefire success. She was up for the part of Monica, the youngest character, whose pregnancy, at twenty-five, didn't hinder her progress in a swank advertising firm. Replacing the temazepam with Ecstasy, and doubling her daily Prozac dose, Malory pored over the script endlessly, day and night, until she knew the whole thing inside out.

Flox was impressed. 'It's yours,' he said, of the part.
'You think?'
'Absolutely. You're absolutely perfect for it.'
They cracked open a couple of beers, and toasted success. Malory cried tears of happiness.

'You do realise that this is, like, it?' she asked him. 'If I get this part, that's it. The big time. All my dreams come true. I'll be rich, famous!' Nervously, she brought the can to her lips and drank.

'And I suppose that's when you'll leave me?' Flox said, a slight edge to his voice.

Malory let out out a playful shriek and jumped on her boyfriend, nuzzling her pre-op nose into his neck and showering his chest with butterfly kisses. She spoke in a squeal: 'I'll never leave you!' she insisted. 'You're mine! Without you, baby, I'd never have gotten this far. I owe you everything.' A look of sudden seriousness shadowed her face. 'Flox, I love you.' She kissed him deep and hard.

In the weeks preceding the audition offer, Malory had been going through Flox's screenplay, perfecting her English accent so that she could play the part of Julie Clark, the London-born aerobics instructor who falls for the porn actor whose brother is among Hollywood's most bankable stars. 'You'll still find time to play Julie in your hectic schedule, won't you?' Flox asked warily.

'Just you try and stop me!' She giggled, took his hand and led him to bed.

The champagne was the biggest and most expensive bottle in the shop. Flox put it on his card. Back at home when he managed to force out the cork, it shot straight through the window — which later proved a major bone of contention with the landlord. The contents frothed out and two mouths attacked it then met in a Moët & Chandon kiss. Malory was crying tears of joy again, while Flox had goosebumps on his arms and neck.

'I told you you'd get it,' he said, nibbling her left ear.

Malory had returned from New York just a day earlier. Within thirty minutes of her arrival at home, the telephone rang – the good news had spread.

The celebrations began in earnest. First they clinked glasses to Malory's good fortune, and drank to their future together. Then they jumped into Malory's VW bug and drove to Malibu where they and their ex-pat pals drank and popped pills well into the night, Malory promising to fly everyone out to New York for the show's first recording. The money, she'd already learned, was going to be obscene. 'I'll be rich!'

Flox's heart beat that little bit faster in anticipation.

It unfolded before his eyes in a fantasy made real. She'd be able to introduce him to all the right people, to the movers and shakers of Manhattan's media set. They'd love him, his insouciant Britishness, his ragged charm. Offers from off-Broadway would fan themselves before him like a deck of cards. He'd make his movie début in a low-budget independent flick, his smouldering glare suggesting technicoloured talent within the grainy black-and-white of the film. His career would pick up pace, and he'd run with it. YES! YES! YES! He poured another glass of bubbly and drank deep. His dream was coming true. He was floating. And then he, too, cried tears of happiness, and normally Flox never cries over anything.

The following afternoon found the jubilant couple by the departure gates at LAX, both having made it somehow to the airport on time despite a thunderous hangover and feral scorchmarks left by the drugs. Malory had creatively camouflaged the disaster area that was her face with a thick layer of makeup, but Flox looked dreadful, and hid behind sunglasses. As the last call for her flight came over the Tannoy, they embraced passionately.

'One week, baby,' she said, her eyes welling prettily. When she blinked, a single tear spilled down her cheek with such design it was practically art – she had acquired authentic movie tears through much practice. She cupped her boyfriend's drained face in her slender hands.

'I'll miss you,' he replied, battling against a lump in his throat.

'I'll call you tonight and every day. If I can call you more I will, but no matter how busy I get, baby, I'll be thinking of you always.' She kissed his mouth delicately. 'And when you fly over, I'll take you to all the parts of Manhattan you missed, okay?'

'You'll need a lot of time off, then,' he said, teeth gritted, and forcing a smile.

'I'll get it, don't you worry,' she said, as another couple of tears, one at each side, made slow descent. 'This may be my big break, but nothing is more important than my heart's true love.' Her lower lip quivered. 'You.'

She planted one final kiss on his mouth, and Flox stood rooted to the spot, watching her retreating form. At Passport Control, she turned and offered him one last wave. She looked ravishing but daunting, her label-conscious attire concealing a soft, warm interior that only Flox knew existed. His heart swelled, then deflated with trepidation. He walked over to the giant windows and waited. He watched the plane taxi, take off, and rise up into the blue sky, above the smog. Then he turned and left, clutching the car keys she had left for him – along with her treasured bug – as a token that this parting was temporary and, she joked, so that he wouldn't easily forget her.

Flox would never easily forget Malory Cinnamon.

Even when the calls didn't come, when the days became weeks, the weeks months, and the years an unending, torturous eternity.

At first, he found a multitude of plausible reasons why she didn't call. Her schedule must have been wildly hectic. The pilot, after all, required a lot of attention and concentration – which Malory hardly possessed. He placed innumerable coast-to-coast calls himself, but never got connected. Suddenly, Malory had people around her, people whose job, it seemed to Flox, was to prevent her being bothered by outside disturbance. Regardless, he still punched the speed dial upwards of forty times a day, and spent the rest of his time waiting by the silent telephone, begging it to burst into life. He developed a form of agoraphobia: he could not leave the apartment in case she called. He'd acquired an illogical mistrust of the answerphone, and continually refused invitations from friends to go out and get drunk. He stopped shaving, as men do in these situations, and called in food and drink. He stewed in front of the television, and smoked so much marijuana that paranoia crept up the walls around him. The rings around his eyes were the kind that normally circle a bathtub.

Matters became even more desperate a few days later when he was woken, one morning, by the landlord – a heavy-set man with more hair on his eyebrows than on the top of his head, and a thick post-war Polish accent – who let himself in and demanded that the property be vacated immediately. Since Ms Cinnamon had cancelled her standing order at the bank, rent was no longer being paid. Consequently, Flox had no business being there any more. 'You got till noon,' he barked, as Flox sat upright in bed, wiping sleep from his eyes and the remnants of a taco from his mouth.

This was the cherry on the icing of the crumbling cake. The good times were over, his love affair with LA curtailed.

During the next few weeks, every other strand of Flox's Stateside life began to unwind. He moved into a house on Venice Beach with his British friends, where relationships quickly became strained, as if the reason for Flox's presence heightened their own failures as well. Arguments were frequent and ugly. One lost her job, another became disillusioned with LA's fakery and longed to return to Grimsby, and Flox's work on his screenplay ground to a halt. When he read it over one evening, loose, dog-eared pages strewn with ballpoint corrections in one hand, a spliff in the other, it revealed its true colours: it was worthless, full of clichés, bad grammar, and little actual story. He loped over to the kitchen sink, dropped in the pages, lit a match and let it fall. All his hard work and effort burned out in little more than five minutes. This, he thought, was somehow symbolic.

The following morning, before sunrise, Flox packed his bag and moved out, conscientiously avoiding the farewell

Spin Cycle

ceremony. He wandered down an empty boardwalk, the Pacific grumbling alongside him, avoiding the assortment of stray dogs, disabled veterans and elderly keep-fitters *en route*. He picked up a copy of the local free newspaper and, over a cappuccino and waffles, perused the for-rent pages. This was a pointless exercise given that his tattered nylon wallet was now down to its last forty bucks and, unless he started getting paid for attending auditions, it was not about to become plumper. Conjuring up a sliver of hope, he found a cash machine and tried to withdraw some money, but it swallowed his card. Disused face muscles contorted themselves into a sour smile, and Flox coughed out a short, sharp laugh. So this is how it feels to be destitute, he thought. For the next two nights, he slept in his former girlfriend's bug, then drove it resignedly to a second-hand car dealership and exchanged it for just enough money to cover the cost of a flight home.

Flox left America on a bright Friday evening. He spent his last afternoon not reconciling with the friends he'd made over the past few months but in a sterile food court in the Beverly Center, alone. With a plastic knife and fork, he speared soft chunks of microwaved lasagna, pushed them into his mouth, and sucked at a Mountain Dew. Then, when he'd deposited the leftovers in a bin, he took the escalators back to ground level and waited forty-five minutes for a cab to take him to the airport.

As the plane raced down the runway Flox closed his eyes. While he was tempted to watch his adopted city recede into the distance, he didn't feel strong enough to cope with the pain it would doubtless bring. As the plane reached cruising altitude and the refreshment trolley appeared, he decided to drink himself into oblivion.

Footnote. Over the subsequent eight years, Malory Cinnamon was famous on both sides of the Atlantic. *Central Park Six* became a series and ran for four successful seasons until she bowed out at its peak to become a movie star. She appeared in a run of moderately successful romantic comedies that proved hugely popular in video shops on Saturday nights among young women in happy relationships. She was also involved with a series of attractive actors, which kept her in the tabloids. While Flox did his utmost to avoid her, there was no escaping her forever smiling face: it was never out of the gossip rags. And whenever he came across it, it never failed to hack away at another chunk of his dilapidated heart. But the agony remained strictly his; he told not even his close friend Danny of their relationship, because some things are best kept private.

Four

Danny was grieving over the death of his relationship, and didn't return to work for more than a week. After that fateful Saturday night, he sank into a trough of self-pity from which he could find no reason to crawl out. He stewed in front of the television, allowing his eyes to glaze over and his brain to download. For the first three days, he didn't dress. His diet slimmed to little more than consecutive cups of coffee, which made his eyelids twitch and his limbs tremble. On the fourth day, he attempted a bath. The fifth, he played back messages on the answerphone, discovering several from his manager at work. Between moments of extended inactivity, he hunted for photographs of himself and Amy, a previously happy couple who had once enjoyed their time *together*. Acutely aware that he was in the midst of a depression, he decided to play it for all it was worth. He gorged himself on chocolate, played only the kind of music that kept beat to a funeral march, and willed himself to cry, under the assumption that tears would prove cathartic.

Come the morning of the eighth day, Danny fell out of bed early enough to consider going to work. In the bathroom, he stood beneath the drizzle that masqueraded as a shower, and revolved under it for ten minutes. Then he felt almost ready to face the cruel world. He went back into the bedroom, temporarily immune to the sub-zero conditions, dressed, grabbed his Walkman and left the house, intent on walking the four miles to work, thinking that the exercise would do him good. His choice of music, however, had been unwise: after four minutes of lovelorn lyrics, he substituted the pavement for a crawling bus, his smile for a frown.

On arrival at the record shop his mood failed to lighten: he found its familiarity – which had previously never failed to comfort – now bordering on the repulsive. Its red and black criss-cross patterned carpet was wearing as thin as the rug in his room, and he thought he could make out his own footprints in it. At the counter, he lifted the flap and went round to the tiny workspace where the stony-faced manager, Clive, greeted his arrival much like he would a demand for alimony from his former wife. His thin eyebrows scaled three inches up his chickenpox-scarred forehead. 'Well, well. Look who it is.'

Danny said nothing, just nodded curtly, a dwarfish, mute *hello*.

'And where have you been? That's if you don't mind me asking, of course,' he said. 'It's been – what? A week now? No phone call, no returning of messages?'

Danny shrugged. A telephone behind Clive started to ring. He barked at Darren to answer it.

'I'll need more of an excuse than that, sunshine.'

Clive's eyebrows pointed down like arrows. 'You left us right in the shit. Barbara had to do your shift every day, and you know she's been revising for her evening-course exams.'

Suddenly Danny felt terrible. 'I'm sorry,' he said, wishing that she was there now so that he could apologise directly to her. 'I've had . . . a few personal problems.'

Clive bridled. His shoulders twitched nervously beneath his acrylic jumper. 'Danny, son, a question. Do I ever miss a day over personal problems? Do I? *Do I?* No, I do not. And that's because I've a shop to run here and because I'm a professional, which you, clearly, are not. No matter what goes on at home, we've still got orders to place, customers to serve, CDs to file.' He started pulling agitatedly at his ear. 'None of these duties suddenly stopped because of your personal problems, now did they? No, they did not. Instead, poor Barbara had to fill in for you. But, then, I suspect you don't really care, do you? You selfish little . . .' Saliva had gathered at the corners of his mouth, and he spat when he spoke. 'Get out of my sight.' Running a record shop was tough work – but someone had to do it.

An hour later, the shop had a steady stream of customers, many of whom were carrying heavy backpacks. Waitresses from the coffee shop next door flicked through the dance compilations, and a tramp was asleep in the tiny window display, as he was most mornings. Danny's daily rituals – serving, filing, cleaning – now filled him with a sensation close to despair. Was this really all his life amounted to? As he squeezed between the customers, placing CD cases in their racks, every little bump, every tiny knock annoyed him. And when he reached the front of the shop, where the snoring that emanated from the stinking heap on the floor was almost as loud as the music that came from the speakers, Danny felt hatred mainline through him. He leaned towards an exposed, crusty ear. 'Fuck off out of here! Go on, piss off, you old bastard,' he said. The tramp groaned, stirred, and got slowly to his feet, mumbling confusion beneath his beard.

Later, as if to make amends for this, Danny helped an attractive young woman, whose wayward hair and crooked glasses suggested that order was something forever outside her reach. She approached the counter with her arms full of CD cases, most of them compilations of recent chart hits. As she let them fall on to it, inches away from where Danny was leaning and watching her with interest, some scattered and fell to the floor.

'Oops,' she said, and bent to retrieve them, banging her head and emerging with a red bruise just below her hairline. 'Ouch. Sorry.' Then, looking down at the pile of CDs between them, she felt an explanation was needed. 'Party,' she said, blushing slightly. 'I'm having one tonight, but none of my records at home are suitable, so I thought I'd better buy these.' She curled a loop of blonde hair behind an ear, and smiled.

Danny smiled back, and immediately felt he could fall in love with this woman. She exuded an awkwardness he found beguiling. So unlike Amy, he thought. Her blue eyes swam. Her cheeks were rosy. She looked like she was embarrassed easily and blushed often. He wanted to be part of her life. He ran each of the albums through the till — six compilations at almost fifteen pounds each, and two greatest hits at sixteen. When he hit the total button, the screen read £121.94.

The young woman let out a yelp of shock. 'Gosh,' she said, blushing again. 'That's a lot.'

She counted the money in her tatty wallet, banknotes stuffed alongside till receipts and faded yellow Post-it notes. Thirty-five pounds, along with some loose change. Instead, with evident anxiety, she handed over her faded Switch card, the thin plastic coating peeling, the signature fading, practically invisible. Danny read her name. Felicity James. It expired in twenty-seven days.

'I'll need a new one soon,' she said, following Danny's eyes, 'but this one should still work. I hope.' She crossed her fingers, and Danny noticed that the middle one curved slightly to the right. Double-jointed? He swiped the card through the machine, and waited while it churned and clicked into life. He looked up at Felicity, who was gazing at the CDs with consternation, and smiled again. He felt warm inside. Some moments passed, more than usual. Felicity frowned, and scratched her left temple. Eventually, the machine refused her the use of the card for this transaction. Her right eye twitched. 'Um, I've been overspending recently. Maybe that's it.'

Somewhere inside his chest, Danny's wounded heart lifted and expanded. He checked over his shoulder to see if the manager was lurking. He wasn't. 'Never mind,' he told her, his voice barely above a whisper. 'We've got a discount on all CDs, starting tomorrow.' This wasn't true. 'But for you I could make an exception.'

A light went on behind Felicity's eyes. She straightened her glasses, and her cheeks reddened. 'Oh, right. Well, thank you, thanks very much indeed. Um, how – how much, exactly?'

'As of tomorrow morning,' he said conspiratorially, 'all these albums will sell for five ninety-nine.'

Embarrassingly, her card still refused to go through, so in the end Danny knocked another fifteen pounds off the total until she had enough cash to cover it. She thanked him profusely. 'You're very kind,' she said.

'Think nothing of it,' he said, with a cavalier flourish more typical of Flox in predatory mood. 'Enjoy your party.'

At lunchtime, he crossed the station concourse and went upstairs into the antiseptic food court where he bought his usual jacket potato topped with tuna and sweetcorn, and sipped a lukewarm cappuccino. Today, as in the shop, he felt asphyxiated by the familiar surroundings. It can't be beneficial to one's life, he thought, to sit on the same plastic green chair, eating at the same plastic table day after day. Suddenly, he felt queasy. He pushed away the potato and fled, running down the escalator two steps at a time.

For the next ninety minutes, he walked through the teeming rain around Pimlico's back-streets, labyrinthine avenues where impressive Victorian houses sat awkwardly alongside peeling housing estates. Outside a launderette on Lupus Street, a young couple were screaming fat, nasty words into each other's faces, their proximity broken only by a pram, the young baby within testing its awesome lung capacity.

At the pub opposite, a row of newspapers, some broadsheet, most tabloid, sat up in a row across several tables, behind which men made inroads into a liquid lunch. In a greasy spoon further down the road, Danny watched a small, manageable fire engulf, then swallow an already blackened frying-pan. Within seconds, the cook had successfully extinguished the flames by pouring over it a saucepan of boiling pasta. He walked on, in the steadily pouring rain, getting increasingly soaked, heavy drops pouring off the bridge of his nose and dripping on to his protruding tongue. He eventually arrived back at the shop sometime after three.

Clive was waiting for him. 'Ah, Danny!' he began. 'So good of you to join us. You're a little bit late, aren't you? I wonder why? No, let me guess. You got lost after your sandwich and wandered down to the Covent Garden branch by mistake, right? Happens all the time, sunshine, all the time.'

Danny said nothing, and pushed past him. A moment later, he assumed his regular position behind the counter and was about to serve a customer brandishing three CDs.

'And what do you think you're doing?' Clive asked him.

Danny, with all the deadpan delivery he could muster, told him in slow, faltering words that he was serving this gentleman. The customer grinned uncertainly.

'No, you're not. Go round the back and wait for me.'

The customer tutted and checked his watch. Danny sighed, went to the back as instructed, then changed his mind. He picked up his jacket, which he had hung to dry in front of the rattling fan heater, and put it on. He walked back through to the front, where Clive was in the process of handing over change, and lifted the flap.

'Where do you think you're going, sunshine?'

Danny shrugged. He hadn't, until now, given it much consideration. 'Cinema, probably.'

'If you leave here under these circumstances,' Clive announced, with the modicum of authority invested in him, and much to the glee of the shop's customers, who were now paying full attention, 'you'll not be welcome back. Do I make myself crystal?'

Two young women, who were glancing through the hip-hop section, said '*Oooh!*' in sarcastic unison, and Clive flushed, but stood firm. Danny walked up to one, whispered something in her ear, and pointed to Clive. They both laughed girlishly into their hands, perhaps louder than was strictly necessary, and Danny swaggered to the door. Before leaving the premises for good, he turned to face his manager and smiled a final goodbye. For the next quarter-hour, through the still-wet streets of Victoria, Danny walked on air, exhilarated and free.

Later, he found himself in a cinema in Leicester Square. Over popcorn and a succession of fizzy drinks, he watched two films back to back, losing himself first in a generic action flick, then the gentle hysteria of a Hollywood romantic comedy. The second film starred his favourite actress, Malory Cinnamon, who, for almost an hour and a half, failed to realise that the man of her dreams was right in front of her the whole time. The film plundered every romantic cliché, but Danny was hooked, and by the closing credits, he could not ignore the lump in his throat. When he brought his hands to his face, he found tears.

Danny was in awe of Malory Cinnamon. Her beauty was panoramic: chocolate-drop eyes, cheekbones like clifftops, a delicate nose, long, full lips, a gift from a generous god. Her neck was swan-like, her brown hair lustrous, and her figure poured like wine into any outfit, irrespective of the quality of the garment: she looked as beautiful in Versace as she did in a pair of dungarees. Danny sucked at his straw, closed his eyes, and wished himself transatlantic bound, into the arms of a goddess such as she.

Afterwards, he walked out into the freezing early-February night, pulling his still damp jacket tight around his body. It had stopped raining, but a slight frost seemed to cling to the air and coated his skin in a fine layer of invisible ice. He strode briskly up to Tottenham Court Road, then walked down to the Central Line, where he waited ten minutes for a tube. His eyes scanned the adverts for beer, cars, holidays, computers, the Internet – some of which Amy might have worked on. When the tube arrived, Danny got into the penultimate carriage, which was empty save for three other passengers, two men and a woman. On the seat next to him, he found an abandoned copy of the magazine Flox worked for. He picked it up and started leafing through it.

Flox's day had also been confrontational.

An argument, long brewing between the theatre and cinema editors, erupted moments after the morning meeting in which nothing of any pressing concern was, as ever, either discussed or resolved. Nathan and Neville were accusing one another of tit-for-tat theft, a pencil here, an eraser there, the occasional stapler; pettiness personified. Nevertheless, it led to a showdown that remained strictly verbal: neither was able to form a fist, much less throw one with either direction or impact. To Flox, they were like a couple of squabbling elderly women, and their bickering led him to thoughts of murder.

While trying to ignore their whining, Flox had been working on his latest idea. In addition to dreams of celluloid infamy, he continued to consider himself a writer of as-yet-untapped talent. He'd semi-completed three manuscripts since the age of eighteen – one a futuristic cyberpunk novel, one an allegory of mental illness, and one about drug-taking football fanatics – but each had been rejected by upwards of thirty agents and publishers. As a result, he now viewed such people with the kind of hatred usually afforded to Nazis, and he had reached the stage where he felt close to throwing in the towel. But recently a friend had introduced him to the concept of recycling: 'Musicians do it all the time,' he said – and, indeed, when Flox took a look at the charts, he saw that it was full of regurgitated cover versions that didn't build on the originals so much as *karaoke* the hell out of them. If they can get away with it, he thought, then so can I – in literary form. Thus, Flox was now in the process of completing a thinly disguised cover version of Bret Easton Ellis's *American Psycho*. This rewrite was set on the sodium city streets of London and was titled *The Capital Slayer*. *American Psycho* was perfect cover-version material: it prompted immediate revulsion in everyone, and existed under a spotlight of considerable, unshakeable notoriety that kept it infamous. However – and Flox thought he knew this for a fact – it was also a book (and, subsequently, a film) that few people had actually read; instead, they loathed it via perceived wisdom. And it was this that made him believe he could now make it his own.

Although it was clearly the hare-brained idea of a man approaching the end of his tether, its extreme foolishness refused to dawn on him, and the concept of copyright remained as alien to him as mathematics GCSE. He'd told Danny of this plan, but Danny had poured undiluted scorn over it, so now he spoke about it to no one. He would not be discouraged.

In order to have maximum time to concentrate on his opus – the plot was already there, courtesy of Ellis, but the typing took a lot of time – he had had to cut corners at work: for the past couple of months, then, his listings had remained effectively unchanged, but for the dates. So, according to his column, the Dust Bunnies were playing at the Borderline every Wednesday without fail, even though the singer had died shortly before Christmas in a motorcycle accident. And Aerosmith, currently on tour in the Far East, continued to play Wembley Arena twice a week. But as no one actually read the magazine, this went unnoticed, not least by the editor who hated popular music and always gave Flox's section a wide berth. While his colleagues diligently keyed in the ever-changing details of myriad cinema, theatre and art programmes, Flox had *American Psycho* open beside his keyboard and was feeding his computer screen with Ellis's words as quickly as his fingers could locate the correct keys. Right now, he was on page 300. Another ninety-nine to go.

He found it invigorating, therapeutic work, and although Ellis had written it as satire, Flox took it seriously. He related to Patrick Bateman's violent intent, his inability – his refusal – to suffer fools any longer. The rage Patrick Bateman felt, Flox felt too. For the past few years, he had spent his working day surrounded by people who took petty stupidity off the Richter scale. Each day, he was forced to stifle soul-stripping screams of frustration. At night he ground his teeth and woke in the morning with shards of enamel on his tongue, both fists clenched and a frown on his forehead. *American Psycho* was an outlet: he liked to imagine that, while he was typing, steam poured from his ears. Once this book was completed, he was going to reinterpret *Fight Club*.

Now he hit the keyboard forcefully, testing the springs beneath the keys, but still his concentration wavered. Three feet away, Nathan and Neville continued their duel of words.

'Give it back.'

'Don't be stupid. You're imagining things.'

'No, I am not. Give it *back*.'

And so it went on, throughout the morning.

Shortly before lunch, Nathan flicked an elastic band at Neville, which hit him above his eye. Neville yelled in pain and picked up a stapler to retaliate.

Slowly, as if every movement was being photographed, Flox got to his feet. He flipped *American Psycho* shut. His face bore no sign of emotion as he walked round his desk towards Nathan, who watched him, biting his lip with yellow teeth. Flox placed a hand on the back of Nathan's shirt and gripped it. With one mighty yank he brought Nathan to his feet, then dragged him towards Neville, whom he picked up in a similar fashion. He was taller than both men, who now dangled from either of his hands like puppets. Everyone else in the office watched in silent shock as Flox dragged the pair outside, into the rain, then dumped them like yesterday's rubbish.

'You're both grown-ups,' he said, 'so sort it out like men. Punch seven shades of shit out of one another, then come back in. But I warn you,' he pointed at them in turn with a finger that pulsed with purpose, 'when you come back inside, I don't want to hear another word about who stole what from who.'

Whom, said Neville to himself.

Alone, Nathan and Neville stood side by side, sheepishly, neither knowing quite where to look. The older man cleared his throat several times and, under his breath, complained that his arthritis always played up in rain. Nathan busied himself by tucking his shirt back into his trousers. They stood under steady rainfall for a further five minutes, too timid to make the first move back into the office.

Eventually, Neville took control. 'Oh, come on, this is ridiculous. Who does Quentin think he is? Let's go back inside.'

They walked in, Neville first, Nathan trailing, and resumed their positions behind their desks. Flox glanced up briefly, then resumed work on his literary masterpiece. When he was sure Flox wasn't watching, Neville waved at Nathan to get his attention. Then he gave him the finger.

Nathan went blue in the face with frustration, and snapped a pencil in two.

* * *

As usual, the platform at Lancaster Gate was empty, but just as the doors were about to slide shut, a frantic figure jumped from the stairs and landed in Danny's carriage with a thump. Pleased with this near-Superman feat, he regained his balance, screamed '*Yes!*' at the top of his voice, and demanded applause from his audience of four. Undaunted by the silence, he swung his acoustic guitar from his back until it lay across his stomach then began to play. He was tall, probably in his mid-forties, with spidery dreadlocks that sprouted from his head like irregular roots, and a cluster of thick freckles that gathered around his nose. He was dressed like a court jester and at first glance seemed harmless enough, but the unbalanced glint in his eye pointed to a madness that had little to do with either drink or drugs.

He could have turned left in the carriage and serenaded the man and the woman at the far end, almost opposite each other, their noses in books, or he could have stayed where he was and sung to the sleeping man in front of him. Instead, he turned right and skipped towards Danny, who took even more interest in the contents of Flox's magazine.

The song was impromptu, off the cuff, and rarely managed a rhyming couplet. Its main lyric concerned young men on late-night tube trains reading worthless magazines. Danny's eyes darted up intermittently to meet his entertainer's, and he forced his rigid face into a brief smile as his discomfort mounted. The song continued until they had pulled out of Queensway and ended just after the tube lurched to an unscheduled halt between stations. The jester bowed his head theatrically. Danny offered another wan smile before resuming reading. The jester opened his palm, thrust it forward, and kept it there until Danny looked up.

'You like my song?' asked the jester.

'Yes, very good,' said Danny, in monotone. He experienced a premonition. This was going to turn nasty, he was almost sure of it.

'Well, then, give me money. Twenty pounds.'

'I've got no money. Sorry, spent it all.' Danny tensed.

The smile slid from the jester's face, and he bared a library of crooked teeth. Danny glanced around him, towards the other passengers. No one looked up.

'You messing with me?'

'No. No, honestly I'm not.' Danny took a deep breath.

'I hate people like you,' said the jester, his voice rough around the edges. 'It's all me-me-me with you lot. You trying to tell me you've got no money? No money at all?'

Danny explained that, yes, he had *some* money, but not enough to give him.

'Typically fucking selfish of fucking people like you!' The jester's voice was booming now. Danny's hands were trembling, and he clutched at them, trying to keep them still. Despite a vague notion that young men are supposed to challenge and defend themselves in situations like these, he was too frightened to do anything. As he met the man's stare once again – two large brown eyes, a tangle of crows' feet at either end – he felt his insides hollow.

The jester jabbed at his shoulder with a finger. 'Man, I fucking hate people like you.'

Danny, attempting to keep calm, turned a page of the magazine, then looked up. 'Listen, I'm sorry, I don't have any money,' he began. 'What else can I say? I don't want any trouble. I just want to carry on reading my magazine.'

A hand swooped down, ripped the magazine from Danny's grip, and threw it across the floor of the carriage.

'Get up, cunt. You've pushed me too far now.' He swung his guitar on to his back.

Danny swallowed. 'Look, I really don't want any trouble here.'

'I said *get the fuck up*.'

'All right, okay, I think I do have some money. Here—'

The jester punched him just below the cheekbone, hard, then pulled him to his feet and headbutted him square in the face. Danny dropped to the floor, and the jester began to kick him repeatedly. By now, the carriage's three other passengers were watching in horror. Danny took kicks to the face, ribs and legs, his body curled into a foetal position, his eyes tight shut. Suddenly, the tube lurched forward and pulled into Notting Hill. The doors opened.

'You dirty fucking cunt,' the jester sneered. 'Don't you ever patronise me again. Understand?' He delivered another kick to the base of Danny's spine, then calmly stepped off the tube, his guitar bouncing on his hip.

Danny opened his eyes and blinked. Then, with an effort, he pulled himself into a sitting position. His shirt was covered in blood. His face felt soft, lumpy. His body ached. Slowly, he turned his head to look at the other passengers, who stared at him with expressions of pure, frozen fear. They had read of attacks such as this in their newspapers, and now they had witnessed one. They remained rooted in their seats. Holland Park station came and went. The woman reddened, and turned away. A man's voice floated down to him. 'You all right, mate?'

At Shepherd's Bush, he got off and made his way slowly up the stairs towards the escalators, which carried him up towards the dark, wet streets of west London.

Five

Excerpts from a diary

Some time in early February – who the hell cares what day it is? Time: 4 a.m., the dead of night. Things are going bad, rotten. I am not – repeat – NOT in the best of health right now! I am on a downward slide. Insomnia strikes again. It has been 3 weeks 4 days and 11 hours since Helena last took me out for lunch (the bitch). What? Am I not important enough to her any more? She was the one who told me to take those roles anyway so, if anything, it's her to blame not me. Whatever. These last 15 months have been a real learning process for me (she said, trying to accentuate the positive). 1: I will never be in an action movie with Hulk Hogan again. 2: I will stop mixing champagne and Prozac. 3: I will start to meditate, get Helena to introduce me to Deepak Chokra, and stop crying all the damn time. (Also, I will try to learn more about Scientology ... maybe that is the way forward?)

February 14 (alone all day — no cards, no calls)
Rented Phenomenon *on video with John Travolta. Scientology is definitely the way forward. (Possibly.) Note to self: Read L. Ron Hubbard.*

February 18
Still no Valentine cards — not even from my fans. Fickle assholes! Read L. Ron Hubbard. Is it me, or does that guy just make no sense whatsoever? Like, what is he on? I read three lines of him, and all I got was just blah blah blah, some kind of psycho-pseudo-babblespeak that goes way above my head, like as high as the clouds in the sky. Always did wonder why Travolta had that strange glint in his eye. Now I know. And excuse me, but Nicole Kidman? Need I say more?

February 27
Am writing this with my left hand on account that my right hand is in bandage. Again. Yes, dear diary, I had another interface with a pane of glass. Yeah, I know: ouch-o-rama. The usual, I guess: flew off into a rage, punched a window. What's the matter with me? No more writing for now because my left hand doesn't work properly, and anyway, I need it to wipe away the tears.

Tantrums were becoming her speciality. She could throw them at a moment's notice, regardless of her surroundings. In small, select circles, she was already famed — and, she thought, widely reviled — for this. Unlike most of her life, however, the tantrums weren't scripted. They came to her blind, descending on her like epilepsy, and she was powerless against them. She would scream, stamp her feet, cry, and pull at her hair extensions until they came out in handfuls. Then she would storm out of the nearest exit, and walk, no matter the costume, no matter the neighbourhood. Then, later, she'd be forced to return, metaphorical tail between famous legs, and apologise to everyone, the entire crew. This way, her shrink had informed her, she would earn the respect right back. On the surface, her apologies were always accepted. But she never dared look beneath that surface, because she knew only too well what lurked there.

This morning, she awoke in mid-tantrum, which was a first. As she lifted her head from the pillow, she realised that the strange whining sound that had jolted her awake was emanating from within her. She sat up, and flung the pillow to the other side of the room. On the way it knocked to the floor the alarm clock, a tall glass of warm water, and two bottles of prescription pills. Then she slumped forward and allowed the early-morning crying jag to work itself out. There was no one in the house to rush to her aid. The bed was empty of male company, and the cleaners wouldn't arrive for another hour. By the time the tears had dried, she felt exhausted and wanted nothing more than to return to a chemically assisted sleep.

But today that was not possible. This was her last day in the sprawling Hollywood Hills mansion. Earlier in the week she had received instructions that she was to be out by midday at the latest. Right now, it was a little after eleven. She forced herself upright, then shuffled off into the *en suite* bathroom, shed her silk pyjamas, and stepped under the shower.

Thirty minutes later when she turned off the taps, she felt better, and brave enough to peer into the mirror – above which hung a plaque that read: YOUR REFLECTION IS JUST A STATE OF MIND. The face that stared back at her had puffy eyes and a thin slice of mouth where yesterday there had been ripe lips. Any remaining trace of all-over tan had disappeared down the plughole in the shower cubicle: she was deathly pale. She was now thin rather than slim, and the definition of ribcage suggested an eating disorder.

The whine resumed.

Two years ago, Malory Cinnamon had moved into this rambling house, high in the Hollywood Hills with an auspicious view, to announce to the industry that not only had she arrived but she was now ready for the big screen and all its associated trimmings. Her New York-based sitcom, *Central Park Six*, had made her famous and sought-after, and she had quit when her LA-based agent told her that the movie offers were streaming in. She'd heard of this house, up for immediate rental, on the grapevine. It belonged to a young, successful television actress who was in the process of ploughing her riches into property for *security* – the current buzzword for the sage Hollywood youth. Malory took the place without viewing it. When she arrived, however, with just one removal van of belongings, she was taken aback. Despite the grandeur of the estate and the enormous windows that looked out on to the homes of her rich and famous neighbours, inside the place was a tip.

The living room was so large it didn't know what to do with itself. There was a long, low sofa that ran round the perimeter, an overstuffed bookshelf containing the works of Danielle Steele, Jackie Collins and Naomi Campbell. There was an old piano in one corner, and a coffee table, on which sat a book of black-and-white photographs. The uncarpeted floor, strewn with rugs, was littered with pages from soap-opera scripts, but the smell that emanated from the kitchen should have had a lid on it. On one side of the living-room floor, a trap door lifted to reveal a flight of stairs leading down into a cavernous bedroom that contained a regal four-poster bed. There was just one window here, which looked on to thick shrubbery as the garden had been neglected for some time. The tap in the *en-suite* bathroom dripped, and several tiles were loose. Damp festered in one corner.

Nevertheless, the place had character, and its location couldn't have been better. Within a month of moving in, Malory had enlisted a squad of Mexican cleaners to sort it out. Carmelita, a squat woman in her late forties with facial moles, was in charge of the team and she ruled over them with strict discipline. They whipped the house into shape, making it not just habitable but modestly luxurious, a most desirable temporary residence for a rising Hollywood starlet. (When Chuck Fielder married her, on that beach in Barbados, with just a few handpicked guests and several hundred loitering *paparazzi*, he moved out of his bachelor pad and in here with her, bringing with him his own abundant clutter — much of it mental — and it soon reverted to its chaotic original state. But when he moved out — not much more than six months later, the schmuck — she and Carmelita restored its female ambience, and calm was restored.)

And now she had to leave. Her landlady, two years her

junior, wanted instant repossession as her current daytime show had just been axed. She refused to give Malory the mandatory three months' notice, and threatened that if she wasn't out in a week, she'd run to the tabloids to reveal just what a terrible tenant the temperamental Malory Cinnamon had been.

With Carmelita's help – she'd arrived earlier than scheduled out of concern for her employer – Malory was ready by twelve, and now stood on the doorstep in an awkward embrace with her maid. Carmelita said she'd miss her very much, and that even though she was being kept on by the returning owner, she was sure she'd turn out to be a nasty piece of work. 'You much better, *nicer*,' she said. Malory thanked her for the compliments, and for all her help these past couple of years, then ran down the winding steps to the awaiting cab before tears ruined her makeup. While her belongings went into storage, Malory Cinnamon was aware that a statement had to be made here. This was the kind of town where people noticed what went on, and were prone to gossip. It would do Malory no good if it was believed that she was homeless, so she checked into a vast suite at the Chateau Marmont, a hotel that took great chunks out of anyone's fortune but did wonders for the reputation.

She opened the giant fridge in the suite's kitchen, took out an ice-cold Budweiser and rolled it across her forehead. She took a gulp, then slunk into the master bedroom, propped herself against a mountain of plump pillows, and made a telephone call to someone who knew someone who would be happy to deliver to her room a very particular type of gift.

While she awaited delivery, Malory allowed herself the luxury of another shower. It was a quiet, hot day. She had no pressing engagements – she was between films, and hadn't signed on any dotted line for some time now – so had nothing better to do. Afterwards, back in the bedroom, she stood naked before the full-length mirror, which prompted the depression to hurtle back. Her breasts, once of average size, pert, and blessed with dark, alert nipples, were large and bulbous, almost fat. Her nipples had lightened, and were no longer as responsive to touch as they had been. If you looked closely – Malory wouldn't allow anyone's eyes within a twelve-inch radius – you could just make out the crescent-moon scar around each areola. When she jumped on the spot, both breasts stayed where they were.

She had had the operation eight weeks earlier as a present to herself when the son-of-a-bitch she'd married stormed off with someone else. Traumatised, she had decided that bigger breasts would make her feel better than anything she could purchase on Rodeo Drive. She told no one, and even as the doctor was drawing uneven lines around her breasts with a thick black marker, she still had no doubts.

They came later.

It took over two weeks for the swelling and scarring to go down, and a further three before she could look at them without hyperventilating. On Monday of the sixth week, she took them to Helena Finklestein, her agent, for appraisal. Helena Finklestein was a small woman with a large name, and more jewellery in her mouth than on her fingers. Her teeth dazzled onlookers with their bright white sheen and four gold caps. When fully upright, she stood no taller than a circus performer famed for his lack of height, but her stacked heels and a tank-like character afforded her a presence that even giants would bow before. She had hooked up with Malory when *Central Park Six* was half-way through its second season and the Hollywood offers were gathering pace. Since then she had landed Malory several respectable roles.

Helena liked Malory Cinnamon. While she knew that she would never carry the same weight as other, more serious actresses, she realised that someone like Malory would be offered perfectly good roles in films that made money on video, and, as long as she kept her anger in check, she'd remain employable for several years yet.

Malory called her agent that Monday morning and was told that Helena had a window shortly before lunch.

When she arrived at the sumptuous office, Helena air-kissed her from ten feet away. Malory was nervous, but also excited. 'I've got something to show you,' she said.

'Well, go on, I'm watching.' Helena sat down and ushered her PA out of the room with an impatient wave.

Malory undid the buttons on her white silk shirt, then opened it. She unhooked her front-loading bra and let her new purchases bounce free. Bouncing, however, was the last thing they did. Instead, they stood to firm attention with a discipline they'd never previously shown.

Helena Finklestein's painted-on eyebrows shot towards her hairline, which came down to meet them, and she opened her mouth wide enough for each gold tooth to catch the light and sparkle. She swore, in Jewish. 'Oy vey, *oy vey*! What in the name of Joan Rivers have you done to yourself?'

Malory fought back confusion, beamed, and thrust them out still further.

Helena got to her feet, which wasn't immediately obvious as the desk was almost as high as she was tall. She held her face in her hands and moaned like a mother in mourning. 'You foolish girl! You foolish, *foolish* girl! What have you done?'

Malory's lower lip trembled, which was normally the sign for Helena to backtrack and embark on some rapid diplomacy. But today she was unrepentant. 'ARE YOU MAD? COMPLETELY OUT OF YOUR MIND?' She was shrieking like a banshee. 'Silicone is *out*, baby. It's strictly last millennium's thing.'

'But – but—' Malory was spluttering. She wanted to list the names of all the other actresses she was sure had recently gone under the knife, but words wouldn't sit still on her tongue.

Helena shut her eyes. 'Put them away!'

She went over to her oak-panelled drinks cabinet, and poured herself a large vodka tonic, gulped it, then climbed back on to her leather chair. 'Unless you get rid of those preposterous air-bags,' she fumed, 'the only jobs I'll be able to get you are tacky cable TV shows. Either that, or you'll be running up and down beaches in a tight red swimsuit. And movies? You can forget about movies! Now, please, correct me if I'm wrong, but is that what you *really* want?'

Malory's mouth hung loose. She felt like a painting that was melting in spiralling heat. She wanted to scream.

Helena leaned forward and placed both mottled hands, palms down, on the table before her. 'Malory, think hard.

Concentrate. Hollywood today is three things: it's slender, it's blonde, it's *natural*. It's the era of the girl next door. Pamela's out, Gwyneth's in. Think about it.' She whipped her little body back into the chair and raised a finger to her lips, which, years earlier, she'd had injected with fat from her behind.

'Are you telling me I should have them out?' Malory said, with mounting fear.

'Sure, absolutely, you bet. No option, really.'

'But I hear it's very painful.'

'Every sacrifice is painful, darling.' Helena shrugged. 'Now, if you'll excuse me, I have a lunch date.'

Malory Cinnamon had come to Hollywood in pursuit of a dream, and had found it where millions before her had failed. She was one of the chosen few, and had lived life in a lap of luxury she had thought previously existed only in imagination. In her five years here (post *Central Park Six*), she had worked almost consistently, both on television and the big screen, and, as a consequence, she'd met almost every star famous enough to warrant a stalker. She'd been to all the parties – thrown by producers, studios, recently promoted A-list actors – and innumerable charity events, for cancer, Aids, or those less fortunate than the rich. Up close, the famous faces were even more perfect than their two-dimensional counterparts, proof enough for Malory that streamlined design had weighed heavily on God's mind during their creation. But behind the toothpaste-and-conditioner façade were streaks so evil that no one dared turn his or her back in another's company. Competition was endemic, public criticism a way of life. And while she tried to insinuate herself into such company, Malory never felt that she truly fitted in. And as the breakthrough proper continued to elude her, so the greetings from winsome young waifs – her peers – became more forced, more haughty, *bitchy*. She felt the token object of derision and, were she not such a hot piece of ass, she was sure she'd be scorned by her male counterparts, too.

Her marriage to Chuck had, at first, seemed like a genuine gift from above. They had met on the set of *Felicity Beach*, but by the time the credits had rolled in cinemas, ten months after filming, he'd already left her for a younger model whose recent big-screen début was causing a minor sensation and whose star was in greater ascendance.

Even the business of filming had begun to sour for Malory. Everyone in this town was obsessed with dimensions. *My close-up must be more close-up than hers. My left profile is better than my right; my nose appears slightly shorter. Hers is a larger trailer than mine. I want my name above the title, in a larger font, and it should be underlined also, prefixed with 'and'. I want a car with six doors, a jet with twin propellers. I want the island besides Jagger's. I want more girls, more lithe young boys, the finest cocaine, the largest table, a bigger fee, the leading lady.* Malory could never get herself into this frame of mind.

Acting alongside a venerable actor who had made his name playing wealthy middle-aged American males on the edge of a breakdown was not the honour she had thought it would be. This star, like so many others, was discourteous and too self-important ever to give her – someone who had come from *television* – the time of day. Once, during the shoot, she mentioned his own rise from television, years earlier, and his sneer felt like a fork jabbed into her side. When that film had wrapped, he'd thrown a party at one of his beachside residences. Mysteriously, Malory's invitation had taken a wrong turn in the post, and arrived on the morning after the event. She cried for three days.

In five years, she had completed nine big-screen movies, three TV movies, one TV police drama and two comedy pilots that never landed a series. Her most successful cinematic offering, *The Girl Who Dreamed*, had taken just twenty-two million dollars at the box office, which ensured she'd never sit next to Tom Hanks at the Golden Globes (she'd yet to be invited to the Oscars, much less nominated). One TV film, however, *A Fatal Disease*, about a young mother dying from cancer – in which Malory had shaved her head in Method preparation – was repeated regularly on one cable channel, usually in the dead of night for insomniacs with a penchant for weepies. In brief optimistic moments, she believed that her true time was still to come, that she hadn't already peaked with the New York-based sitcom, which industry types had already forgotten about. Occasionally she felt confident that one of her small-budget movies would go on to become a sleeper, word-of-mouth ensuring that her sensitive portrayal didn't go unnoticed. Overnight, she would become the new female sensation and command a million-dollar fee. But mostly Malory found herself obsessed with the film *Sunset Boulevard* and related uncomfortably to the Gloria Swanson character, in a world where every tomorrow was just an empty shell of yesterday.

Thus, with few real friends upon whom to unload her

insecurities, Malory became increasingly reliant on the empathy she found in bottles of expensive red wine. Also, in a variety of clubs with some of her former television co-stars, she experimented again with a drug called ketamine, which had been introduced to her years earlier by a young Englishman. Place one of those babies on your tongue, and the following day becomes nothing more than a rumour. Instead, when your blinking finally resumes a steady rhythm, an entire week will have gone by.

Consequently, she hadn't worked for months.

There was a sharp knock at the door. Her dealer. She invited him in, and they sat at a glass coffee table. He spread his wares in front of her and she chose some cocaine, half a dozen ketamine pills, and a stash of marijuana. She paid in cash. Later that evening, she indulged behind closed curtains and a sign on the door that read DO NOT DISTURB. She didn't surface for over a week, and made no new entries in her diary.

Ten days later, Malory decided that action was required. She got up, pulled open the curtains, and light penetrated the suite. The sofa looked bleached, while her dwindling stash of drugs, scattered carelessly on the glass table, looked strangely guilty. Dust motes plunged through the windows and danced before her in great streams. Malory moved through them slowly, barely lifting her feet over the luxurious carpet. Her face was still folded in sleep, her eyelids struggling to remain open.

She opened the french windows and took in great gulps of fresh air, sat down outside and composed herself. Then she turned on her mobile phone. Instantly it chimed, alerting its owner to the presence of several stored messages. One was from an acquaintance in television, requiring her dealer's number, the remaining twenty-seven all came from an increasingly hysterical Helena Finklestein, demanding to know why she was refusing to return calls. The first handful were about auditions, the rest queried her disappearance and complained of the inconvenience it brought. Not once did Helena ask after Malory's welfare, she just repeated the word *inconvenience* until it became an irritating mantra.

When Helena Finklestein had talked herself out, Malory dialled a series of digits that had once been familiar to her. She put the phone to her ear and listened to the clicking of connecting lines from state to state. Her mother picked up.

'Hi,' Malory said, awkwardly. 'It's me.'

The older woman was silent, and Malory could almost hear her brow furrow. 'Who?'

'Malory.'

'Malory?'

'Alicia,' she said, elaborating.

Static bounced across the line, the faintest of echoes. 'Alicia?' her mother asked.

'Yes, Mom. Hi. How are you doing?'

'Are you eating properly?' she asked.

They talked for over an hour, until the phone's battery was dying and the tissues were soaked with tears. Malory had done most of the apologising, her mother most of the reprimanding. Before saying goodbye, the actress promised she would come see her real soon, to try to make amends and build bridges. But before then, she said, mindful of the self-help programmes she'd watched over the past five years, she had first to find herself.

'You're speaking to your mom now,' her mother chided, 'not your therapist. What in the hell are you talking about, exactly?'

Malory told her that she just had to get away, as far away from Hollywood, the industry, as she could. Immediately her mother worried about money, but Malory assured her that she had enough to be getting on with. 'I've thought about this a lot, Mom, and I have to do it. I need to travel, set myself free. When I come back, we'll hook up, okay? I love you, Mom.'

It was her mother's turn now to cry. She told her how much she loved *A Fatal Disease*.

'What about *The Girl Who Dreamed*?' Malory asked optimistically.

'I don't think I saw that one.'

Back in the suite, Malory flushed the remaining drugs down the toilet and destroyed any lingering evidence of the habit that, as of today, she was determined to kick. She had a bath, dressed, packed, and checked out.

The taxi shuttled her off to LAX. Because he recognised her, the driver allowed her to light a cigarette in the back seat, as long as she kept the window open and directed all cancerous fumes out into the traffic. In Europe, they were a lot more understanding of smokers. In fact, over there, it was very much the other way round: they frowned on those who abstained. In Europe, everybody smoked, and they smoked with a panache that Malory, ever the actress, found she was looking forward to perfecting.

On the flight over, she had her neck and hands massaged by the on-board physio. Then, after watching one of her more recent films on the in-flight programme, she tilted the wide chair back until she was practically horizontal, then curled up into an S shape, and slept soundly. Ten hours later, she opened her eyes and caught just a glimpse of the Eiffel Tower as the plane banked, preparing to land.

Malory Cinnamon went to Paris because all upwardly mobile Americans, at some point in their therapied lives, go to Paris.

Six

Flox stole the magazine because, as of right now, he had decided on a strict regime of spontaneity. It helped pass the time. He'd gone into the shop to buy some menthol-flavoured chewing-gum, but had seen the magazine with the nearly naked woman on the cover, and thought, *Why not?* As he made his way to the automatic doors, his sphincter clenched in expectation of the alarm he was sure would go off as he stepped over its invisible threshold. But no sound came, and he carried on walking, smiling widely. Elated, he made his way to the bus stop, then saw a black cab. His arm shot out, Nazi-style, to flag it down.

'Where to?' the driver asked.

Flox relaxed into the shiny black seat, and told him to drive north. The driver, with exaggerated weariness, draped both arms over the steering-wheel, and craned his fat neck round to face Flox's near-horizontal form in the back.

'Look, mate, this is a taxi, not a bus. You tell me where

you want to go, I take you. That's how it works. I am not driving north like some ponce waiting for your directions at whim, do you understand me?'

Flox smiled again, for no particular reason. He pulled himself up into a seated position, his gaze locked on to the driver's the whole time, and ran a hand through his hair. Who knew what he was going to say next?

'I'm sorry, you're right. Can you take me to, um . . .' Flox paused, as the Northern Line's map raced through his mind, and he counted off several stops. '. . . Finchley Central, High Barnet branch, please?'

The driver turned his large bulk round, muttered obscenities beneath his breath, and pulled out sharply into the traffic. Flox settled back into a position of considerable comfort and started to read the stolen magazine.

It was a weekday afternoon, and Flox was playing truant from work because he simply couldn't face the office. Not in his current mood. He had taken Danny's mugging badly — worse, probably, than Danny had. When Danny had returned home with a face full of blood and bruises, any lingering respect that Flox might have harboured for the human race vanished. He had stormed around the house swearing and punching things — he needed an outlet for the violence boiling inside him, and was afraid that if he returned to work Nathan would prove too tempting a target. Instead, he paced the hall, thrusting his fist into patches of damp plaster.

Danny, meanwhile, was falling to pieces. Until just recently, he'd fancied himself set for life: girlfriend, job, few demands, pleasant daily routine, annual holiday. But then, one by one, everything had fallen away from him

– and now this brutal mugging. Was this really the way life was supposed to be – a litany of misery?

That night, Flox had stormed about the kitchen, seething. 'I can't believe nobody did anything to help,' he spat. He went over to one of the drawers, and pulled out a yellowing notepad that had lived in the house far longer than they had. He found a pencil stub and sat at the table. 'Can you remember what he looked like?' he asked, hunched over the paper, ready to draw.

'Flox, what are you doing?'

'You're going to describe him and I'm going to draw him. Then I'm going to hunt the fucker down and kill him.' Flox had an A level in Art. Caricatures of former flatmates and girlfriends were strewn liberally about the house.

Danny threw him a withering look. Flox, his face flushed with purpose, appeared deadly serious.

'I'm deadly serious,' he confirmed. 'Now, let's start with the nose.'

A few days passed, and things reverted seemingly to normal. Danny, however, found himself too scared to leave the house, and instead pottered about it miserably. Jobless, he stared vacantly at the television set and limited his thoughts to the love he had lost. Slowly, his bruises healed, and the mugging was filed away in a dark part of his memory. He learned to accept it as one of the downsides of living in the capital.

Flox, though, felt on the brink of change. Action, of as an yet undetermined nature, was clearly called for.

Now the taxi made slow progress towards Finchley Central, and Flox watched as the meter reading climbed higher and higher, feeling a perverse thrill that his wallet contained no more than four pounds in loose change. He'd never been to Finchley Central, and until now had never felt compelled to check it out. He watched various high streets come and go, the same chain stores, the same antiseptic ambience. He watched mothers battle with pushchairs and shopping-bags, and children in school uniforms loitering in places they shouldn't have been frequenting at all. Eventually, Finchley came into view and confirmed his suspicions. It was a miserable pocket of 0208 suburbia, its bland façade appropriate to its wan inhabitants. The streets were littered with Mercedes, BMWs, and nippy little motorscooters in bright pastel colours. He made a retching noise, which alerted the taxi driver.

'Where do you want to be dropped?' he asked.

It was a good question. Flox looked around. He didn't want to be dropped anywhere round here. In fact, he wanted to get out of Finchley Central as soon as possible: its tedium surrounded him like a suffocating gauze. He leaned forward and was about to tell the driver to take him back into town but something else came out of his mouth.

'Just up from the lights, next left,' he said.

As luck would have it, the lights were red, so the taxi pulled up. Flox found himself shifting along the seat towards the kerbside door and slowly curled his hand around the handle. He applied pressure and squeezed. It clicked, popped open, and Flox was on the pavement running, the wind in his face, adrenaline pumping through his body, Nirvana's 'Territorial Pissings' pounding in his ears.

Behind him, he heard a shout. He turned round to see

the driver clamber out of his vehicle and give chase. This pleased him greatly. With his head down and both fists punching the air, Flox ran faster down a slight hill towards the tube station. He slalomed in and out of a crowd of people, the entrance now within his sights. The taxi driver, meanwhile, wasn't making quite such successful progress – regular fry-up breakfasts had clogged his arteries and now slowed his pace considerably. Flox had reached the stairs and was taking them two at a time, hitting the platform with a thud, and jumping into the open doors of an awaiting train. When he landed, heavily, people seated on either side peeked over the headlines of their newspapers and looked at him with mild curiosity: public fracas were the domain of the inner city, not Finchley Central. Flox offered them a shy smile and shrugged his shoulders.

The taxi driver had by now reached the top of the stairs and was running down them heavily. His eyes were on stalks, his hands clenched, and sweat was pouring off him. He was shouting unintelligibly and pointing towards the train. Once again, newspapers were crumpled down towards laps and eyes peered out. They watched a fat man, whose gut was straining at its belt, lumber down the stairs like a walrus. The noises that came from his mouth were either cries of agony or angry directives; no consonants, just slurred vowels. Flox tensed. *Come on, come on!* he begged the tube driver. *Close the doors – move!*

Suddenly there were beeps, and a recorded voice told everyone to mind the doors. The taxi driver was on the platform. His trousers were sliding down the crescent moon of his stomach, and three buttons had popped open on his white shirt. His stomach was pale and fleshy, wet with sweat. The doors shut just as he thrust an intervening hand between them, trapping four fat fingers. He winced with pain. The train didn't move, the doors didn't open, and Flox's heart played the xylophone against his ribcage. He counted to ten. Other passengers watched in amazement, but still the doors didn't open, and although only moments passed, for Flox they lasted an uncomfortably long time. The doors juddered, slid open a fraction, then snapped shut, the taxi driver having removed his fingers. He made full eye-contact with Flox, muttered unheard words in his direction. Flox winked at him, which provoked an avalanche of swearing and raised fists. The train pulled slowly out of the station, and the taxi driver receded from view, now doubled over, his fat hands on thick thighs, breathing heavily. Flox squatted on the floor, and laughed to himself. Gradually, the commuters' heads disappeared behind their broadsheets as central London crept towards them.

At Camden Flox alighted and strode down the high street feeling omnipotent. He walked up towards the lock, passing an endless parade of shoe shops left and right, each window filled with the latest arrivals from America. He looked down at his boots, an old pair of Doc Martens, and spontaneity took over once more. He chose an emporium, and went in.

The shop was full of European students, girls and boys no older than fifteen. Few appeared to speak English, and all seemed obscenely excited at the prospect of purchasing a brand new pair of Nike trainers. Eventually, he found a seat between two Italian girls in Limp Bizkit T-shirts, and loosened the knots in his laces. With an effort, he removed his boots and flagged down a harassed assistant. While he waited, he studied his Doc Martens. They'd been an almost permanent part of his wardrobe for the last four years, and he'd grown as attached to them as if they were an old dog. But then a dazzlingly bright pair of box-fresh trainers came into his field of vision. Ocean blue, striped with electric white, and a rim that would glow neon within the darkness of a nightclub, they were terrifically expensive. As he slipped them on, his feet felt as though they were encased in clouds of pure comfort. He stood.

'Bounce,' said the assistant encouragingly, 'and watch what happens.'

Flox found himself a little space in the shop that wasn't overrun with screaming kids, and began to jump on the spot. An incredible thing happened. His entire body appeared to inflate, upwards. Suddenly, he was taller, more mobile. He felt a surge of air emanating from the base of his heels, and by the third bounce, he felt like a human trampoline.

He looked at himself in the mirror.

He grinned.

He ran out of the shop.

And kept running, across the road, in front of oncoming traffic, and towards the canal. For the second time that day, he looked over his shoulder to find somebody in pursuit, but this time the chaser was a strapping security guard with menace on his face. Flox ran faster still, then hung a sharp left, down the slope and along the canal. His thighs were burning, and he realised that stamina was now something he lacked. School had ended over a decade ago, and since then his muscles had turned to putty. The only thing that kept him going was pure white fear. He clambered up a metal staircase and emerged in the back-streets of Primrose Hill. He ran across the road, narrowly avoiding collision with actor Jude Law, who was doing press-ups on the pavement while Sadie Frost, Jonny Lee Miller and Anna Friel stood around him applauding. He continued to weave between streets and around corners until he was sure he'd shaken off the security guard, and his heart threatened to burst out of his chest. He took off his jacket, and when both legs had stopped trembling quite so much, walked unsteadily towards the nearest newsagent, where he purchased a can of Coke, like any normal, law-abiding citizen.

Back outside, he peered at his reflection in a car window, his newly acquired trainers giving him an aerodynamic quality even when motionless. He was happy with his acquisition. He crossed the road, and walked through one park then another before he arrived in Oxford Street where he jumped on a bus that took him home.

He paid for the ticket, but did so spontaneously.

Several weeks later, Flox insinuated himself into a poker syndicate that met after hours in an east London pub. Poker wasn't strictly his game, and neither was this kind of environment, but he was drawn to its grimy cinematic atmosphere, the clear and present danger, the insalubrious players, the sweet sensation of risk. Once a week, he'd lose large chunks of his meagre savings, but cocaine took the edge off the loss, and he'd leave shortly before dawn, walking the empty, unfamiliar streets through pouring rain, ignoring the creeping feeling of desolation and barely aware of the gaping hole in his pocket where previously had sat an absolute bundle.

He lost all his money rapidly and could only make the weekly card games via trips to a local loan shark first, convincing himself that he needed the next game in much the same way that a junkie does his next fix.

Seven

The phone call was quick, devastating. She had cancer, and she was going to die. There was nothing anyone could do.

Danny walked unsteadily into the kitchen, his face a mask of pain and confusion. His neighbour, Sanjay, was in the middle of making them both a light evening meal on the Baby Belling, but on seeing Danny's face, he abandoned the cooker and rushed to his side. 'What's the matter?' he asked.

Danny looked down to the kitchen table and saw a full cup of coffee there. He picked it up, brought it to his mouth, and took a few tentative sips. It was cold.

Sanjay put his arm round Danny's shoulders. He didn't know what was wrong, but he knew that it wasn't good. He asked again, 'What's happened? Tell me?'

'That was the hospital,' he said.

'Which hospital?'

Danny shrugged. 'They phoned to tell me about my mother. She's got cancer.' He looked up at Sanjay. 'I didn't even know she was ill. And now she's going to die.'

Sanjay didn't know what to say so he hugged him tighter. Danny looked over his friend's shoulder at the garden door. It didn't quite fit the frame, and the wind was whipping in. It was dark outside, early evening, and cold. Until the phone call, it had been just another ordinary, empty day, Danny fulfilling his role admirably as one of life's unemployed. Today's news would do little to pull him out of his quagmire. The lady he'd spoken to – a nurse? doctor? – had told him that his mother had been admitted over a month ago with jaundice. She was in a pretty bad way, but hadn't wanted them to contact her son because she didn't want him to worry, which was just typical of her. They'd done a series of tests, which revealed that another series was required. After that, she was referred to an unspecified *specialist* who conducted further tests. The results of these had been compared to those of the others, and after several doctors had discussed the matter, they felt able to offer a conclusive diagnosis. And that diagnosis was cancer. The pain she had suffered for over six months was caused by a malignant growth in her liver. It was particularly virulent, and by the time the hospital had learned what it was, it had spread to her lungs. An educated guess suggested that the colon was next, or maybe the bowels. It was, therefore, inoperable. Chemotherapy *was* an option, but in this case it would not be able to cure, merely slow the progress of the disease. Also, it would make her very ill, and she was weak enough as it was. After some consideration, his mother had decided not to go through with it, and merely to accept her fate. She was depressed, very low. 'But she's being brave,' Danny was told, and she had eventually agreed that the hospital could let her son know.

'Apparently she only has about six months, maybe less,' he told Sanjay. 'I know we haven't spoken for a while, but she never mentioned anything to me at all, ever.'

The words hung in the cold air like speech bubbles. Sanjay led him to the nearest chair and got him to sit down. He sat opposite, and kept hold of Danny's hand, as Danny stared emptily into the middle distance, anguish written all over him.

And then, into this silence and disrupting it, came Flox. He carried several bags of food. 'Chinese takeaway!' he announced. 'My treat.' Then he surveyed the scene in the kitchen. 'What's up?' he asked.

The following morning, Flox went to work under a cloud of cataclysmic aggression. He felt fury and sheer astonishment. He stood on the tube, strap-hanging, and felt as if he might explode. Would he have felt any worse if it had all happened to him, and not Danny? If it had been he who had lost his girlfriend, his job and now his mother, with a brutal mugging in between? In a perverse way, perhaps he would. At least then there would be full justification for all the rage that swam around inside him. Instead, Flox had to stand by, effectively impotent, and watch it all happen to his best friend. The word *why* rebounded inside his skull like a rubber ball. Around him a hundred thousand other commuters were sardining themselves in this cramped compartment for the sake of what? Work? Flox started muttering out loud unaware of just how close he was to becoming the nutter on the tube.

Several stops later, he disembarked and stormed up the escalators, pushing people out of the way, spoiling for a fight. When he arrived at the office, everyone was busy at their desks and he had to suppress a lunatic cackle. The atmosphere in here was close, stuffy, the air-conditioning working overtime, and Flox pulled at the neck of his jumper. He sat down at his desk, but fidgeted ceaselessly. He called up his regular file, and blood rushed into his head at the sight of it. There was no way he could spend another day like this, in this environment, with these people. He lit an illegal cigarette, and screwed it into the corner of his mouth. The editor glanced at him, ready to scold, but changed her mind when she saw his face. This was a more extreme Flox than even she was used to dealing with, and she decided to seek out the publisher at lunchtime. Flox had to go.

Flox flexed his fingers. He went through every line of blurb that explained why attendance at a particular concert was recommended, and deleted it all. Then he wiped the venues. By the time he had finished, there was nothing but a blank screen, a vast ocean of white. When the next edition hit the streets in less than forty-eight hours' time, the music section would be conspicuous by its absence. There would be two pages of nothing. Since Flox was exclusively in charge of his section, no one would bother double-checking his pages before they went to press. They wouldn't realise the glaring omission until the magazine was out. This made him feel inexplicably happy, like a child committing its first act of minor vandalism. He called up *American Psycho* and deleted all his precious work. Then he attacked his dog-eared paperback, ripping out the pages and tossing them into the bin.

When he stood up, propelling his chair backwards, Nathan, who had been watching him, ducked instinctively. Flox turned to face his noticeboard on the wall behind his desk, and removed every scrap of paper, every photocopied feature, countless business cards, and dropped them all on the floor. He walked round to the other side of his desk and swept off pens, pencils, staplers and piles of paper. The computer followed, sending sparks of electricity flaring into the air. A dictionary and thesaurus tumbled after it.

No one spoke. They just watched him in stunned silence. The editor found she was shaking, and to calm herself, she made a mental list of what she had to buy from the supermarket that evening. A friend was coming over, and she wanted to get some brown rice. Neville slipped away to the toilet, from where he had little intention of returning. Tears filled Philomena's eyes: Flox's *chi* was all over the place, and she worried for him so.

Flox walked to the coat stand and retrieved his jacket, which he put on. He looked at each of his workmates in turn, leered, and left. Outside, he put up his collar and walked past a news-stand where the day's headline concerned a dictator facing charges of genocide. He had employed a team of lawyers so expert that people were now worried he would shirk the blame altogether, and that ultimately the charges would be dropped. As he turned into Oxford Street, Flox felt sickened at a world that could strike down the innocent with cancer while letting the guilty get away with murder.

Eight

Several decades earlier, the hospital walls had been painted off-white and now, untouched by brush ever since, were the colour of yesterday's porridge. Watercolours by former patients tried in vain to brighten the place a little. Danny stood in the lift lobby and waited for one of six to arrive. He wrung his hands and paced the linoleum floor. A family of five Orthodox Jews arrived and preceded him into the lift. Husband, wife, and three children, they stood silently around the walls, allowing Danny space in the middle. He looked at the large, bearded man and the woman, whose ample bosom jutted out before her. They and their small, mute children were dressed almost entirely in black. They looked sombre, funereal. All Danny could hear was rhythmic breathing, and the occasional shuffle of feet. He cleared his throat and one of the children mimicked him. He swung round to face the culprit who looked at his brother and grinned. The older boy cleared his throat too, followed by his sister. Muffled giggles ensued until the father mumbled something that returned them instantly to silence.

At the seventh floor, the family alighted, allowing Danny to complete his journey alone. When the doors opened, he walked out, turned left, and froze as he reached the entrance to the ward. Nurses walked by. A visitor sat on a solitary plastic chair, staring into space. Someone was talking into a public telephone, a hand cupped around the mouthpiece. Danny took a deep breath and walked on. At either side of the corridor small rooms contained four beds each. He walked the length of the ward, then turned back, confused. Where was she?

Eventually, he found her, and couldn't quite believe what he saw. They'd last spoken about a month ago, maybe two, and he hadn't seen her since . . . September? She'd spent last Christmas with friends so, yes, it must have been. He walked up to her bed, and saw that she was sleeping. Christ, he could hardly recognise her. Her hair, once rich and brown, was now grey and wiry, shorter than he remembered. The cheekbones of her youth had returned, but her skin was loose, sunken. Her eyelids were huge, her lips pale, and her breastbone sharply defined beneath a thin hospital-issue nightgown. She breathed deeply and regularly, seeming very far away.

He pulled up a chair to sit down, but it squeaked loudly across the floor, and his mother woke up. She opened her eyes and saw her son. Tears came, and she blinked them back, smiling weakly. Danny took her hand and held it tightly. An immense pressure pushed inside his throat. She asked him how he was, and the irony cut deep.

The woman in the next bed let out a cry of pain and shouted at Danny to push the call button. He did so, and felt an immediate wave of relief when the nurse arrived.

Somebody else, another patient, coughed hard and brought up so much phlegm that Danny winced.

His mother smiled. 'As sick as dogs, every last one of us.' The smile vanished. 'I'm sorry to have burdened you like this. I didn't want you to find out – I'm sure you've enough on your plate as it is.'

Danny's voice caught in his throat, and he willed himself not to cry.

'So, tell me all your news,' she said, her eyes bright. Clearly, she did not want to talk about the cancer, so Danny did his best. He told her all about Amy and how busy she was at the moment. Yes, they were happy; no, no plans to marry yet. And certainly no children.

'I'll never be a grandmother,' she said. 'Shame.' She asked about his job. She wanted to know about the flat, his friends, if he was happy in life, and was pleased to learn that he was.

Danny wanted to talk about her, but this was not on the agenda. When he asked why she hadn't told him earlier of her illness, her eyes crimped at the edges and she appeared to deflate, so he was forced to steer the conversation back to himself. She seemed keen to know that she was leaving her son in safe hands, and Danny did his best to play the role, speaking in affirmatives. He wanted to tell her that he loved her, that he was sorry not to have been in touch more often, and that he wished things could have been different. But he didn't – couldn't. He simply held her hand and answered her questions. She smiled constantly at him, only turning away when the pain rose. Suddenly, she would squeeze his hand and her body would convulse. Danny looked at the needle poking from beneath a plaster on her skeletal arm. He followed the plastic tube up to the bag, and watched the clear, translucent liquid drip slowly down into her.

A nurse approached her bed bearing gifts. 'Time for your medication,' she said.

With Danny's help, his mother forced herself into a sitting position, her face twisted in a grimace. He fetched her a glass of water and watched her take four pills, two blue, one white, one yellow. Then, she lowered herself and sighed heavily. Her head was in an awkward position on the pillow. It looked uncomfortable, but she didn't attempt to move it. Her eyelids flickered shut, and within minutes she was asleep, in temporary respite from a pain that had yet to do its worst.

Quietly, Danny stood up to leave. His footsteps on the dull yellow linoleum were soft, almost silent. In the lift, two nurses discussed boyfriends, and a small girl dropped her lollipop. She cried until her mother produced another from her coat pocket.

Outside, rain fell.

Job descriptions changed, and the weeks scrolled by. Spring arrived, and Flox began temping in earnest, taking any job that was offered as long as it paid well. He was now determined to make as much money as possible, then hopefully double it at his weekly card game, before making an emphatic life change. He planned to take Danny with him, but decided to keep this to himself for the time being.

The work was fruitful – and it had to be. The loan shark, to whom he was indebted to the tune of several thousand pounds demanded that he never miss a repayment.

He worked every hour possible: in offices manning the photocopying machine; making deliveries in the financial district, answering telephones, reorganising filing systems. It was tedious work that he could only perform in a state of almost total brain shutdown. Occasional fringe benefits helped him keep going, such as the mini hi-fi equipment he managed to steal from one of many warehouses he worked in while loading lorries throughout the night. His social life withered, then evaporated altogether.

And Danny?

His flatmate had also found a new job, one that not only kept him busy, but ultimately ensured both men's eventual escape.

Nine

Initially, the mother was wary. 'I must say,' she said, 'I was rather expecting a girl. 'You're the only boy I've seen.' She rolled her tongue across immaculate teeth. 'But I must admit I'm intrigued. A male nanny! Whoever would have thought of such a thing?'

For two successive summers, just before leaving his teens behind, Danny had been a counsellor at an American camp. An only child, he had quickly taken to his new 'family'. On both occasions he had spent eight of the most hectic, exhausting weeks of his life attending to a bunch of screaming, hyperactive kids, and had loved every minute of it. So when, after an unsuccessful visit to the job centre, he saw an advert in the window of the local newsagent for an experienced nanny he thought he'd give it a go.

And now here he was, sitting before his potential new employer. So far, so good.

Colette Godin – tall, elegant and with a certain similarity to the Holly Golightly-era Audrey Hepburn – was a thirtysomething lecturing artist who lived, with her gynaecologist husband Philippe and their two young children, in an imposing four-floor house in Holland Park. Her parents, and her husband's, were upper-middle class French with homes in France and England, but viewed the British with disdain. She drove a brand-new cherry red Volkswagen Beetle, while Philippe, ten years her senior, had an austere Mercedes for work, and a classic Citroën DS Pallas for the weekends. (Her lover buzzed around town on an electric green Vespa.) The family had two crab-coloured Siamese cats, a cleaner who visited daily, and the telephone numbers of many respected local psychiatrists.

The house was enormous, like nothing Danny had ever seen. The dining room, which dissolved into a stainless-steel kitchen, revolved around a large antique oak table, upon which sat an elaborate candelabrum that dated back to Napoleon. Overhead hovered a silver chandelier that had once belonged to Victor Hugo; it winked and twinkled gold when the light was on. Colette made coffee at a breakfast bar designed by Conran.

'From Chimanimani,' she announced. 'You'll never have tasted anything quite so aromatic.' She placed the mugs on a silver tray. 'Come. Let's take these upstairs.'

Danny watched her bottom jiggle up the stairs. Underneath sheer black Lycra, he could make out a white thong which clung to her firm cheeks like an illicit secret. Her T-shirt – tight, white – rode up to reveal a tanned back. She clearly kept herself in shape, and a number of self-portraits adorning the walls suggested self-obsession elevated into an art form.

'You'll make such a change from our usual,' she gushed, as she sat down on a creaking leather sofa in the living room. 'Most of our home help has tended to be blonde and Swedish. Female, too.' She gave a short laugh. 'Philippe may not warm to you immediately, but don't let that worry you. He's a bit of a stickler for tradition. And blondes.' She rolled her eyes. 'Anyway, tell me about yourself.'

The living room was home to everything but dust. Artful clutter abounded. The glass coffee table looked like something out of a museum, and the walls groaned under the combined weight of framed black-and-white photographs and multicoloured paintings. African carvings billowed on the mantelpiece; Venetian masks smirked on top of an ancient bureau. A grand piano occupied one corner. The *chaise-longue* looked like a frozen snake's tongue. There were mirrors everywhere, and the lighting was soft, the carpet softer.

At around four, the front door opened and an avalanche of noise erupted into the hall. The departing au pair — blonde, Swedish, and so beautiful that Danny ached in the knowledge that she'd always be someone else's girl — herded in the children, Viggo and Victoria, ten and seven. The Siamese cats, Tai and Chi, hovered around them, weaving in and out of legs, tails erect and quivering.

'Darlings,' said Colette, 'this is your new nanny. Say hello to Uncle Danny.'

Viggo fashioned his top lip into an Elvis sneer, while Victoria stared at her shoes. The Swedish slice of heaven stifled a giggle, and afforded Danny a withering look that contained a message he failed to understand.

'Can I go upstairs, please?' Viggo asked.

Colette ruffled his hair. 'Viggo is obsessed with computer games,' she told Danny. The child rushed off, but Victoria remained glued to her mother's side.

'I leave now,' said the Swede who, Danny noticed, Colette hadn't introduced. 'See you tomorrow.' Colette frowned as the girl went out.

She did not ask Danny for references. She listened to his life story, his experiences in America, and judged him perfect for her children. 'You have a good aura,' she told him.

His day began shortly after the daytime Australian soaps finished, mid-afternoon. It ended later and later each day, often not much before midnight. He'd arrive in Holland Park on foot, let himself in, then help himself to delicatessen meats and cheeses from the fridge. Next, he'd restore a bit of order to the children's rooms, then Beetle over to Bayswater to collect Victoria from school. Victoria always sat in the back of the car, and remained quiet, sucking her hair. Her day had been always either *good* or *fun*. It took only two days for Danny to be convinced that she was an angel. A smile from those cherubic features made his day.

Victoria was everything Viggo wasn't. Viggo, Danny decided, was hateful. His role on earth was to annoy, a teenager before his time. The Elvis sneer rarely left his lips. School angered him, non-animated television infuriated him, his sister, mother, father and nanny were poisoned thorns in his side. He loved the shock value of swear words. Everyone was a *fucker*, a *fucking wanker arsehole*, a *paedophile*. When Danny asked him what a paedophile was, exactly, Viggo would reply, with no little authority: 'A fucking wanker arsehole, *obviously*.' Viggo never had a good day at school. He was forever in trouble, and always angry that something had happened to spoil, as he once explained to Danny, my *eekilibiyum*. One afternoon, a concerned teacher took Danny aside in the car park and asked him whether Viggo had ever been diagnosed with ADD. 'Attention Deficit Disorder,' she explained, 'is actually quite common with the, um, children from more affluent families. Are his parents . . . *absent* a lot?'

Danny confirmed that this was indeed the case. The father was hardly ever at home, and when he was, he retreated into his study with paperwork and a bottle of vintage red. He believed strongly in discipline, but was rarely around to administer it personally. Instead, he left notes around the house for the children to learn by heart. These he would entitle RULES; parenting by proxy.

1. *Do not talk over whoever is speaking at the time.*
2. *Lights are to be turned off when leaving the room.*
3. *All laundry is to be taken down to the basement and placed in the laundry basket.*
4. *All homework assignments are to be completed before friends come over or television is watched.*
5. *You are to remain seated throughout all meals. Even if no adults are present.*
6. *During your homework, you are not allowed to be disruptive or loud. You must not fidget. However, between subjects you may take a short break with my permission, or from whoever is in charge at the time.*

7. You are to listen to whoever I've put in charge of you in my absence.
8. No answers will be given to questions to which you already know the response.
9. You must understand that if rules are broken there will be consequences.
10. When mistakes are made we can all learn from them.

His wife found the lists ridiculous, but she was out a lot too. Evenings would often find her at an 'exhibition' but in fact, as Danny soon learned, she was off with her lover.

While Victoria seemed happy enough to watch wildlife programmes on television, or read *Harry Potter*, with a cat on her lap, Viggo would storm around the house demanding attention. He'd bother his father in the study until the doctor sent his son, wailing, to his bedroom. When Viggo realised no one was going to console him, he'd march into the TV room and change channels to antagonise his sister. Danny, smack bang in the middle of this maelstrom, would attempt to bring order, but was ultimately helpless. Viggo's tantrums would continue until his father, shouting obscenities, stormed out of the house to drive endlessly around the block, like a dog chasing its tail.

So, yes, it was entirely likely that Viggo was suffering from ADD.

Danny became a stranger to the house in Shepherd's Bush. His new family took up almost all of his time. The money — cash in hand — was useful, not least as he continued drawing dole and housing benefit. Also, the sheer concentration it took to look after two children *and* their dysfunctional parents kept his mind occupied, which was exactly what he needed. He visited his mother in hospital three times a week, but otherwise, his waking hours were spent in Holland Park. He was forever exhausted, utterly drained, and when he went home he'd crawl upstairs to bed, and sink into sleep within seconds.

Routine had been reintroduced into his life. He was not *happy* exactly, but he was content, and contentment was all he craved just then.

Ten

'There is a level you should never allow yourself to fall beneath. I have fallen beneath it. Well beneath it. I'm a shameless whore, pond scum, the loser of all losers. Look at me – I look . . . Christ, I look *appalling*.'

Flox was standing by the bathroom sink, naked, oblivious to the cold. He was peering at his reflection in the mirror and talking to himself. With mounting desperation, he saw bloodshot eyes, pale skin, spots, erratic hair. He picked up the whisky bottle that was perched on the edge of the bath, and took a swig. It was dawn on a cold Friday morning and he had been home just two hours. He was getting ready for work. The night before he'd lost yet more money at the card table, and was now as close to broke, properly broke, as he'd ever been. Quite how he'd make the next repayment to the lone shark was something he had yet to work out. Due to his consistently bad behaviour on his temporary assignments, Flox had burned bridges at practically every agency, all of whom refused now to keep him on their books. So he'd been forced to get a regular full-time job.

He cleaned aeroplanes at Heathrow. Shifts lasted twelve hours a day, six days a week, irrespective of weekends, bank holidays, outside lives. Flox had been there just three weeks, but already it felt like a lifetime. He got up at five each morning, and was in an empty Piccadilly line train half an hour later. After two security checks, his day began at seven. A lunch hour was not permitted; instead, sandwiches were grabbed whenever it was convenient. There were six teams of seven, and everyone wore a purple-and-beige uniform that resembled an all-in-one romper-suit for the insane. His colleagues were mostly middle-aged Asian women and students, and they each worked their way through approximately thirty aeroplanes a day *ashing* – passing through the plane, removing rubbish and emptying the ashtrays of any in which smoking was still permitted. Speed was of the utmost importance – planes often landed, refuelled and took off again within forty minutes. It was terrible, mind-numbing work. But the worst part, for Flox, was cleaning the toilet cubicles. He was convinced that passengers pissed over the floor deliberately to upset him. Once he found shit smeared over the mirror, and was reprimanded because it took him more than fifteen minutes to hack it off with a plastic spatula. 'Chop-chop,' the group leader, a small Asian woman in her fifties, barked at him.

When they finished a plane, they convened in one of the airport buses to await the next arrival, which might come in thirty seconds or thirty minutes. Here, few people spoke. Instead, most caught up on sleep, or read a newspaper.

Flox merely scowled out of the window as the smell of aviation fuel turned his stomach. Inevitably, he learned of the presence of a dealer within the ranks who, after the shift, would lead him to a small, pebbledashed house in Hounslow and furnish him with whatever he could afford. He didn't yet turn up in the morning off his face – security was too tight for that – but he made sure that the long, lonely journey home flew by courtesy of some uppers.

Drunk, high, depressed as hell, Flox was in a bad way. And getting worse.

Eleven

Sanjay had good news, and wanted to celebrate. He had landed a part in a new play at the Lyric. His ambition for fame, which he'd harboured for so long, was now about to be realised.

Whenever Sanjay Kapoor called round, and he often did, his presence lent the house a kind of youthful glamour more associated with the silver screen. With just Flox and Danny in it, the place had all the seediness of a Tom Waits song; Sanjay gave it an air of exotica, as if Hanif Kureishi had suddenly shown up with a typewriter stuffed under his arm and semen on his lapel, with stories to tell. At just twenty-five, he was younger than Danny and Flox, and far more driven than either of them. It was as if success almost sought him out. He'd arrived in London from some dowdy suburb two years earlier, hungry for experience. Refusing to follow paternal footsteps into medicine, he was determined to become an actor. His rebellion – and an argument of epic Bollywood proportions – meant that he no longer spoke to his father but he maintained an intermittent telephone relationship with his doting mother who believed in him with the same faith her son did.

And Sanjay, indeed, was, destined for greatness.

A shining example of sensitive masculinity, he was exactly six feet tall, with thick black wavy hair, piercing brown eyes, a sharp nose, well-defined cheekbones and a mouth to which both men and women felt an irresistible pull. He wore Egoist, smoked cheroots and devoured literary fiction.

On arrival in London, he had moved into an Earl's Court youth hostel, and within a week had landed himself a job at a fashionable Japanese restaurant in Soho where he befriended several others who aspired to either the catwalk or the stage. The tips were plentiful enough to ensure that he could sustain himself without his father's help and he moved into the first of a succession of flatshares.

'For the experience,' he'd say. 'I want to meet people, *real* people, and to do that, you must live among them.' Sanjay had once read a biography of Laurence Olivier, and had been deeply affected by it.

In between waiting tables, he'd also appeared in countless fringe theatre productions and had had walk-on parts in several TV police and hospital dramas. His star was in the ascendant.

The play had attracted rave reviews when it opened a month earlier in a far smaller theatre in Slough, and the first night at the Lyric was already sold out. *Time Out* was due to attend, sitting alongside the *Guardian*, the *Independent*, the *Daily Telegraph* and, regrettably, the *Daily Mail*. Nevertheless, Sanjay was exultant. He'd already celebrated with the cast several nights earlier, and with friends from the restaurant he worked at during the day, but now he wanted to take out his two friends from next door.

'Come and see the play on our second night, Friday. I've got the weekend off, so we can hit the town afterwards – my treat.'

Danny was only too eager for a bit of escapism, and once he'd convinced his flatmate – who viewed Sanjay with barely disguised jealousy, envy and, consequently, hatred – Flox was too.

That Friday night both made an effort by dressing up, and during the interval, they bought tubs of vanilla ice-cream. When the curtain fell for the last time, almost a hundred minutes after it had first risen, they gave Sanjay a standing ovation.

'Not bad, not bad at all,' Flox was forced to concede backstage.

'You were brilliant, Sanjay,' added Danny. 'You had real presence.'

Sanjay blushed. Then, on a natural high, he dragged them out and into an awaiting taxi.

'Where are we going?' Danny asked, full of anticipation.

'A club I know.'

Flox watched from the window as London's West End came and went, the taxi leaving it all far behind. It continued on past Euston, then crawled up the Pentonville Road, prostitutes waiting at the kerb, left and right. Now, growing suspicious, he wanted to know exactly where this club was.

'We're almost there,' said Sanjay. 'Patience.'

The club, which was situated down a dark alley off the main street, and next door to a poisonous-looking kebab shop, was called Pop*Tartz*. Despite the early hour – it was barely ten thirty – there was already a large crowd waiting to get in, consisting mostly of young, muscular men all poured into tight bright T-shirts and clinging vinyl trousers whose job was to conceal nothing and accentuate everything.

Flox gawped. Then he shock his head. 'Oh, no, no way. Sorry. I'm not going in there. Not my scene, I'm afraid.'

'Oh, come on,' said Sanjay. 'Don't be a spoilsport.'

'Absolutely not,' he said, both hands raised. 'Look, if you're bisexual, as you always claim to be, why can't we just go to a straight club?'

'This *is* a straight club.' Sanjay indicated the crowd, which he now saw was full of biceps, tattoos and testosterone. 'Well, okay,' he conceded, 'it's both. But I promise you, you'll love it.'

Danny grabbed one of Flox's arms, Sanjay the other, and together they dragged him forward. Courtesy of one of the young actor's friends on the door, all three were allowed to jump the queue and go straight in. Inside, it was dark and hot. Sweat was pouring off the walls, and everyone was in a state of undress. The music was hard and fast, a throbbing, pulsating, hi-energy techno that made diaphragms vibrate. Flox did a full 360, but all he could see was uncomfortably attractive young men with their abs on display. Sanjay disappeared, and returned a few minutes later with three bottles of beer. He leaned close to Flox's ear and shouted, 'Come with me.'

Upstairs, kitsch music from the eighties tumbled from the speakers. Everyone was singing along at the top of their voices, but the atmosphere was brighter and less overtly gay. And, to Flox's relief, there were several women, all gorgeous, all gyrating wildly, in tiny hotpants and patterned bikini tops. He allowed himself to relax, and soon located his initial prey. He zoomed in, handed over sixty pounds in crumpled tens, and came away with a greedy smile and a new currency in his hands.

They danced deep into the night, Sanjay attracting the lion's share of attention, both male and female. Flox was lost in his own personal rhythm, and everyone on the dance-floor gave him a wide berth as he pirouetted about enthusiastically.

Trouble only flared much later.

Danny's watch appeared to be sweating, and the cloudy glass front refused to reveal the time. He thought it must be close to four. He'd been dancing for hours, and his muscles were screaming for mercy. He found himself a free corner, and slumped down in a crouch, clutching his knees to his chest. The floor beneath him was sticky and the seat of his trousers stuck to it. The club was still fairly full, but the dance-floor was emptier now. People had coupled off with one another and were dotted around the perimeter, all locked in an embrace. Eventually, craning his neck, he spotted Sanjay, who was in the middle of a clinch with a woman who, from behind, looked quite stunning: slim and tall, her hair tied up in tiny bunches. She was wearing a denim bra and a short skirt that rode up to her hips, allowing everyone a glimpse of her shimmering gold thong. Beads of sweat trailed down her tanned back, and Danny watched with a mixture of hunger and envy. Flox was still dominating the floor, persisting with his bizarre dance.

Someone approached Danny and asked, over the music, if he had a light. Danny shook his head, but the man – big, bald, with eyes like pistons, and dressed in leather chaps – sat down beside him, his giant calf muscle touching Danny's. He tried to spark up conversation like a damp match striving to light.

'Look, I'm not interested,' Danny said, into a large studded ear. The man shrugged, and moved on. Danny closed his eyes and allowed the music to rock him back and forth.

Suddenly, he heard a shout, a girl's name – Sharon or Shirley. Maybe Shelley. Danny looked up and saw a young man of average height bustle through the crowds, pushing people out of his way. He was wearing a suit and a mac flecked with raindrops. His hair was soaked, and his face was the face of someone drunk and angry. He shouted the name again – Shelley – then located her. Anger turned to rage, and his cheeks reddened. Seconds later he was tearing her away from Sanjay. She tripped over his feet and fell, legs in the air. Instinctively, Sanjay tried to break her fall, but was stopped short by the man, who blocked his path with an outstretched hand. He jerked his head forward and caught Sanjay on the cheek, just below the right eye. The skin broke, and blood poured down his face. Then the man grabbed him by the neck and thrust him up against the wall. The music was still pounding, but everyone had stopped dancing to watch the unfolding commotion. Meanwhile,

Shelley had staggered to her feet and now jumped on to her boyfriend's back, screaming at him, then grabbed his hair and pulled it. Sanjay looked stricken – he was a lover, not a fighter. He held up his hands to his face, desperate to prevent any further damage, or his understudy would have to take his place on Monday night.

Even from across the floor, Danny could see that he was trembling. But before he could get across to protect his friend, someone else was intervening. Flox had a crazed look about him as he separated hunter from prey. He punched the boyfriend square in the face, and followed that with a sharp headbutt, and a knee to the groin. The man slumped to the floor. Seconds later, before Flox could do further damage, he was manhandled out of the club by two large bouncers, who deposited him on the wet pavement outside. Danny and Sanjay, still trembling, pulled on their jackets and followed.

'Are you all right?' Sanjay asked worriedly. 'I'm so sorry.' He explained that Shelley had told him she'd split up with her boyfriend, but not that it had happened only an hour earlier. 'Are you hurt? Oh, God, I'm really sorry.'

Flox got to his feet and gave a loud whoop. 'This is turning out to be a terrific night,' he said, checking his watch. It was a little after five. 'Come on, let's go get ourselves some breakfast. I'm ravenous.'

They took a cab back to Hammersmith where Flox knew of a lorry-drivers' pub that opened early and offered London's largest feed for a fiver. Still reeling with adrenaline, all three delved into large platters of fried everything. Flox swept back his long hair to reveal the blossoming bruise that had felled the suit, and Sanjay began to feel proud of his own wound.

'Been years since I had a proper scrap,' Flox said. 'Shame he didn't put up a bit of a struggle.' He pointed a fork at Sanjay. 'But I'm proud of you, Sanj, she was absolutely gorgeous. You're not totally bent, then?'

Sanjay allowed a sheepish grin to spread across his face. Great drama practice, he thought.

After walking off breakfast around Shepherd's Bush market, they decided to go swimming at White City, and bought trunks and goggles there with the tickets. Breaststroke was an effort on full stomachs, but when the wave machine kicked in, Sanjay's stomach flipped and he vomited into the water. Several hours later, over a pub lunch and more beer, Flox was still in tears of laughter over their ejection from the pool and the lifetime ban imposed on them by the duty manager.

'It's really not funny,' insisted Sanjay.

At Flox's insistence, they made their way to Stamford Bridge to watch the football, bought some ridiculously priced tickets from a toad-like tout, then took their seats behind one of the goals.

'I can't see a thing,' Sanjay complained. He had never been to a match in his life. While he claimed to detest football, by half-time he had conceded to a more than passing attraction for the many Italian players dressed in blue. 'Massive thighs,' he noted. Flox and Danny spent their time cheering and singing, and they all staggered out high on a euphoric sense of victory.

'A drink, I think,' said Flox.

Later that evening, now almost thirty-six hours without sleep and after a large Indian meal that turned their stomachs into poisonous wind machines, they dragged their feet along some patches of wet grass in a park they'd never previously visited. In fact, they weren't even sure what part of London they were in. All that was clear was that it was dark, as cold as January, and home seemed a long way off. Flox farted voluminously. Each man was somewhere between catatonic drunkenness and chronic hangover; either way, they were nowhere near sober, but the night air was crisp and sharp, and kept their battered senses alert. At one point Flox stumbled on a large rock, then stooped to pick it up. He cradled it in his hand, somehow reassured by its weight. An idea sprang to mind.

Presently they found themselves in a quiet street lined with trees, discreet semi-detached houses, and new hatchback cars from Scandinavia, most of which had flashing alarm signals on the dashboard. Flox peered into each and eventually found one without a blinking light. He measured the weight of the rock in his hand, then threw it at the passenger-seat window. The sound of shattering glass filled the quiet night. He opened the door, and ordered the other two to get in. Stunned, they did as they were told and Flox fiddled with some wires under the steering-wheel. Sparks flew, the engine turned over, and they were out on the main road, the speedometer needle racing towards fifty. As they turned sharply on a roundabout, Flox let out an almighty warrior cry, laughing so hard that saliva flew from his mouth on to the windscreen.

Sanjay and Danny, in the back, exchanged a look that would have been filled with even more horror had they not been so intoxicated. Then the police siren wailed.

Flox thrust all his upper body weight into a right turn, and accelerated. Danny turned to look out of the back window. Nothing, the coast was clear. But relief lasted less than a second as blue neon flashed aggressively into view.

'Shit! Flox, get us the fuck out of here!'

Sanjay caught Flox's gaze in the rear-view mirror: his friend's eyes were wide and he was grinning with pure exhilaration. A bus was approaching, filled with Saturday-night stragglers. Immediately Flox swerved into its path. The bus lurched and changed lanes. More horns blared. Lights went on in bedrooms up and down the street, but Flox hung another left, powered down the sleepy road and pulled up sharply in a small cul-de-sac.

'Out!' he roared.

Three doors flew open and they all ran, two sheep following their lunatic leader. They raced down a little path lined with shrubbery, which led them out to another quiet road and then on to the main road. Here, they slowed to a walk. The bus was still there, its emergency lights on, the driver hunched over the steering-wheel, shaking his head. The police car was nowhere to be seen. Flox jogged over to the bus doors, rapped his knuckles on the glass, and put both hands together as if in prayer. Reluctantly, the driver opened the doors, and three young men, all flushed and sweating, paid their fares, went upstairs and sat down. Opting for caution, they stayed on the bus till the end of the line, then took a mini-cab home.

* * *

The next morning, Sanjay called round and joined them, cautiously, for coffee. All three sat in the freezing kitchen, teeth chattering.

'So,' began Flox. 'Did we have fun last night, or what?'

The others exchanged loaded glances. Sanjay spoke first. 'Look at my *face*!' he said. 'The director's going to kill me when he sees this.' He pointed to the plaster that sat high on his cheek.

Flox shrugged. 'Big deal,' he said. 'There's nothing wrong with a few war wounds. Think of it as a souvenir of a great night out.' He changed tack. 'Anyway, we still have the whole of today to fill. What shall we do?'

Sanjay shook his head. 'Sorry, you'll have to count me out. It's too dangerous, and I've got too much at stake right now. Last night was wrong. We could have been in serious trouble.'

Danny concurred. 'He does have a point, Flox. You know, joyriding and all that.'

Flox shrugged again. 'Fun though, wasn't it?'

Danny and Sanjay smiled. 'Yes,' said the actor. 'Too much.'

After Sanjay had returned home to attempt to minimise the gash on his face with makeup, Flox and Danny went out on a pub crawl, beginning at an ancient hostelry in Chiswick and working their way along the Thames towards the centre of town. With each new drink, the gloom that hovered around Flox's shoulders descended. This kind of depression was not unusual in him, and when it hit, it hit bad. Anyone in his company suffered from the fallout, and today that dubious honour fell to Danny, who felt like an unpaid psychiatrist.

Flox's dream, he argued, was a simple one. 'What I don't understand is, *why*? Why hasn't it happened to me? What is so different from me and whoever happens to be on *Top of the Pops* or at the local cinema this Friday? That's what I want to know.' The stars of today, according to Flox, were not like they used to be a generation earlier. Back then, stars were born with star quality intact, the kind of glamour you didn't develop but possessed naturally. 'Look at Cary Grant, Grace Kelly, Dean Martin,' he said. 'They were *never* ordinary people. They were *special*. But these days practically everyone has access to celebrity, even if it's just for fifteen minutes.' He named several current boy bands. 'It's easy to be famous – all you need is a haircut, an accent, false tits. Even the decent ones – people like Robert Carlyle, Tim Roth, Liam Gallagher – they may have talent, but they are still fundamentally *ordinary* people. They are *attainable*. Just like you and me. Only we're on this side of the fence, the wrong side. Why can't I jump over? How come they've managed to make their mark, and I haven't?'

At the next pub, he revisited the theme.

'Aside for my time in America, which would have been perfect if . . . Well, anyway, aside from that, the most fun I've had in years was last night. Do you realise that? And do you want to know why? *Danger*, that's why. Things could have turned really nasty there, and I loved every second of it. It made me feel . . . *alive*.'

Danny sighed heavily and looked at the clock above Flox's head. It was late.

Eventually they abandoned the pub crawl to attend to the insistent rumbling of their stomachs. They took a cab back across town and went into a cheap, bustling Cantonese restaurant in Acton, where they made their way through a variety of meat dishes that came coated in a Dayglo gluey sauce. Flox was still dominating the conversation, his monologue revolving around the redeeming wonders of danger. Between great mouthfuls of food, he was suggesting that the pair of them indulge in danger together, the implication being that Danny's life, too, could do with a little injection of excitement.

'Look, last night we were a great team,' he said, urgently. 'Sanjay was hopeless, a wet blanket, but then Sanjay is Sanjay. But you and me, we were perfect, completely on top of it. And that was without preparation, either. We just winged it in perfect synchronicity. Doesn't that tell you anything? It tells us that we *are* a great team – that we could do anything.'

Danny was tired. 'Right, Flox, whatever you say.' He ordered another beer.

'No, I'm serious!' Flox insisted, and reeled off several suggestions. They could dabble in some more joyriding, for example. They could rob the local post office where the elderly couple behind the counter were almost comically dozy. They could attempt a little Internet crime, as long as someone taught them how. They could go on shoplifting sprees, timeshare scams, burglary. Entrapment. Kidnapping.

'Kidnapping?' Danny had gone off his food, and pushed his plate to one side.

Suddenly, any hint of levity left Flox's voice, and

he became increasingly grave, then tetchy, irritated that his flatmate wasn't taking him seriously. Which was ridiculous, because Flox was deadly serious.

'Yes, kidnapping.' He endeavoured to explain.

Twenty minutes later, they were at the tube station, pacing around the open-air platform. It was dark, close to midnight. A night-time freeze was creeping in, around ankles, up spines. Danny shivered. Flox droned on.

'Yes, kidnapping. Think about it. We could do it so, so easily. We kidnap your kids, bring them back home, and demand money with menaces. From what you've told me, the parents are so loaded and screwed up that they'd pay immediately, if only to avoid any drawn-out hassle. They'd probably blame themselves for it, for not being around more, and for not being proper parents. They pay, they get their kids back, and we get rich and disappear. Simple.'

Danny shook his head, and walked off briskly towards the end of the platform. Flox caught up with him, pulling him back by the shoulder. 'Look, obviously we'd plan it thoroughly, but I'm convinced it could be done – and that we'd get away with it. You never know, it might even do them a bit of good, make them better parents. And, let's face it, those poor kids deserve better parents.'

He was like a terrier with lockjaw. He wouldn't give up. He kept on blabbering away, his words smacking against one another like dead fish, coming up with more reasons why it would work, why they should do it, and what they'd do with the money afterwards. Clearly fuelled by the staggering amount of alcohol he'd consumed in the last forty-eight hours, his words sounded to him like pure logic, and he wasn't going to stop until he had made Danny see sense, see reason — *agree*.

But, right now, all Danny saw was a mounting rage. Drink swam around his head and sloshed inside his stomach. He looked past Flox and saw the other commuters dotted around the platform. According to the announcement board there were still eleven minutes to go before the arrival of the next tube. Underneath this, he saw a tramp walking close to the edge, muttering to himself. Elsewhere, couples hung on to each other for warmth, and single travellers read books under striplight. The minutes clicked by in anything but sixty-second spans. Seven minutes until the next tube, then six, a figure it appeared to stick on. Five took an age to arrive, four even longer. And still his drunken friend talked on. Danny could smell his breath — sweet and sour, soy sauce, beer. Rancid.

Something inside him broke. 'Right, that's it!' He grabbed Flox by the lapels of his jacket, pulled hard, and shouted directly into his face: 'Drop it now! Shut the fuck up! You're insane — and you're pathetic.'

He let go, and tried to create distance between them, but Flox blocked him. Danny pushed at him, and was pushed back. Then, with a firm, open palm, Danny hit Flox on the shoulder and propelled him sideways. With a clear route ahead, he started to run. This wasn't easy, because with all the alcohol his vision was distorted and he wove an erratic path. The tramp stopped and staggered to the right. He tilted his head back and appeared to drink from a brown paper bag. Danny tried to veer round him, but too little and too late. They collided. He heard the tramp say something beneath his beard, and there was a muffled grunt, but he carried on running. The faces in front of him now looked his way, and in every one Danny read fear, panic, shock. He chanced a look over his shoulder and saw two images: the tramp falling towards the train tracks, and Flox racing after him, his mouth twisted in either an ugly grin or a howl of pain. Everything inside him told Danny to stop, turn around and offer help, but he ran faster and faster, without knowing why. Blind panic? Flox hollered behind him, another of his war cries. Tears streamed down his face.

At the top of the stairs were the ticket barriers. Instinctively, Danny hurdled them. Half-way over, his foot snagged on something, and his trajectory came to a prompt halt. He fell to the ground with a sharp thud, felt pain lance his nose. Over his shoulder, he watched Flox hurdle the barrier with ease, screaming like Tarzan, then run out of the station. Danny scrambled up and followed. Once outside on the street, he watched Flox go one way, so he went another, and carried on running, two guilty men swallowed up by the complicitous cloak of night.

Twelve

Excerpts from a diary

Monday 7 March
Been here one week now, and am having the best time. France is rilly French, just like the movies (French movies). Checked into a nice hotel right in the center so that I feel in the thick of things. As of today, I'm on a diet to complement my new hairstyle and new outlook on life. I'm also completely off the drugs and I will have no more than one glass of wine a day – okay, maybe two, but no more. This is the new me. I'm changing for the better! Tomorrow I go to the doctor to have these damn silicon sacs removed. Help! I hate my boobs!

Tuesday 8 March
The doctor was 2 die 4!! So suave, so sophisticated! I was lucky to get an appointment this quick, but I think my desperation helped (I wish it was my fame, but nobody in this damn town seems to know who in the hell I am!). He (his name is Henri Dupont) was busy

for weeks, but when I showed up in person at the end of last week at his surgery with tears streaming down my pretty little face, he obviously knew that this was an emergency case, and so he made an exception and squeezed me in. I was so grateful (but not like that!). He took me into his office and I explained to him that I wanted a breast reduction. He looked at my chest area and asked me, in a deeply sexy accent – he has a wedding band on his finger, shame!!! – why, because they looked all right to him. How sweet! Anyway, I told him everything – especially about Helena's reaction – and he nodded as if he understood perfectly. Then he asked me if he could see them, my boobs, that is. I think I went a bit red in the face (he was so handsome and I guess I haven't had a boyfriend in such a long time) and slowly, maybe even provocatively, I undid the buttons on my silk chemise. Luckily, I had on my best Victoria's Secret – red lace balconette, front-loader. I undid it and they just kinda stood there, as if to attention. As I looked down at them, it was like I saw them with Helena's eyes for the first time. Hey, like all girls, I'd like firm boobs, but this was ridiculous. They do look stupid, and sooo fake. Plates with nipples! At that moment, I wanted my old boobs back more than ever, no matter what size. Henri was sweet about it. He placed his warm and masculine hands (hairy but fortunately not on palms!) on each and felt the silicone. I could feel it moving around inside me. Ew. Oddly, the experience wasn't even slightly erotic ... perhaps because they were to me now sooo fake? He said that the surgeon had done a good job, but that if I wanted the silicone removed then he could do it for me real easy and that my boobs (but he called them breasts, naturally) would return to their original state and no one would ever be able to tell they'd been messed around with in the first place. (The scars — tiny ones — will be under my armpits. Maybe I'll stop shaving, like Julia?) I was so grateful and relieved when I heard him say that, I burst into tears again!

So anyway, he booked me in for an appointment next week — which is now today. I'm writing this is my private hospital bed in recovery — and guess what? I feel fine! MESSAGE TO BANK ACCOUNT: this operation was rilly expensive, so the moral of the story is, I guess, don't interfere with nature. Its cheaper! But whatever, I'm so glad they're back to normal. Breast is best! At least, I hope they're back to normal. At the moment, I've got thick bandages around my entire chest area. Its pretty sore actually, kinda like a couple of bad bruises, but the doctor told me to expect this and not to worry. The pain would go in a few days. I only came round about half an hour ago, and I still feel kinda dizzy. Henri told me that everything went perfectly, and that I should now spend one night here to fully recover. Which is fine by me, because this place is almost as fabulous as my hotel: TV, hi-fi, room service, the lot! He has a lovely bedside manner, Henri. I wish he was my gynaecologist! (That was a bit gross — I blame the prescription drugs!!)

I'm going to sleep a bit now. Will write more soon ...

Midnight: I've just woken up, and I'm still here in the room. It's dark and quiet around here now. I feel a bit better, I think, but I've been suddenly hit by this huge depression. I'm in a foreign country, in a strange city, and I'm all alone.

Sunday 20 March
Today I went to see a double bill at the movie theater. They were playing two old movies called Jean De Florette and Manon Des Sources. The second one had Emmanuelle Beart in it who became famous in Mission Impossible with Tom Cruise. She actually is French! Both movies were unbelievably beautiful — I cried and I cried, especially when Gerard Depardieu died. He was awesome — I never thought I'd find a hunchback sexy, but I did. Afterwards, I felt kinda low because they were both much better than any movie I've ever been in, even The Girl Who Dreamed. They had a simplicity to them, I guess a kind of realness that my movies — in fact, any Hollywood movies — always seem to lack. While I've been making silly little popcorn pictures, Gerard Depardieu and Emmanuelle Beart have been making proper art. Why can't I be a French actress?

 On the subject of art, I've been to lots of galleries and museums. Only some of them were boring. Most, like the Louvre, were really ... engrossing. Also I've been reading novels, which I haven't done since I can't remember when. I found a small second-hand bookshop that has American editions, which was a major relief for me — 1, because, obviously, I don't speak or read French, and, 2, I've been kinda lonesome recently and I need something to occupy my mind. I'm always on my own, and I've never much been on my own before. Although, I must say, I have had a lot of offers from

Spin Cycle

French men. In fact, they never leave me alone and are very persistent! There's a couple of bellboys at the hotel who are always making eyes at me and bringing room service even when I didn't order it. Maybe they think I need company ... which might be true (if I'm completely honest, dear Diary). There is also the head waiter at L'Escargot, a few of the taxi drivers outside the hotel (who always smell of nicotine and garlic), the guy at the café with the pencil mustache, the grocer with the beret, and a whole bunch of guys at the swimming pool and sauna — which is segregated (unfortunately). Although I'm very flattered, none of them seem to actually recognize me. They just see a pretty face — which I guess is all right by me (maybe I just miss being famous?). I have yet to take any of them up on their offers because I think I do need to be on my own for a while, until I get my head straight. Being alone is good for you, it's good for the soul. Soul food. Emmanuelle Beart was on her own in Manon Des Sources, if you don't count the goats, and she was all right, wasn't she? And that book by that guy, 100 Years of Solitude — everyone agrees that solitude can be good.

So, yes, being by myself is a very positive thing. I go for long walks through this beautiful city and I try to sort out the mess in my head. Like: where am I going? What do I want to do with my life? Diary, I think I'm making progress. I haven't cried for almost a week, I don't even crave the drugs anymore (much), and my boobs are back to normal and I'm very happy with them. Does this mean I'm actually content?

I just wish I had a dog or something. Y'know, something to cuddle, something to cuddle me back.

Wednesday 27 March
Dear Diary: when did life get so complicated? I think I may be going out of my mind. I'm, like, sooo lonely. I feel more alone than I ever have in my entire life. Last night I made a big mistake and I regret it now. Last night, I made myself up for a night on the tiles. I had the longest bath (nice 'n' hot 'n' fragrant) then I put on my new black Donna Karan, my new pumps and my new leather jacket. I looked swish, très European. And then, dressed to kill, I went out to L'Escargot (which I later discovered actually means snail — ew!). Within what could only have been a matter of minutes — I'm not kidding! — this completely amazing looking guy approached me at the bar and asked if he could buy me a drink. He asked me in French, which flattered me, and when I told him I was American, a light appeared in his eyes and he was hooked. (I could tell.) Before long, we were sharing a bottle of champagne — Veuve Cliqòt, I think. Very expensive, real nice. The table had a candle on it, and he got a passing waiter to light it.

Description: tall, dark and handsome, his skin the color of a deep tan. He wore a beautiful suit, leather shoes, and had a huge Rolex on his right wrist — not the left one, which intrigued me somehow. Age? I don't know ... I never asked (too polite), but I'm guessing he was maybe 40. But he looked great on it — like Warren before Annette. After the second glass of bubbly, I got to asking him why he was here on his own. And, boy, did he have a sad story to tell! He'd just discovered, like a couple of days before, that his wife had been cheating on him. He thought that it – their marriage – was over.

Maybe fate was bringing us together.

He'd moved to Paris from the south 5 years before, but had spent a couple of years in America when he was younger – which is why he speaks English so good (not to mention a sexy accent into the bargain). We talked a while longer, then moved to a table and had the most amazing dinner, which he insisted on paying for. He works in oil, so he is rilly rich. Afterwards, he took me to this amazing bar in Montmartre where they serve ancient wine from these peculiarly shaped bottles. In the corner of the room, there was a concertina player. I'm not kidding, this guy must have been about 100, but he played like an angel, and he even dedicated a song to us. Me and Patric (that was his name – my boyfriend, not the concertina player!) were sitting at a corner table, holding hands, telling each other about our lives, and then we started necking. I felt like a teenager all over again!!

Anyway, long story short, we ended up back at his place – which only happened to be the most incredible apartment I have ever seen in my entire life! It has all these narrow corridors with enormous rooms behind them, filled with antique furniture (one writing bureau he showed me dates back to 1962!!). He has great taste in furniture and decoration ... I wonder whether he does his own interior design? I guess I must have been quite drunk by then, because all my usual inhibitions just disappeared and left me. Diary, we had a bath together! Seriously! Before we'd even, you know, touched each other, we were there in this huge tub, completely naked, with bubbles everywhere. I scrubbed his back and he washed my hair, and pretty soon we were kissing each other's faces and drinking more champagne. Diary, I have never had foreplay like it – it was incredible! Then, he took me into the master bedroom (master!) which, naturally enough, had a giant four-poster bed in it with satin sheets ... and we made sweet beautiful love for almost 2 hrs 45 minutes. (He loved my boobs!)

I came 4 times – 4!!!

And then I slept the sleep of angels.

Okay, so I know I can get a little presumptuous at times, but by morning I was convinced that this was it – I was in love! I mean, we were just so good together, the evening and the night being totally perfect. When I told him I was an actress (he hadn't seen any of my movies, and he rarely watched television but I didn't mind), we had this wonderful conversation about the le cinema, and I told him just how much I love French movies and French actors – Gerard Depardieu and Emmanuelle Beart especially. I have never been able to talk to someone with such ease and have such fantastic sex with them before. Back home, if I can talk to someone in an honest way, they turn out to be gay (example: Rupert), and if we just have fantastic sex, they turn out to be assholes the next day (example: Charlie). But this ... this was special.

After we had both showered we went out for breakfast

to this amazing little cafe in Montparnasse. He knows the best places! And we held hands the whole time over croissants and café au lait. Our conversation was, if anything, even better and more intimate than the night before. In fact, everything was going perfectly ... too perfectly as it turned out.

After breakfast, we were walking through a park nearby, his arm around my shoulder, mine around his trim waist, when all of a sudden this little melody sounded: his cellphone. Still holding on to me, he said, 'Oui' into the voice bit, and then his face went all serious. He actually let go of me and walked away for I guess some privacy. Well, I didn't know what to do, so I just put my hands in my pockets and took in the view, trying to look casual. A young couple passed me, and I think they recognized me. They kinda looked twice as if they were sure and unsure at the same time, and I watched them look back at me a couple of times. I even waved, trying to lighten the sudden awkward atmosphere that had descended all around me. I even hoped that maybe they would ask for my autograph, just so Patric would see. But he was still too involved in his phone call. His expression was very serious. When I looked at him again, what I saw took me completely by shock and surprise. Patric had tears in his eyes: he was crying! Then he shook his head, and it looked like every word he spoke hurt him right in his heart. It was bad news, I just knew it — I have a sixth sense about these things. So I walked off a little, towards a small lake or pond, and I sat down on one of the cold metal chairs there. I watched some small birds — sparrows maybe — sit on the concrete rim of the pond and dip their beaks quickly in and out of the water, drinking. It was so cute, but it also somehow made me feel like crying. There were lots of them, about 10, and they all huddled together for warmth. They were all friends, they looked out for one another. Patric was too busy on his cellphone to look out for me, despite everything that happened last night.

After maybe as much as 15 minutes, Patric came up and sat beside me on one of the other cold metal chairs. He drew it close, and put both of his hands on mine, which were in my lap. I looked at his fingernails, which were manicured and very elegant. I was too scared to look at him in the face, so I kept on watching the birds drinking. I counted them and discovered that there were only 8. Perhaps 2 flew away? And then Patric started talking — for a long time.

Long story short, that was his wife who called. Apparently, she was very sorry for what she had done. It had only happened a few times, she told him, and it was a huge mistake. She wanted him back, for them to try again — if only for the sake of the children. He never told me he had children ... but then he was virtually a stranger to me, as I was beginning to belatedly realize. Then it was like he swallowed a truth pill or something, because everything came out. He told me that he himself had hardly been faithful to her either recently. The apartment was his city place, where he had taken several women over the last 2 years. Their marriage had hit problems when his wife had miscarried their 4th child, he said, and both had sought comfort from the constant arguing in the arms of strangers. But him leaving the family house had been too much, and now she desperately wanted him back. Turns out, he wanted her too, so he had to go. For him, his wife, the children. Tears rolled down his cheeks. He looked so beautiful and so open. He was giving to me, and I could feel his pain. Yes, Diary, I was hurt, but I could relate. He asked me if I understood, and naturally I told him I did. I encouraged him to return home, even though at that very moment my earlier suspicions were now confirmed: I was sooo in love with him.

Anyway, he thanked me for my understanding and told me he'd never forget me. He also said that I hadn't been like the other girls, but special somehow – and, Diary, I choose to believe him. He even said he'd watch out for one of my films on television, which was sweet of him (I recommended The Girl Who Dreamed). Then he kissed me on both cheeks, French style, and walked off in one direction while I walked in the other, which was very cinematic I think. Although I wanted to, I didn't look back. I probably wouldn't have seen him anyway, because all the crying I was doing blurred my vision.

It is now 3 hours later and I'm back in the hotel, alone again on my double bed. I know it was only 1 night and supposed to be just a bit of fun, but I already miss him so much and I feel so lonely without him. I can still feel him inside me, still smell his scent on my fingers, still feel that sense of possibility about him and me as a couple. But whether I like it or not, the man is history, a memory, an opportunity *for happiness I will now never be able to lay proper claim to.*

Letter home

Dear Mom,
Greetings from Paris, France! I'm having a wonderful time here in Europe! The hotel I'm staying at is called Le Parc, which is French for The Park but it's nothing like the one in Beverly Hills (this one is far more grand). It has a swimming-pool, health spa, jacuzzi and steam room. I feel very pampered!

It's rilly (joke spelling) great to be away from the industry. No one here knows me – or if they do they don't say anything, which is fine by me. Just like ~~Katherine~~ Audrey Hepburn in Roman Holiday with Gregory Peck I've had my hair cut so that now I'm virtually unrecognizable. I feel like a new woman. And no, Mom, I haven't met any men just yet, but to be honest I'm not even looking at the moment. I think I need some time to reflect on life all on my own and by myself (can you tell I've had therapy?!). But oh horror! I'm 29 yrs old! I'd better find myself a husband soon. Maybe I can find somebody like Gerard Depardieu (only without the fat!). Y'know, someone handsome and chivalrus (correct spelling?) and debonair and with that amazingly sexy accent!

And how are you? I hope you're well and that the new man in your life is making you happy – you deserve it, Mom. And hey – I forgot to ask you when we were on the phone – is Sundance still alive? I feel so guilty that I didn't ask before. I guess I just took it for granted because Sundance has been around for ever. Tell him hi and that I miss him so.

Mom, I miss you tons! I'm sooo glad we spoke recently – I rilly miss your voice. And I can never apologize enough for losing contact with you the way I did. I think I just needed time to make something of myself without my parents, if that makes any sense. Maybe it was my rebellious time?? I enjoyed Hollywood and I hope you're proud of what I achieved there. But although I have had some success, I've recently had the bad feeling that my time has come and gone – my 15 minutes, as Andy Warhol would say.

Oh, Mom, what am I going to do with my life? Part of me wants to go back to Hollywood – maybe I could produce?? or just hustle harder?? – but another part wants some space to think it all over and consider doing something completely different instead. Who knows? I guess that's why I'm here – to figure things out. Whatever I choose to do, I promise this time to stay in touch.

Anyway, enough of my kveching. As I write, it's approaching 2 in the afternoon. I'm on my hotel-room balcony with the roar of traffic below. After I sign off here, I will write a few words to Pops, then I'll go to the post office to buy a couple of stamps that will take both letters all across the Atlantic to my beloved parents. Then I will find a small romantic cafe (the city's full of them!), and drink French coffee while reading a book and thinking deep thoughts, just like a true American in Paris.

Mom, much love to you and to your new man. I love

you lots and hope to see you real soon. And a big woof to Sundance!
   Bye for now!
   Love,
   Malory (Alicia)
   xoxoxoxoxoxoxoxo!!

After posting her letter, Malory crossed the yawning road, full of afternoon traffic speeding every which way, and took a seat at her regular café. She ordered frothy coffee, pronouncing it *café oo lait*, much to the waiter's wry amusement, and flicked through a second-hand paperback she'd bought a few days earlier. When the waiter arrived with her order twenty minutes later, he silently offered her his handkerchief. It was still too early in the season for hay fever, regardless of her protests. And, anyway, he'd seen it all before. They were real tears, and hers was clearly a depression that no amount of nose-blowing would alleviate.

Thir—

Malory Cinnamon is a very superstitious lady, especially at this crucial time in her life. There is no Chapter Thir—.

Fourteen

Independently, they both decided not to mention the tragic incident with the tramp. Because they had heard no news reports about the death – or was it murder? – Flox was sure that there was nothing to worry about, and that they had had a lucky escape. Anyway, he said, during their only argument on the subject, who said he had to have died? From platform to rails wasn't much of a fall, after all, and he'd probably only sprained an ankle. Danny wondered momentarily whether it was worth explaining the concept of electrocution to him, but decided against it. Danny himself, as the one who had made contact, was plagued with a guilt that never lifted. At night, he suffered horrific nightmares, and during waking hours he felt he should be seeking forgiveness from someone. But who? Certainly not a priest, and he could hardly burden his mother with it. Instead, he reminded himself that it had been an accident, and endeavoured to throw himself into work with a gusto that would keep him as occupied as he could reasonably hope.

And this, luckily, was easy, because in addition to Viggo and Victoria, he now had to look after Cinjun, a friend of Viggo's. Cinjun was almost eleven, and had hair so blond and fine it was almost white. Unless the imminent arrival of puberty was planning to ravage his cherubic features, he had a face that would one day make his fortune. Disarmingly cute, he was a DiCaprio in waiting. Unfortunately, he was only too aware of this and, as the only child of a wealthy couple who had made their fortune in architecture and design, he was heavily pampered and obscenely precocious. He could flash a grin so smug and self-satisfied that Danny often fantasised about smacking it clean off his face. Cinjun was his responsibility three times a week, when the mother was otherwise engaged, from Tuesday through Thursday. Danny picked him up from a private school in Hampstead mid-afternoon, then made a quick, often reckless dash back west to collect his other two charges, who were waiting impatiently for him at the gate. After a quick stop at Falafel King – both sets of parents loathed McDonald's – it was back to Holland Park where the two boys would disappear up into the bedroom to annihilate one another via joysticks for the next couple of hours, while Victoria tended her doll collection and read them stories. When either Philippe or Colette returned, Danny was required to wrestle Cinjun from the computer and drag him, kicking and screaming, home to his parents.

Meanwhile, relations between Philippe and Colette had taken a further turn for the worse. Colette was now openly parading her boyfriend in the family home, claiming that he was merely a student who required extra tuition.

Philippe's response was always the same: he'd tuck a bottle of red under his arm and take himself into the study, slamming the door. At this point Colette and her beau would disappear into the master bedroom for a quiet hour, which was often anything but. During this time, Victoria seemed to retreat into herself even more, her only defence in an increasingly mad and hostile world, while Viggo attacked Danny with bunched-up fists, screaming blue murder. After he'd exhausted himself, he'd often sit down by the telephone and call 'Auntie' Alison – a family friend Danny had met several times – in need of a sympathetic, quasi-maternal ear. Alison was a small woman, neat, homely, and in her early forties, with one grown-up child. She'd known Colette for years, and both children were very fond of her. Viggo was always on his best behaviour with her, and she lulled him into calm over the telephone on many an evening. When he hung up he resumed giving hell to his nanny. On nights like these, Colette would pass Danny an extra twenty pounds before he left. 'You're an absolute darling,' she'd say, and follow it with a condescending kiss on his forehead.

On Saturday morning the first true sign of spring crept into the air. For the first time since September, the sun emitted rays of warmth. Danny was seated at a small table in a crowded café in Shepherd's Bush, a big breakfast in front of him, his head in his hands. The night before had been a long one.

On Friday night he had been forced to sleep at the Holland Park house when one of the regular arguments between Colette and Philippe had spiralled out of control.

It had started earlier in the evening, Colette arriving home later than expected — later than *requested* — despite the dinner party to which she'd agreed to accompany her husband. Worse, she proudly bore a great ugly love bite on her slender neck, which mushroomed above the stiff collar of her crisp white blouse. For once, Philippe stood his ground, determined to face up to his philandering wife. As the screaming match ensued, it quickly became apparent that neither would make the dinner party that night. Instead, they hurled abuse at one another like a couple of tennis players in a never-ending rally. Danny, working against desperation and the clock, got the children dressed, then whisked them out of the front door to the cinema, where they all watched an animated film in which large-eyed characters professed undying love for one another while swinging from tree to tree in some jungle setting. At its conclusion, Victoria was practically choking on her tears, her little chest heaving. Danny thought that perhaps these were tears for her parents, and the situation she found herself in whenever they were home, but all she talked about, throughout their illicit McDonald's Happy Meal, were the characters in the film. Viggo, however, appeared unmoved by such pathetic cartoon nonsense, and inserted ketchuped frys up each nostril, then snorted and had a coughing fit.

Afterwards, Danny drove them home, wary that their parents' argument might have turned physical. When he opened the front door all the lights were blazing, but he could hear no sound, no laboured breathing, no footsteps, no tears. On further investigation, he discovered that the house was empty.

'Where's Mummy?' Victoria asked.
'She's just popped out, darling.'
'With Daddy?'
'Yes, with Daddy.'
'Bullshit,' said Viggo, the Elvis sneer in place.
'Don't swear, please, Viggo.'
'Bullshit.'
'I'm telling Mummy,' said Victoria.
'Bullshit.'
'Come on, both of you,' said Danny, losing patience. 'Bedtime.'
'Bullshit.'
'Danny, tell him to stop swearing,' said Victoria, tears welling.

Danny took Viggo to one side, bent down to the child and whispered in his ear. 'I'm warning you, Viggo. Shut the *fuck* up.'

It worked a treat – Viggo was stunned into silence. In the lexicon of bad language, 'fuck' was far worse than 'bullshit', especially when it came from the lips of a furious adult.

As a reward for their behaviour, which Danny falsely proclaimed to have been good, he allowed Viggo to listen to his MP3 player and Victoria to read a few pages of her latest book in bed. Fortunately, the little girl fell asleep before she'd even managed two paragraphs, and her brother a quarter of an hour later.

Shortly after midnight the door slammed. Danny woke with a jump on the floor of Victoria's room. He tiptoed into Viggo's, relieved to see him still out for the count, a pair of oversized headphones still hugging his head. He removed them gently and placed them on their stand. He didn't know whether Colette or Philippe had just staggered home, and he didn't care. He made his way into the guest room and fell asleep on the bed, fully clothed, enormously tired.

The next morning even before he went downstairs to the kitchen, Danny was aware of a strange atmosphere that hovered over the house like a dark cloud. It was unnaturally quiet, no rustling of newspapers, no babble from the radio. At the breakfast bar, he found Colette and Philippe sitting at either end, staring into space. Both were red-eyed, possibly hung over, tired and emotional. In front of each of them was a plate with one slice of wholemeal toast. Danny felt bile lurch inside his stomach, followed by a grumbling rumble.

'Well, I hope you're very proud of yourselves,' he said. Neither looked up, so he continued, 'Listen, feel free to fuck up your own lives, by all means, but try to remember that you've got children. Your kids are already half-way towards being royally screwed up anyway.' Colette looked at the floor; Philippe grew visibly irritated. 'Every argument you two have in front of them just pushes them closer to the edge. No wonder Viggo has Attention Deficit Disorder.'

'Now look here—' Philippe began.

Danny didn't give him a chance to go on. 'I'll leave you two to sort it out today,' he said. 'See you Monday. And, please, *grow up*.'

As he made his way down the hall, he heard their bickering erupt like lava.

* * *

Spin Cycle

Over breakfast in the café, his own miseries took over. He sat at the only empty table in the place, a piece of charred Formica on wobbly legs. He picked up the dirty cutlery and pierced the fried egg with the knife, expecting the dull yellow yolk to flow over his sausage and beans, but it was solid. He sighed, and pushed it to the edge, where it sat alongside some black pudding. He peered at his plate, wondering what had happened to his appetite.

Above him someone said, 'Excuse me, young man. Is this seat taken?' He was well spoken, his words clearly enunciated, but there was a roughness in his voice that betrayed pain, maybe humiliation, as if he was used to being on the receiving end of abuse. Danny looked up, and as he did so experienced a flash of *déjà vu*. He shook his head, and the man sat down opposite him with almost studied inelegance. Inconspicuously, Danny glanced at him and saw a mass of hair, a wiry beard, a dirty face, thick hands, black fingernails. A tramp. He had on a heavy overcoat, black with grime. The stench coming off him was intense, strong as bleach, thick as dog hair. When he smiled, he revealed a few crooked teeth. But his eyes danced and sparkled with the remembrance of a former life. They were dark blue, and ominously familiar. For some reason, they put Danny in mind of the record shop.

And then it came to him. *Recognition*. Everything around him fell away. This was the man he'd run into, knocked over, and k-killed at the tube station. The man he'd electrocuted to kingdom come. Right, Danny thought, if he's here now in front of me, does that mean he survived? That he somehow survived a hundred thousand volts in a feat of superhuman survival? Or does that mean that he is a g-ghost? Danny held on to the table for support. What should he do? He chanced a look round the café at the other customers, half expecting to see every finger pointing accusingly at him, but no one took any notice. He looked back at the tramp, who continued to smile at him, exuding a strange benevolence.

An awkward silence ensued, which Danny thought he should fill. His tongue fished around his mouth for words. 'Um, are you . . . you know . . . are you real?'

The tramp slurped noisily at his tea and looked back at Danny with a mixture of interest and curiosity. He grinned, and prodded himself with a finger. 'I think so. But, then, I can't be sure any more. Not these days.' He took another long slurp, smacking his lips together beneath his beard. 'Mmm, that's good.'

Danny trembled. This was just too weird. Ghosts don't exist, do they? 'Why can't you be sure?' he asked, then braced himself for the answer.

The tramp looked thoughtful. He scrunched up his features in concentration, gazed towards the ceiling, and scratched his head. 'Well,' he began, 'the other week, something rather unusual happened. I should have died, but I didn't. I'm not sure why.' He met Danny's worried gaze and smiled.

Danny breathed in. 'What happened?'

'I fell – or rather was pushed – on to some train tracks,' he said, almost with pride.

A great pressure immediately lifted from Danny's shoulders. He felt lighter – released. 'Really? Who . . . who pushed you?'

'Oh, you know, just a couple of young men, drunk I

imagine. Apparently, I should have been electrocuted . . . but nothing happened. I survived. So the world isn't all bad, then.' Despite the optimism of the statement, he looked a little sad, lost.

'Can I help in any way?' Danny asked.

Without hesitation came the standard reply: 'Well, you couldn't help a poor man out, I don't suppose? Perhaps spare me some money for a cup of tea.' He looked at his mug, still half full on the table. 'I mean, another tea, after I finish this one.'

Danny immediately took this as an olive branch, an opportunity to right a wrong. 'Absolutely, of course.' He searched for some change, before remembering the twenty-pound note in the breast pocket of his shirt, and handed it over.

The tramp's eyes lit up. 'Well, gosh. Very kind of you, sir. Very kind indeed.' He turned it around in his fingers, then laid a hand on Danny's. It felt cold and clammy. 'A word of advice for a young man such as yourself, if I may,' he said. 'When opportunity reveals itself to you, take it. Don't live a life of regrets.' He nodded gravely at him, and smiled once more. 'Thank you. I won't forget this,' he said, waving the note triumphantly in the air.

Neither would Danny.

Two

Action

Fifteen

The room had a sharp, citric smell to it. The curtains were drawn, and all the windows were closed. Danny walked lightly over to the far end and opened one to its full extent – an inch. He lowered his nose and breathed in deeply, grateful for fresh oxygen. He walked over to the bedside table and removed the source of that intrusive smell: a bunch of wilting flowers. He took them out into the corridor, and deposited them in the large bin in the communal kitchen area. He nodded hello to an elderly woman making coffee for her husband. He opened the fridge and hunted for the litre carton of apple juice he'd bought earlier, poured himself a tumblerful, and downed it in one. Then he returned to the private room where his mother was winding down gradually to the ultimate full stop.

It was late on a Saturday evening, and the hospice was settling for the night. The corridors were largely empty and only intermittent snoring broke the silence. Earlier in the day, while Danny was struggling to keep three children occupied, he had received a telephone call informing him that his mother had taken a turn for the worse. It was unlikely she would make it into tomorrow. At first Colette was furious that he was walking away from his duties when she was so busy, but she relented and allowed him to go.

An hour later, Danny arrived at the north London cancer centre. When he found his mother, he recoiled. Although she was conscious, the woman in the bed was not the one he remembered. She was a shell of what his mother had once been. She looked as though she'd melted into the mattress, leaving behind only a skeleton. She wore a nightdress that was too big for her, and lay unmoving, her eyes wide, staring blindly at the ceiling. If she could hear him talking into her ear, she made no response. He sat in the chair beside her and held her cold, thin hand.

In the early evening, a nurse arrived with a hypodermic and injected more painkiller. Within minutes, Danny's mother had drifted into a deep sleep from which she would not stir. Danny switched off the overhead light and turned on the small lamp beside the bed. He sat down again, in the near dark, and within a quarter of an hour he, too, was asleep.

He awoke some time later with the arrival of a couple of his mother's friends, two middle-aged women he'd never seen before. They introduced themselves awkwardly, then stood around the bed in silence, waiting. The dying woman's chest rose and fell with directionless purpose. In the half-light, Danny was shocked to see that the whites of her eyes were now a muddy brown. It was a stark, shocking sight. He wished they were closed, that he could close them, but he couldn't. He glanced up at the two women, who were crying quietly. He could hear a clock, or watch, ticking. His? When he held his mother's hand again, it was colder than it had been earlier. The woman opposite him began to stroke his mother's cheek. The wheezing became slower, irregular. Then it ceased. Suddenly, she wheezed again, and gave a low, almost imperceptible murmur. Silence, then another wheeze. Her shoulders shrugged, and her features screwed up. Then her shoulders loosened, and she sank back into the mattress. She seemed gone. She didn't look peaceful, she looked spent, ravaged by pain. Through tears, Danny looked up at the wall clock opposite: ten thirty. The two women came around the bed and hugged him tight, but instead of being consoled, he felt awkward. Who were these people?

He made arrangements to come back for the death certificate on Monday morning, and then, politely declining the offer of a lift from his dead mother's friends, he walked down quiet streets with his hands in his pockets and his head down, into darkness.

Flox was in the freezing kitchen making coffee with the kind of anger usually expended in a boxing ring, knocking into and spilling everything. The funeral was now history, behind them by forty-five minutes. As soon as they had arrived home, Danny went out again, closing the door quietly behind him. Sanjay followed Flox into the kitchen, and was forced to listen to his friend's lengthy dissertation on the equation *life = shit*.

At one point, Sanjay intervened: 'Flox, I sometimes

think that your sole purpose on earth is to complain. Are things really that bad for you? Danny I can understand, but you?'

'I can't help it,' came the reply. 'I just feel all this *anger* inside me. All the time. What's been happening to Danny these past few months only makes it worse.'

Sanjay shrugged. As far as he was concerned, Flox was cantankerousness incarnate. Always had been, always would be. But Flox persisted. To illustrate his point, he picked up a book from the kitchen table. 'It says it much better in here,' he said, flicking through the pages. Sanjay bent down to peer at the cover. *Out of Sheer Rage* by Geoff Dyer.

'Isn't that D.H. Lawrence on the cover?' he asked.

'What? Oh, yes, yes, it is. It's a biography about him.'

Sanjay smiled. 'Since when have you been interested in D.H. Lawrence?'

Flox was poring over the pages, looking for a particular passage. 'What? Oh, Lawrence. No, I couldn't give a shit about him, but I like the writer.' He flicked through the pages. 'There's a bit in here all about anger, and it's absolutely brilliant. It's *exactly* what I feel, *how* I feel. It could be about *me*. Wait.' He frowned. 'Listen to this: "That's what I'm doing: shaking my fist at the world. I won't let even the smallest grievance escape me. I'm going to seize on the most insignificant inconvenience, annoyance, hindrance, set-back, disappointment and am going to focus all my rage, anger, bitterness and frustration on it."' Flox looked up and nodded eagerly. 'He says something else as well that's bang on the money. Now, where is it?' Pages flicked through his fingers. 'Here. Here it is. *Capacity for annoyance.* That's exactly what I've got, a capacity for annoyance. I can't help it, Sanjay, I just have this huge rage inside me, and anything can set it off. I'm easily provoked.'

'Wow,' Sanjay said, impressed, 'that was very dramatic. I should introduce you to my director.'

Later, as they were both sitting in front of the television watching Italian football – Sanjay having developed a taste for the sport, as well as for those who played it – they talked about how they could help Danny.

'Well, whatever you do,' said Sanjay, 'be delicate.'

'I'll help him through it,' said Flox. 'I'll help us both through it, through everything.'

The thought of affirmative action swept through him like a hurricane.

Later that night, Flox awoke to a pressing sensation across his mouth and nostrils. He couldn't breathe. He opened his eyes and saw, above him, the figure of a large man. Flox's heart thudded in his ribcage.

Slowly, the large man brought his head down towards Flox's ear. His voice was as rough as sandpaper. 'My boss thought it wise to send you a personal reminder,' he said. Flox looked into his big brown eyes, at the uneven surface of his forehead, the chin thick with whiskers. Everything about the man exuded brute strength, implacable purpose. He spoke again. 'You owe three thousand pounds, and your deadline is Saturday. If we don't see you by then, we'll come looking, and we won't be so friendly next time.' He grasped Flox's jaw, squeezed fat fingers into the flesh around his cheeks. 'Remember, we know where you live.' And with that the large man left the room as stealthily as he had arrived.

An hour later, Flox was still wide awake. There was something soul-destroying about insomnia, he thought, something so terribly lonely about lying awake in the dead of night, alone, while all around you is asleep. He could hear the walls sigh, the floorboards creak, the tiny patter of insect life. Downstairs, he heard the fridge change gear, its rattle and hum ceaseless. Birdsong seeped through the cracks in the window-frame. He was bathed in a cold sweat, and the room was spinning. He felt speeded up, jittery, as if he'd been remixed by Norman Cook. A low depression settled, the acknowledgement that inexpert gambling brought with it all manner of nasty side-effects, such as home visits from scum after dark. This is serious, he realised. A Saturday deadline?

He wouldn't be around come Saturday.

On Monday, Danny went back to work, the cloud of gloom still in place, and Flox phoned his team leader at Heathrow and told her he'd cleaned his last plane. He spent the rest of the day building up conviction, and when Danny returned home, exhausted and ashen-faced, he put his plans into first gear.

'What are you doing with the kids tomorrow?' he asked. It was half-term, so Danny had them from nine in the morning until nine at night.

'Nothing special,' Danny said. 'Maybe the cinema, ice skating, swimming? I don't know, I'll see how I feel. If I can't be bothered to take them anywhere, I'll just dump them in front of the television with some sweets. That'll keep them occupied.' He sounded utterly despondent, which made Flox buoyantly happy.

'Tomorrow,' he began, 'we – you and me – are going to take the kids on a little outing.'

Danny knew what Flox was suggesting. Kidnap. He was back on that reckless, ridiculous idea. But Danny had had a long, arduous day: Philippe had shouted at him, and Colette had screamed at everyone before indulging in a series of covert phone calls, then flouncing off in a cyclone of expensive perfume for the rest of the afternoon. Consequently, the kids had given him hell.

'Fine,' he said, past caring.

Flox could hardly contain himself. He lit up like electricity. '*Seriously?* You mean it?'

Danny nodded, once. 'Whatever.'

'You won't regret this, I promise you. This'll be a whole new beginning for us.'

The tramp's words swam around Danny's head: *When opportunity reveals itself to you, take it.* 'I hope so,' he said.

Sixteen

Tuesday's sunshine, Flox decided, was a good omen. By eight thirty, they had breakfasted and were walking towards Holland Park, not talking, matching each other's stride. They arrived at the house, and Flox took in its size, whistling through his teeth. It stank of money, and he hated its owners. As Danny opened the imposing front door, they encountered a flustered Colette, who was on her way out. 'Hi,' she said, not even looking up. 'In something of a rush. I'm late.'

Danny breathed deeply. 'Um, Colette, we – this is Flox, by the way – we were thinking of taking the kids on a little outing later,' he said.

Colette was barely listening. Clearly, her appointment was an important one, and she collected, dropped, juggled and searched for her things in a symphony of chaos. 'Fine, whatever,' she said. 'But I'm taking the Beetle. You'll have to take the Pallas.'

Danny frowned. That car was Philippe's plaything, out of bounds to anyone but him. 'What about Philippe?'

Colette stopped what she was doing and looked up. She glanced briefly at Flox, then at Danny. She pursed her lips, as if they'd just been smeared in salt. 'Philippe had a *conference* to go to in Hamburg. He left first thing this morning.' She curled her lip. 'He'll be away for a few days, so take it. He'll never know.' She found the keys on a small Georgian side table, and threw them to him. Danny caught them in his left hand, pleasantly surprised by his sudden dexterity.

Colette rushed towards the door, then stopped. 'Oh, and by the way, I may be a little late tonight myself. But don't worry, I'll make it up to you.' She grinned at them, then focused on Flox. He looked as though he hadn't been up long, and he seemed uncouth, rough around the edges. He looked like he could be a little wild. She straightened up and stood erect.

Flox studied her: the wave of her hair, the proliferation of makeup, and the kind of rouged lips he'd like to draw into his mouth and suck.

'I'm in a bit of a hurry,' she said, smiling enigmatically. '*Bye,*' she said, stretching out the word so it sounded as if it ended with at least half a dozen Es.

The door slammed, and she was gone.

'Right,' said Flox, rubbing his hands together. 'Introduce me to your children, Danny.'

Upstairs, Viggo and Cinjun – the latter was spending half-term with his friend while his parents relaxed in Bali – were at war on the PlayStation, attempting to lance one another with light sabres. Victoria was in her own room engrossed in the television. Danny attempted to introduce them all to his friend, but the first two weren't interested, and the little girl was too shy. They went back downstairs, where Flox helped himself to the contents of the fridge. 'Jesus,' he exclaimed, over a New York-style bagel and lox, 'they must be loaded.' He looked around the kitchen and dining-room area. 'How much is this place worth? No, let me guess. Four floors, Holland Park, gigantic back garden. Hmm, easily a mill five, maybe two.' Danny nodded in confirmation. '*Jesus*. Is it all self-made?'

'No, the husband was born into it, and the wife was born *for* it. His great-grandfather was a major landowner in France. There's a painting of the family mansion at Perrier up in the master bedroom.'

Danny took Flox on a guided tour of the house. The frown never relinquished its hold on Flox's forehead. 'God, I fucking hate the rich,' he spat. 'So fucking ostentatious. All this money, all the opportunity that comes with it, and they're still fucked up. It's the children I feel sorry for.'

'Those would be the same children you're planning on kidnapping, I presume?' Danny muttered.

'The very same. Anyway, the kids'll have no clue. It'll only be the parents who'll suffer, and then only financially. It'll teach them a lesson they need to learn.' He beamed. 'I've got a great idea,' he said, rubbing his hands purposefully. 'We're going to have a blast.'

Danny frowned.

'You're not having second thoughts, I hope,' Flox worried. 'Because it's too late. I've got it all mapped out.' He tapped the side of his head with an index finger.

Danny shuffled. 'How much are you going to ask for?'

Flox looked confused, uncomprehending.

'Ransom,' Danny explained, under his breath.

'We'll discuss that later,' Flox replied.

'You do realise, I hope, that this is an imprisonable offence?'

'It will, emphatically, not come to that. I assure you.'

'How?'

'Danny, believe me. I wouldn't put either of us at that risk.'

When opportunity reveals itself to you, take it. 'So what's your plan, exactly? Where are we going to . . . take them – *keep* them?'

This time Flox tapped the side of his nose. 'I'll tell you when you need to know. Meantime, leave everything to me.' He grinned like the madman he might easily become.

They were now in the bathroom, twice the size it needed to be, and Flox was standing fully clothed in the tub to measure its considerable depth. It came up to his knee. He was impressed.

Danny nodded towards it. 'Flick that switch,' he said, 'and it becomes a jacuzzi.' He tried to smile, but he had questions to ask, all of which began: *What if . . . ?*

'You don't know what you're letting yourself in for,' he said. 'And I don't mean the actual, you know,' under breath, '*kidnapping*. I'm talking about the kids. Do you have any idea what it will be like spending a large amount of time with kids – *these kids?* They are a *nightmare.*'

'Danny, you underestimate me. I'm great with kids. I used to be one.'

'You still are,' Danny replied, and they both started to laugh.

* * *

'What's up? What's the matter?'

Viggo and Cinjun had heard the commotion in Viggo's parents' bathroom, and came rushing in to investigate.

'Why're you laughing?' Viggo didn't like anyone having fun unless he was in on the joke.

'No reason,' said Danny.

'Tell me!' he shrieked, and kicked Danny in the shin.

Flox intervened. He bent down and scooped the boy up, throwing him over his shoulder in a fireman's lift. Viggo started laughing and kicking wildly, whooping like a hyena. Cinjun circled in on Flox like a cat does a mouse. 'Me too! Me too!'

The more jealous Cinjun became, the more Viggo roared with laughter. He was the chosen child. When Flox put him down, he attempted to jump on Flox from behind, determined to see the world upside-down again. He flew through the air, landing with outstretched hands on a pair of broad shoulders. Flox's T-shirt ripped at the neck. He felt like King Kong, experiencing attack from all sides. And Cinjun was also trying to climb up him, from the front. Flox's ponytail had come undone, his hair was everywhere. From underneath his fringe, he stole a glance at Danny and grinned.

A voice said, 'What's that on your back?' Viggo was peering beneath Flox's T-shirt at the tattooed snake winding down Flox's spine. 'Cor! That's brilliant.'

Cinjun ran around Flox and jumped on to the bed. 'I want to see!' he cried. 'Let me look!'

Ninety minutes later, as Viggo and Victoria were getting

dressed with Danny in attendance, Flox was rooting around a chest of drawers in the living room, for the children's passports. He flicked through them to discover that they had visited more foreign territories in their few years than he had in three decades. He pocketed them, then sought Cinjun and took him to one side.

'Do you want to play a special game?' he asked him.

Cinjun looked at him with suspicion. 'What game?'

'The kind of game that would make Viggo jealous?'

Cinjun nodded his blond head eagerly.

'Okay, but you have to keep it secret – for now at least. Understand?' The boy nodded again. 'If we drive to your house, would you be able to go in and get your passport without your mother noticing?'

The suspicion returned. 'Why?'

'Because you might need it for our game.'

'Why?'

'Never mind why.'

'Why?' The boy grinned.

Flox sucked in air through his mouth, then counted slowly to ten. Perhaps he wasn't as good with children as he had thought. 'Because we might be going to EuroDisney, that's why.'

'Do you mean Disneyland, Paris?' Cinjun asked, deadpan.

'Yes, Disneyland Paris, whatever its name is.'

Cinjun jumped three clear feet in the air and screamed deliriously. Flox caught him and clamped his hand over the boy's mouth. Slowly, he removed it, but warned him to keep quiet. 'It's a surprise for the others, remember.'

'I've always wanted to go,' he said, breathless. 'I've already been to the two in America. This one probably won't be as good, I'm sure, but I'd love to go.' He looked up at Flox with something resembling fondness. 'You know, I think I prefer you to Danny. He's always so miserable.'

Flox brought a finger up to his lips. 'Shh, I said it was a secret, all right? Breathe one word of this to Danny or the other two and it's off. Understand?'

Cinjun nodded exaggeratedly.

'Now, are you going to answer my question?'

'What question?'

Another deep breath. Christ, this was difficult. 'Will you be able to get your passport without your mother noticing?'

'Of course I will, stupid. No one's at home. Mum and Dad are on holiday. That's why I'm here.'

'Oh. And I suppose you wouldn't happen to have the keys, would you?'

Cinjun dug around in his pocket and produced a set.

Flox grinned. 'Terrific. We're in business.'

Ten minutes later, they all stood in the hall, waiting expectantly.

'Where are we going?' Victoria asked Danny.

Danny knelt down and looked into her eyes. He felt his heart fracture. 'We're going on an outing, sweetie,' he told her.

'Will we have fun?'

'Yes, we will. I promise.'

'I know where we're going! I know where we're going!'

Cinjun sang, and continued to do so until Flox glowered at him, and he quickly fell silent.

'Right, come on, then,' said Flox. 'Let's go.'

The Pallas was enormous, the size of a boat. The two adults sat in the front, while the three children convened messily on the huge bench seat in the back. Victoria had brought several books with her, Viggo was lost in his GameBoy, while Cinjun had a finger up his nose and was looking out of the window.

'We're going to Cinjun's house first. He has something to collect,' explained Flox.

Danny had never driven the Pallas before. It took him a while to get used to it. From the front seat it looked as if the car went on forever in every direction. The bonnet stretched out endlessly, and the back end looked a huge distance away in the rear-view mirror. He wasn't looking forward to parking it, but it drove like a dream.

They made slow progress through traffic-clogged London streets, and eventually arrived at Cinjun's Hampstead home an hour later. When they pulled up, the boy and Flox went in, while Danny and his charges waited in the car. Ten minutes later, they were off again. Danny had seen Flox and Cinjun exchange a complicitous glance before they got back into the car, and wondered what they were up to.

They drove south under Flox's instruction for some time, breaking through the outskirts of London, into suburbia, endless dull stretches of grey motorway, and beyond. After a pit stop at a Little Chef in the middle of nowhere, Flox took over at the wheel.

In the back, the kids were restless. 'Where're we going?' said Viggo.

Danny echoed him: 'It's a good question, Flox. Where *are* we going, exactly?'

They'd been driving south for almost ninety minutes now, hampered only by occasional traffic jams.

Flox made an announcement. 'The seaside!'

Danny looked bewildered, Viggo cheered without taking his eyes off his GameBoy, Victoria whispered, 'Beach,' then drifted back off to sleep, and Cinjun said nothing.

'Where are we going to stay?' whispered Danny. 'Have you thought this through properly? It's going to cost money we haven't got.'

'I'll cover it, don't you worry. We'll get it back, anyway. Think of it as an investment.'

'Yes, but—'

In the back seat, a storm brewed.

'Are we nearly there?' Cinjun said, for the umpteenth time.

'I'm bored,' said Viggo.

'Let me have a go,' said Cinjun, wrestling the GameBoy away from him.

'*No!* The batteries are low.'

'I only want one game.'

'No!'

'*Give it to me!* Flux, tell him!'

A struggle commenced.

'I thought you two were friends?' said Flox, into the rear-view mirror.

Both boys looked at him, confused. 'We are.'

'Well, then, let him have a game,' he told Viggo.

'No!'

'You selfish baby!'

'Flox, don't tease him,' Danny pleaded.

'Piss off, you bastard!' Viggo screamed.

'Don't swear at me, you little runt!'

Viggo kicked the back of Flox's seat.

'If you don't stop that, I'll—'

'Paedophile!'

Flox swivelled around in his seat, taking his eyes off the road. 'What did you call me?'

'Paedophile!'

'Flox!' Danny lurched over, and yanked the steering-wheel hard to the right, narrowly avoiding the kerb and a rapidly approaching lamp-post. Flox slammed a foot on the brake, and the car came to an abrupt halt on the verge. Danny was shouting, 'For fuck's sake! Keep your eyes on the road!'

Victoria had been bumped awake and burst into tears.

Flox resumed driving. 'He called me a *paedophile*, for Christ's sake!' he said to Danny.

'Don't take it personally, Flox. He calls everyone a paedophile.'

'Why?'

'It's his new word.'

Viggo leaned forward. 'Shut up,' he said to Danny. 'Shit for brains!'

With weariness in his voice, Danny told him to sit back and keep quiet.

Flox blinked several times, and shook his head. '*Shit for brains?* What kind of child is he?'

Viggo kicked the back of the seat once more, and

Flox lurched forward towards the steering-wheel. The car swerved again, burning rubber. 'I want to go home, paedophile.'

'Right, that's *it*.'

Flox pulled sharply into the next turning, a small lay-by empty but for a rusting, abandoned caravan, and stopped the car. He got out. Then, with an acute sense of drama Danny decided he'd learned from Sanjay, Flox walked round the car, opened the back door and ordered Viggo out. He snatched the GameBoy from him and tossed it into Cinjun's lap.

'Follow me,' Flox said, and walked away. Viggo, trying not to seem nervous, followed several steps behind. They both stopped, facing one another, and Flox started talking, his words tumbling on to Viggo's round, down-turned head.

Danny watched all this with detached amusement from the passenger seat. Flox's index finger did a lot of talking, just like, Danny thought, his father must have done with him years earlier. Viggo shrugged a couple of times, then nodded. His cheeks were bright red, and even from a distance, Danny could see that he was fighting back tears. Telling-off over, they walked back to the car together.

'Onwards,' said Flox, slamming the door and revving the engine.

Some time later, the Pallas, having steadfastly avoided any nearby beaches, joined the queue of vehicles waiting to board the Eurotunnel train. Danny turned to Flox, his face full of questions.

'Paris,' Flox whispered to him.

'*What?* P-Paris? Why?'

'Distance.'

'*Distance?*'

'Look, Dan, I got myself into a little trouble back home. I need to get away for a while, because if – well, you don't need to know the details. Please just believe me.'

'What kind of trouble?'

'Serious trouble. I've no choice, really. And, anyway, it's better this way for all of us.'

'Is that a fact?'

'Well, if things don't quite go to plan with the kids, then at least we've got all of Europe to disappear into.'

'What plan? You haven't told me about any plan.' Danny was beginning to panic.

'Don't be pedantic. Distance for me right now is a requirement. Just trust me. I know what I'm doing. It'll all come together.'

There was silence for a moment. Then Danny's frenzy returned. He spoke barely above a whisper: '*I haven't got my fucking passport! Nor have the kids! We'll be turned back before we've even got anywhere!*'

Flox smiled like a sage old grandfather, wise to details that young folk didn't know existed. 'All under control.' He grinned, patting bulging pockets.

Danny sank back in his seat, helpless and defeated. Victoria climbed into the front and sat on his lap. She touched his burning cheek. 'Are you all right?' she asked.

He looked down at her, and smiled. 'I'm fine, love.'

'You don't look fine to me. Viggo, doesn't Danny look funny?'

'Danny always looks funny,' Viggo said, and kicked

Flox's seat once more. He stuck out his tongue. 'I want to know where we're going!' he added.

'Disneyland Paris! We're going to Disneyland Paris!' Cinjun sang.

Danny swivelled round. 'What did you say?' he asked.

'Flux told me.' He beamed, pointing. 'We're going to Disneyland!'

'It's Flox, not Flux,' Flox corrected. Then he added, under his breath, 'Big-mouthed little bastard.'

Danny looked witheringly at his partner in crime. 'Disneyland?'

'Trust me,' came the reply, and he drove the car on to the train.

Twenty minutes later, industrial northern France emerged at the end of the tunnel. It was drizzling, the sky was grey and miserable, the land flat and unremarkable. Off in the distance, a pale shaft of sunlight attempted to open up the spring sky, but bullying clouds gathered round and closed it off. Flox guided the Pallas carefully off the ramp and out on to the open road, headed for the capital.

Victoria looked out of the window with a quizzical expression on her face. They seemed to be driving on the wrong side of the road. 'Are we in a foreign country?' she asked.

'We're in France, you idiot!' Viggo shouted.

An hour later the three children were fast asleep. When Flox and Danny entered into conversation now, there was no interruption, no flapping ears. It was bliss.

'I've a question,' said Danny, at the wheel again. 'Where

are we going to get the money to take three screaming children to bloody Disneyworld?'

'Disney*land*,' Flox corrected. 'And I've already told you, I'll take care of it.' He lowered his voice, just in case. 'We're not going to Disneyland. I just said that as an excuse to shut up the blond one.'

Danny was incredulous. 'You really don't have a clue, do you? You think that kidnapping and holding to ransom a bunch of kids is easy. That until we get the money – and that will *never* happen – we just dump the kids in the back of the car and sit tight. Flox, you're a fool.'

Flox snorted. 'And you're a major defeatist. Nothing is possible as far as you're concerned, you miserable shit.'

'All I'm saying is you don't understand the ramifications.'

'Ooh, *ramifications*. Big word.'

Danny ploughed on. 'You've told them we're taking them to Disneyland. If you don't take them now, then you've got unholy chaos just waiting to unleash itself in your face. And I'm telling you, you won't be able to control it – it'll be nuclear-powered. And where do you intend us to stay? Or do you expect it all to be over within a matter of hours?'

Flox felt a sudden tightness in his bowels, a repetitive clenching. Was the futility of it all dawning on him? No, of course not. He would not give in – refused to entertain negative thoughts. He instructed Danny to pull into the next service station. Fifteen minutes later, they parked the car in a deserted forecourt, and left the children there, asleep and locked in. Inside, they ordered strong coffee. Then Flox embarked upon a speech that successfully feigned purpose and positivity.

'Here's how it will be,' he said. 'We'll check into some cheap motorway motel. Then, later tonight, I'll put a call in to the mother, Colette. I'll tell her that her children have been abducted, along with the other one. I won't mention your name, and she'll have no idea who I am – we barely spoke this morning. I won't enter into any conversation with her. I'll just tell her that if she wants to see her children safe and well again, she'll have to wire some money over. I'll have decided on a bank earlier. Once I've collected the money and left the bank without any fuss, an hour later the children will be handed over to airport staff who will ensure their safe flight home. Because the parents are rich and guilty of neglect and everything, they'll cough up, and I could demand millions, but no. All I'll ask for is a hundred thousand, no more. My guess is she'll panic so much, and feel so guilty for deserting them in the first place, that she'll hand over the money no problem. All she'll want is for her kids to come back to her alive, and for them to forgive her *indiscretions*. She won't want to bother with negotiating when there are extra-marital affairs to be had. It'll be over in no time.'

'It won't work,' Danny said.

'It *will*,' Flox replied, insistently. 'Just wait and see.'

Seventeen

On the outskirts of Paris, in a nameless suburb that seemed to consist only of small, low-level concrete hotels, car parks, fast-food restaurants, and a bank, to which Flox beat a path immediately, they checked into a cheap *pension*. Danny remained in the car with the children while Flox handled things at Reception, requesting a room with two double beds for two people, for one night. Then, after he had signalled to them from the window, Danny smuggled himself and the children upstairs without any of the staff seeing. The children didn't question his strange behaviour; instead, they enjoyed the subterfuge. They thought it all a big game. However, in the small grey room – the television had only three channels, and universally poor reception – the excitement soon waned.

'I *want* to go to Disneyland! I *want* to go to Disneyland!' Cinjun, standing on one of the lumpen beds, was rocking backwards and forwards, repeating his mantra endlessly.

'Me too!' Victoria was suddenly wide awake. Cinjun had told her of the many wonders of the Magic Castle and a hundred Mickey Mouses wherever you looked. Viggo, meanwhile, was in a poisonous mood. He looked like his father in miniature. He was grouchy because his GameBoy had died, and no one had any emergency Duracels.

'What time is it?' Danny asked Flox, impatient for this to end.

Flox consulted his watch. Despite the amount of time they'd been travelling, it was still only early evening. 'Too early.'

'I'm hungry!' Viggo said.

'Me too!'

'And me!'

'So am I, actually,' said Danny. 'Let's take them downstairs to the restaurant.'

'All right, but I get to choose the food. I don't want you lot to go costing me a fortune.'

'You're a liar,' said Viggo, accusingly, on the way down. 'You're not paying for any of this. My parents are. They *told* me.'

Flox looked at Danny and raised his eyebrows. 'Did they now?'

They sat in an American-style booth that overlooked the car park. Each ate a burger and fries, and drank a large glass of Coca-Cola, which came with bendable straws.

'Not fizzy enough,' said Viggo.

'My fries are soggy. And what's this?' Cinjun thrust a curious finger into the creamy white sauce, brought it tentatively to his nose, then wiped it on Viggo's forehead. 'Spunk!' he cried, in apparent jubilation. Viggo, incensed, slapped him, then began rubbing furiously at the unidentified white stuff with a napkin. Cinjun punched his ear.

Danny intervened. 'It's mayonnaise,' he explained, separating the two.

'Well, it's not good enough. I want proper ketchup.'

'Come on, Cinjun,' said Flox. 'When in Rome . . .'

'We're not in Rome, idiot,' said Viggo. 'We're in Paris.'

'Call me idiot one more time, and I'll suffocate you with those fries. Understand?'

Cinjun giggled, then punched Viggo's leg. Viggo kicked Victoria under the table. 'Ouch!' she cried, then bent down to clutch her leg and hit the tray containing her food, which landed in her lap. Her Coca-Cola, meanwhile, had spilled on the table and was spreading fast, falling over the edge and drenching Flox's trousers. He shot up, his chair toppling over behind him. Beetroot red with anger, he leaned forward and slapped Viggo's head. The boy's neck snapped back and he burst into tears.

'Paedophile!' he screamed.

They now had the attention of everyone in the restaurant. This wasn't good.

Danny roared, *'Flox, sit down!'* Then he brought his voice down to an acceptable level. 'Viggo, stop crying and I'll buy you some chocolate, but you must promise not to kick your sister again. All right?'

'What about me? I want chocolate too!' Cinjun whined.

'I can't take much more of this,' said Flox, fists clenched, knuckles white. 'I'm going to make the phone call now before . . . before I *kill* the little shits.'

Victoria's jaw dropped. 'Danny, he said the S word.'

'Who's he calling?' Viggo wanted to know, as he watched the hunched figure retreat.

'No one,' said Danny. 'Just a friend.'

'Does my mum know we're here?'

Danny stammered momentarily. 'Of course she knows. It was – it was her idea because she and your dad are so busy at the moment. They wanted us to take you on a little break. But you know this already, don't you? You told us earlier that your mother gave us enough money to spend on you. Right?' He continued, 'Your parents wanted you to have a little holiday, which was nice of them, wasn't it?'

'I hate my parents,' said Viggo.

'Don't say that. You know it's not true.'

'It is true. Anyway, they hate me, so why shouldn't I hate them?'

'They don't hate you.' Danny was out of his depth here, drowning fast.

'Do they hate me as well?' Victoria asked, her voice fragile, tremulous.

'They hate both of us, idiot, you more than me,' said her brother, and Victoria began to cry.

'Viggo! Shut up!' Danny said.

'Your parents are horrible,' said Cinjun. 'Mine are much better.'

Viggo punched Cinjun, who took a gulp of his drink and spat it into Viggo's face. Screaming resumed, and a waiter rushed over. 'Sir, ees zere a prow-blem?' He was tall, thin, with a pencil moustache, and a grave expression.

'No, sorry. My cousins are a little hyperactive, that's all.'

'We're not your cousins,' said Viggo.

'Well, pleeze, quiet.'

'Look!' cried Viggo, pointing. 'He walks like a flamingo!'

'Thank you, thank you *very* much. I thought you were all old enough to behave properly,' Danny said to Viggo and Cinjun, both of whom grinned victoriously.

'Why did you say to that man that we're your cousins?' Viggo asked.

Defeated, Danny groaned. 'Oh, just shut up, will you?'

Eventually, Flox returned just as Danny was thinking that they should up the demand to two hundred thousand. These children were *fucking* hard work. But the smile of satisfaction on Flox's chops was conspicuous by its absence. The phone call, evidently, hadn't gone quite as smoothly as planned.

'The bitch wasn't in,' he fumed, through taut lips.

'Do you call all your friends bitches?' wondered Viggo.

Upstairs in the room, Danny washed Victoria's stained dress in the sink while she sat on the bed in vest and pants reading a book. Then, he called the answer-machine in Holland Park and discovered a couple of messages. He accessed them. Both were from Colette. 'Danny, sweetie, I'm going to be late tonight because of work. I'm terribly sorry, but there's nothing I can do. This is really important to me, I'm sure you understand. Take some money from the drawer and treat the kids to McDonald's. Don't worry about Cinjun. He's with us for the week anyway as you know. Bridget's always saying how much he likes you, better than any nanny he's had before.' Pause. 'Listen, must dash. I'll be late, so don't wait up.'

The second message had been left an hour later. She now sounded quite drunk. 'Dan-Danny. Things going kercrazy – hic, oops! – over here. I've gotta stay with some pospective... prospective... pros-pect-ive clients who are just dying to wine me and dine me and talk over, you know, plans. WhatcanIsay?' This was followed by muffled laughter, and the sound of wet kissing. Low laughter could be heard, male laughter. 'Anyway, had a bitta drink. I – I don't think I should drive home tonight. My ... perspective clients have said I can stay in the spare bedroom – I'm at their house right now in fact – so maybe I'll do just that, yes? You don't mind, do you, darling? No, no, I'm sure you won't, don't. Speak to you in the morning. First thing. Lunchtime, maybe. Love to the kids. Hic. Oops! Hiccups!'

Danny closed his eyes, and rubbed them with thumb and forefinger. He imagined himself climbing Everest barefoot. Reluctantly, he looked at Flox, who was seated on the end of one of the beds, the children surrounding him, watching a French talk show. He motioned him to follow him into the bathroom. There, they huddled together and Danny imparted the news. Flox let out a groan. '*Fuck!* What a complete bitch!'

Cinjun stormed into the bathroom, Viggo not far behind. 'When are we going to Disneyland?' he demanded.

'Tomorrow, first thing,' said Danny, intent on instant placation, some peace, some quiet.

They had no choice.

It was a restless, uncomfortable night. Flox and Danny took one bed, the children the other. Because the two boys couldn't stop bickering, talking and farting beneath the covers, Victoria crawled out into the other bed and quickly fell asleep between her two kidnappers. Flox didn't like this at all: her close presence made him feel guilty. Victoria was an adorable little girl, and he couldn't help but warm to her. All this would have been so much easier if he could have hated her as much as he did the boys.

The following morning, the children awoke at the crack of dawn, and dived on to the adults' bed, screaming, '*Disney*land! *Disney*land! *Disney*land!' Flox woke from one nightmare straight into another, and felt his heart race as he opened his eyes to see Viggo's contorted features mere centimetres from his, his mouth wide open, a jumble of vowels pouring out at volume.

Danny reacted similarly. Shaken from a deep slumber, he imagined the world was ending, such was the commotion. In a panic, he jumped from the bed and landed on the floor before realising where he was and what was happening. Amid the carnage, Flox looked at Danny, whose eyes said it all: this had been a stupid, *stupid* idea. He made a beeline for the telephone, then punched in the now familiar digits and waited for connection.

When the machine picked up again, he slammed the phone down so hard it fell off the small bedside table and landed on the floor with a loud clatter. The children looked at him, momentarily silenced, then resumed their chant: '*Disney*land! *Disney*land! *Disney*land!'

Breakfast, in the restaurant downstairs, was predictably chaotic, with coffee, Coke, and croissants flying in every direction. Later they caught the bus with several other hotel guests to the theme park.

Flox winced when he handed over his credit card to cover the entrance cost for two adults and three children. This wasn't so much a kidnapping as a bloody half-term holiday, and he felt acute embarrassment. Once through the gates, the boys ran off into the crowd, but Victoria walked between Flox and Danny, holding their hands tightly and pulling them forward. She wore a huge smile that was almost larger than her face. The first ride, all agreed, had to be the rollercoaster, a gigantic, gravity-defying contraption that traded under a name neither Danny nor Flox caught. It lasted one hundred and twenty seconds, and was all screams, whoops, G-force and tears.

The day was an endless procession of queues, hot dogs, popcorn and soft drinks, and countless trips to the toilet. By the time the sun sloped off towards the horizon, exhaustion had set in.

'Never will I have kids of my own,' Flox told Danny, his calf muscles putty. *'Never.'*

For them both, the exhaustion was compounded by a sense of increasing desperation. The day had been regularly punctuated with attempts at the all-important phone call, but they never got an answer. Colette had disappeared. Back at the hotel, after another eventful and costly evening meal, Danny tried one more time, thinking he would pass the phone to Flox if Colette answered. She didn't. Instead, two more messages had been left, and he listened to them both. The first was from a family friend, and the second from the missing mother. Holding his breath, Danny listened to her voice and the message she relayed. As he replaced the receiver, he felt like a flat tyre.

Given that Philippe had, in Colette's words, 'disappeared into Germany's back and beyond, probably rediscovering his latent homosexuality', she had decided to take a little time off herself. She'd gone to a health farm in Devon, she explained, and she'd taken a friend, which probably meant that they'd travelled there by Vespa. Scattering apologies like confetti, she promised to make it all up to Danny financially upon her return later in the week, or maybe at the weekend. She stressed that she'd only done this because – and here she lowered her voice to a whisper, presumably to protect the children, given that they only picked up on loud noises – 'I feel at the end of my tether, and need a short break to collect myself'.

'Fuck it, then,' said Flox. 'Let's try Cinjun's parents.'

Cinjun's parents, Danny reminded him, were away for the week too.

'No problem,' he said, refusing to be thwarted. 'We'll just have to hold on to them a little bit longer.'

Even as the words left his mouth, they felt hollow. Together they looked at the children sitting on the edge of the bed arguing over what to watch on television. The boys had a little game of tug-of-war going with the remote control; Viggo gave it a forceful yank, lost grip, and it smacked Victoria's forehead. High-pitched screams filled the room. Cinjun dived towards the television and changed channels manually. Viggo lunged at him.

'Or maybe not.' Flox went red in the face, while a rocket exploded inside his cranium.

Flox was up to his nose in bubbles, submerged in steaming hot water. Danny sat on the toilet seat, his head in his hands. He didn't say anything; he didn't need to. Out in the bedroom, the argument had stopped and the children were feeling the pull of sleep. A peculiar sense of calm — albeit temporary — existed. Flox's big toe stretched up, and turned on the hot tap slowly, filling the bath towards overflow.

'I'm sorry, Dan,' he said quietly, avoiding eye-contact. 'I really had faith in this, you know? I thought it would work — it *had* to. But it's all a big mess, and I apologise.'

'Back in London, you said you needed distance because you'd got yourself into some kind of trouble. What trouble, exactly?'

Flox avoided the question by ducking his head under the water and stayed like that for almost two minutes. When the craving for oxygen became too great, he resurfaced, gulped down air, and wiped foam away from his eyes.

'We've got to get rid of them, haven't we?' he said. 'The children.'

'Get *rid* of them? How?'

'Well, we've got to send them back.'

'You mean *take* them back?'

'No. No way. We're not taking them anywhere, ever again. We're *sending* them back. Come on, Danny, think about it. London has nothing for us any more — we could even be in trouble when the mother finds out where we took them.'

Danny rested his chin in the heel of his hand, and considered this. 'Where would we go?'

'Anywhere. The world is our playground now. Let's go and have an adventure.'

'And what do we do for money?'

'We'll get by. Meantime, think about the best and safest way to get rid of the kids.'

Danny thought he had an idea. He would try to enlist the unwitting help of Viggo. He had to get in touch with 'Auntie' Alison. She was their only hope. Tentatively, fingers crossed behind his back and hope in his heart, Danny wondered aloud whether Viggo could remember her number off the top of his head. The boy ran his fingers through his hair, squeezed his eyes tight shut, and eventually, after several drawn-out ums and aahs, he answered, 'Course.' Then came his most frequently employed word: 'Why?'

'I need it.'

'Why?'

'Because I need to speak to her, that's why. Now, can I have it, please?'

'Why?'

'Viggo, you realise that I fantasise about torturing you, don't you, you little sh—'

'Fuck off.'

Change of tack. 'Look, I'm sorry, I was only joking. I need her telephone number because your mother asked me to give her a call.'

'Why?' The sneer was in place.

Smiling, Danny turned to face Cinjun instead. 'Cinjun? Would you like some chocolate?'

The boy took his eyes off the television screen and nodded. Danny fished around inside his pockets and eventually came up with a couple of KitKats. He put one back in his pocket, then unwrapped the other, and snapped it in two. Half he handed to Cinjun, the other half to Victoria; only the latter said thank you. Then he joined them on the bed to watch television. Viggo sat on the other bed kicking his legs metronomically against the base. Danny monitored him from the corner of his eye, watching him fight temptation.

Viggo sidled up to him. He held out his hand, Oliver Twist-style. 'Give me some.'

Danny didn't even look at him. 'Give me the number.'

'Give me the chocolate first.'

'No.'

'I'm going to phone my mother.'

'Fine.'

Viggo looked confused, but decided to act nevertheless. With Danny's help, he dialled home only to find no one there. Victoria joined them, wanting to know where her mummy was. Danny told them she was working late tonight, and when he had spoken to her earlier in the day — while they were on a ride at Disneyland — she had instructed him to phone Alison, which was why, he explained, he'd asked Viggo for the number. Stress lines slowly evaporated from the boy's forehead.

'Chocolate.'

'Phone number.'

'Batteries as well?'

'Deal.'

So grateful he almost burst into tears, Danny instead remained calm, picked up the telephone, unravelled the cord, and stretched it until he reached the small hall where he could have some privacy. Alison picked up on the fourth ring, and he reintroduced himself. Her voice was sunny, bright. He explained that he had taken the children, under instruction from Colette, to Disneyland in Paris while she and her husband were away from home, separately. Alison made sympathetic noises, saying that she'd heard they were going through a sticky patch. Danny went on to explain that earlier that evening he had received word of a family emergency in Milan, where he claimed his grandparents lived (they actually resided in Clacton and spoke no language but Estuary). His presence was immediately required, and he had no choice but to drive there as soon as possible. Obviously, he couldn't take the children with him. Alison understood. Now came the delicate part. He turned his back to the living room, and spoke quietly. Colette hadn't given him enough money to cover such unforeseen emergencies – why ever would she? – but Danny was unable to meet the cost of three air fares home. Furthermore, he was unable to reach Colette, who hadn't left a forwarding number. So he was in a bit of a fix. Could Alison, if at all possible, cover the cost of the tickets and bill the parents at a later date? He wouldn't ask it of her in normal circumstances but, he insisted, these weren't normal circumstances. He simply didn't know what else to do. Then he fell silent, and waited for a reply – which was immediate. Of course she'd cover the cost, she said, absolutely no problem. She was incredibly gracious and understanding. Yes, she'd love to help, and would happily look after the children until their mother got home. She took the details, and said she'd call back as soon as everything was arranged. When he had hung up, he sat on the floor, overcome with relief. Flox and Danny were off the hook, out of the woods, for now.

'Why are we going home so soon?' Viggo asked.

Danny told the children effectively what he had told Alison. Victoria looked worried, and said she hoped everything would be all right. Flox added, unnecessarily, that they'd seen what they'd come to see anyway, so why hang around any longer? 'The holiday's over, *Damien*,' he told Viggo. Viggo stuck out his tongue at the sarcasm, which he had registered if not quite understood, then gave Flox a V-sign. Flox smiled. If this were a film, he'd probably feel a tug of emotion here, and would be forced secretly to admit that he'd miss him when he was gone. But this was no film and he couldn't wait to be rid of the little bastard.

The morning brought with it a final insult, a fitting conclusion to the escapade. Despite the sudden onset of warm weather, the Pallas refused to start. It coughed, choked and died, so they were forced to take a cab to the airport – and pay the astonishingly vast fare for the thirty-minute ride. But what the hell? Flox was in celebratory mood. Granted, things might have turned out much better, but they might also have been much worse. He still had his distance, and for this he felt both grateful and safe. Once the plane took off, the children with it, and they'd had the car repaired, all of Europe was at their beck and call, a tantalising proposition whichever way you looked at it.

The airport was hot and sticky. Half of Paris was off on holiday. The queue for the check-in desk was long and slow. By the time they had worked their way to the front, they were handed three pre-paid tickets, one for each child. At the passport barrier, Danny went down on his knees and clutched Victoria to him in a hug.

'See you soon, eh?' he said. She nodded, split between the excitement of going home and the sadness at leaving her nanny. Flox ruffled the two boys' heads, because that's what men do to boys who have yet to learn how to shake hands, and then watched with undisguised glee as an airline representative took them under her wing and towards their gate. Just before they disappeared into the departure lounge, Victoria turned round and waved. Her smile drew Danny towards her. He felt as if he was about to lose something very valuable.

When they joined the queue at the taxi rank, the two free men exchanged looks, their faces open, optimistic.

'What next?' asked Danny.

Eighteen

Oh, to be in Paris in the springtime. All the trees are in bloom, and the sun falls on the rooftops like so much snow on a winter sidewalk. The scent of flowers fills the air. Young and carefree Parisians walk with a lightness in their step and they smile at the slightest provocation, full of the euphoria that comes with the arrival of warm weather in a city as romantic as this. Beauty comes out on parade, gentlefolk take to the promenade. Sunglasses, previously lazing as a fashion item on top of a blonde head, come down to shroud the eyes, adding mystery to the female whose nose they bridge. Bumble bees drink nectar from nature's wine glass in parks, and light shimmers across the lake upon which swans glide and—

Oh, forget it.

Malory was practising the art of positive thinking. She was trying to feel good: about herself, about her environment, about life, but negativity was creeping around her like ivy. *The Road Less Traveled* was attempting to shed light on her path, but mostly it was plunged in permanent shadow. She'd been here almost two months now, and had immersed herself in a diet, a regime, of utter relaxation and rejuvenation. Chicken soup for the soul. And although she received plenty of male attention, she remained lonely and piqued. Why didn't they recognise her? She was just another attractive woman, but she wanted to be more: she wanted to be spectacular, to nudge greatness, to be acknowledged. She wanted to be an Irene Jacob to France's premier angel, Emmanuelle Beart; instead, she was merely Malory Cinnamon ... to whom, exactly? Pamela Anderson?

She spent empty afternoons trawling the city's wide streets and avenues, the austere museums, the plush cinemas. If she hadn't seen every movie Daniel Autiel had made in the last five years, then she had missed only the uncredited cameo roles, because Paris's movie-theatre district was terrific on repertory. If she had gained nothing else from her vacation so far, then she had certainly come to appreciate and love French cinema. It was so different from Hollywood. Where American movies were all about cars and muscles and explosions, *les films de France* meandered on, hindered neither by plot nor action. The large screens were filled with endless tumbling hills, running streams, pronounced Gallic noses, and winsome feminine beauties who floated through scenes like silk through air. A movie would begin, unravel slowly, then fade towards an end, and *nothing actually happened*.

And she *loved* the dialogue – which she followed courtesy of subtitles. More often than not, Daniel Autiel and his fellow actors seemed to talk in tongues: their lines revolved around philosophy, destiny, metaphor, a kind of ornate naval-gazing that made little sense but spun a magical web of sedate intrigue; and the action, what there was of it, often revolved around a kind of love and sex that had little in common with the soft focus, cut-to-male-stand-in's-buttocks variety that Malory was used to.

Also, it wasn't unusual for a movie just to finish abruptly, without even the hint of explanation, conclusion. The screen faded to black, no cliffhanger, just a final close-up, for example, of a pair of beautiful blue eyes gazing off into the distance, or white teeth biting into a ripe red tomato, or even, on one memorable occasion, a lithe young man's bare French penis, swaying gently in the morning breeze, then the letters FIN. Cue end credits. Malory would leave the auditorium, stumble out into the afternoon sunshine, dazed and confused, but rapt in the wonder of film.

She loved the romance that bled through every scene; the ravishing beauty of the actors, both male and female; the accents – listening to the French language spoken by somebody like Autiel was like allowing chocolate to melt on her tongue then trickle down the back of her throat. During the screening of one movie, a highly charged erotic drama that Malory caught one quiet Thursday afternoon with an audience of just four in a huge theatre, the sexual atmosphere that tumbled from the screen like a soft avalanche aroused her senses so much that she felt moved to some discreet public masturbation – another first for her.

But, like any ordinary individual, there was only so much daytime movie-going Malory could take. She felt that life was passing her by, her presence increasingly superfluous to the world's needs. One afternoon, on a humid platform down in the Métro, her train rattled into the station. She placed both feet at the platform's edge and leaned imperceptibly forward. If she jumped now, into the path of the speeding train, what would happen? Would she be missed? By whom? Sighing heavily, she stepped back and kept the possibility of suicide alive for another day.

And so she tried a little self-improvement. She attended art exhibitions, ticked off all the museums she had visited, and those exhibitions she still wanted to see. She bought books, but, unlike back home in LA where they sat unopened on bookshelves, she read them from cover to cover, and sometimes even enjoyed them. She drank herbal tea at expensive roadside cafés. She ate carefully at Greek restaurants in the Latin Quarter, where she ordered low-calorie salads: today's figure eight could well be tomorrow's fortune. She watched CNN on the hotel television, took long hot baths, cold showers, went to bed early and slept in late. Breakfast was a brioche and a *café noir* taken on the balcony, as she watched a hundred thousand cars going in a hundred thousand directions, each clearly needed someplace, while she was needed nowhere.

The day was hers to do with as she pleased. As were the endless weeks. A thought she struggled with almost daily: Am I going out of my mind?

Kidnappers no more, Flox and Danny had now willingly reverted back to being law-abiding citizens which, if you discounted the theft of the Citroën Pallas, which had since been expensively repaired, was exactly what they were.

After they'd got rid of the children, they checked out of the motel and drove into Paris, eventually settling in a cheap guesthouse that clung for dear life to a small corner of the Latin Quarter. Up two flights of stairs, and down a corridor that invited claustrophobia, they found space in a peculiarly shaped dorm that was home to eight bunk beds. They took the two in the far corner, next to a giant, dilapidated communal wardrobe. Flox was on top, Danny underneath, the pair separated by two inches of mattress. Home comforts were few: there was a micro-kitchen, but its state was such that few dared use it for anything other than heating water. Rats resided beneath the floorboards and the television in the lounge area didn't work.

However unpleasant it was, they decided that it was a step up from sleeping in the car. But only just. On his second night there, Flox experienced his first golden shower when, belatedly, he noticed a gaping hole at the bottom of the urinal. As he peed, the stream bounced off the ceramic, through the hole and on to his feet and legs. Unable to stem the flow, he stood there repelled, but realised the futility of complaining to the staff, a bunch of ignorant bastards concerned only with a constant clearing of their nasal passages, while watching a succession of dubbed daytime soap operas in what they aptly called the mess room.

From day to day, they lived as frugally as they could, for the little savings they had left were evaporating fast. Food was a necessity, as was alcohol to wile away the time, but even though they budgeted, they still went through the francs at a worrying rate.

A week passed, days punctuated by few noteworthy events: trips to the cinema, the propping up of many a Latin Quarter bar, riding the Métro without paying, purchasing some fiendish Moroccan hashish from a man with a handlebar moustache and sunglasses in Montparnasse, being ordered out of the Louvre, a Greek restaurant, and a lesbian bar, due to the effects of the fiendish Moroccan hashish, shoplifting Orangina from a twenty-four-hour supermarket without detection, a race down the Champs-Élysées, up the hill in Montmartre, football in the park, an excursion up the Eiffel Tower, nightly contemplations on the Pont Neuf, sleeping fitfully till early afternoon, drinking, bickering, fighting, and plunging ever closer to a dark and dangerous debt, a spider's web of depression. Flox's anxieties returned: he couldn't breathe properly, a pain above his eye spread to his skull, a lump in his throat was a regular feature of his waking hours, and would not diminish. Cancer? Headaches raged.

And all the while, Danny was plagued with guilt and worry over the children. A recurring argument with Flox revolved around whether he should place a call to Holland Park, just to make sure. Flox insisted this was a mad idea – 'We've stolen their car, remember?' – but Danny could not rest until he knew they were safe and sound, whatever the repercussions. One midmorning, while Flox risked a shower in the guesthouse, Danny made a quick dash to a phone booth on the corner, armed with a handful of change. Gingerly, he dialled the number and awaited connection, breathing fast.

Colette answered. 'Hello?'

'Colette, hi, it's Danny . . .' What to say next? How to play it? 'How are you? And how are the children?'

'Danny! For heaven's sake, where on earth are you? Why did you take the kids to France?' Her words came out in a rush, but she didn't sound angry. Instead, she sounded almost relieved – thankful. 'Lovely idea, though. They had a wonderful time – I'm so grateful to you.' And here she dropped her voice a pitch. 'You helped me in a time of real need.' The whisper was strained. 'But where is Philippe's car? He's been going out of his mind. The man is intolerable! And where are you? Paris or Milan?'

Danny breathed in deeply. He was relieved that the children were safe, but unclear as to how to tackle the subject of the stolen car. Gut instinct told him to stick with the original excuse – ailing elderlies in Italy – but before he could launch into any elaborate alibi, the extension was snatched up.

'DANNY? YOU BLOODY BASTARD! WHERE IN GOD'S NAME IS MY FUCKING CAR?'

Dejectedly: 'Oh, hello, Philippe. Look—'

'You've stolen my car, you bastard! You absolute fucking bastard!'

Colette: 'Philippe, for God's sake! There is no need to talk to Danny like that. I'm sure he has a perfectly reasonable explanation if you just—'

Philippe: 'When I require any of your words of wisdom, my *darling*, I shall ask for them. Otherwise, stay out of it.' Then, to Danny: 'I know where you are. I have already informed the authorities, and they are probably out looking for you as a result, right now. The car is registered in France, and because it's a classic model, it won't be hard to find. So don't get too comfortable. But let me warn you: if there is so much as a scratch on it, then I shall have your guts for garters! You'll be sorry for this, I'm telling you. I'm going to trace this call. You'll be sorry . . .'

Colette: 'Danny, don't listen to him. He's been a complete nightmare recently, so just ignore him. Philippe, the children have already told you, he had to rush to a sick relative somewhere, so just be patient. I swear, you care more for that car than you do for either me or the children. I've had just about enough.'

Philippe: 'And you care more for that bloody . . . bloody *fool* on that moped.'

Danny looked around the cramped confines of the telephone box. The plastic windows had graffiti scrawled all over it, as did the bright orange panelling. He looked at the little screen displaying the francs deposited, the figures clicking down like an inverse stopwatch rapidly. In his hand he held several more coins, but made no movement to push them into the slot. Meanwhile, the argument raged down the line. Danny experienced sudden loathing for both of these people, and although he pitied the children even more, Victoria especially, he knew that there was nothing he could do, that their fate lay outside his control, and that he had to let go. He looked at the Pallas, sitting outside the café opposite their temporary residence, and then, as the two voices continued to bicker at his expense, he slowly replaced the receiver.

As he stepped out of the booth, he saw Flox emerge at the street-level entrance to the guesthouse, his hair still wet. He ran across the road. 'I knew it,' he said. 'You called them, didn't you?

'I had to.'

'And?'

'The kids are fine, but Philippe has alerted the police – the French police, I think – that we've stolen his car. He said he was going to have the call traced. I think he knows we're still in Paris.'

'Terrific.'

'Now what?'

'I guess we'll have to leave Paris.'

Danny looked down at his hand, in which he was still clutching the remaining coins. 'Shall we call Sanjay? Just to say hello? Knowing him, he's probably been going out of his mind with worry since we disappeared.'

Flox looked at his watch: it was a little after eleven in the morning, ten at home. 'Think he'll be in?'

When Sanjay heard their voices, he swore loudly. 'What the fuck is going on with you two?' he asked. He sounded panicky.

'Why? What's the problem?'

Sanjay explained that the previous night their house had been burgled. Ransacked, trashed. The windows had been smashed, as had every piece of furniture. Threatening graffiti that mentioned Flox by name had been scrawled all over the walls. The police had arrived within forty-five minutes but by then the perpetrators had fled. Neighbours on either side, including Sanjay, were questioned, and the police had concluded that the attack had been personal. They wanted to know whether the missing inhabitants – Flox and Danny – had enemies. They also wanted to know their current whereabouts, but Sanjay was unable to tell them anything.

'Well, sorry, mate, but it's going to have to stay that way,' said Flox, wrestling the phone away from Danny and pushing him out of the cubicle. His face was very pale. 'This is just a quick call to let you know we're fine but we've had to go away for a while. Sorry I can't tell you anything else but, believe me, it's for your own safety.'

Before Sanjay had a chance to respond, Flox slammed down the phone.

'Are you now going to tell me what kind of trouble you're in?' Danny asked him.

Flox ignored him, walking towards the nearest bar. 'Well, I guess that confirms it,' he said. 'We're not going home.'

For purely financial reasons, they were unable to leave immediately. Flox said he'd come up with a plan, but Danny became increasingly agitated. With the absence of anything more taxing to occupy his mind, he became convinced that Philippe *had* traced the call, and that the French police were currently combing the city for the stolen car. It was only a matter of time before they caught up with them, after which extradition would surely follow. And then? Court, judge, jury, jail. The kidnapping of minors, the holding of them to ransom, the heartlessness of the crime. They'd throw away the key, undoubtedly.

Matters hardly improved when, poring over a week-old copy of the *News of the World*, Danny read a story about a husband and wife sentenced to nine years' imprisonment for kidnapping a foster-child. His blood ran cold. The mere sight of a *gendarme* sent him into freefall panic. Paris was closing in around his ears. They had to leave. It was imperative.

Nineteen

Dutch courage, Flox called it. It was shortly after eleven thirty in the morning, early even for them, but the successive beers and whisky chasers were necessary, practically medicinal. Flox threw one back after another, and Danny followed suit. Alcohol sloshed around in their stomachs, with only a solitary brioche for company. After the next round, they would be officially penniless, all their savings gone. There were only two options left to them. One was to sell the car, but without the car, what would they do for transport? Neither had the patience for coaches or trains and, anyway, how exactly does one go about selling a stolen car? The second was more ominous, but also more reasonable, given that they needed to escape.

'Right,' said Flox, after their final beer. He turned to Danny. 'Here's what we do.' He removed from his pocket a small tin and a packet of Rizlas, and started rolling discreetly.

Danny listened, shrugged, nodded, gulped, offered no argument, nodded again, finished his drink, and got up to follow Flox back to the guesthouse. He felt mildly drunk, but nowhere near enough for what was about to happen.

Save for a South African, sleeping off a hangover that wouldn't ease until the evening, the dorm was empty when they returned, every bed unmade. Danny, as instructed, went in. The South African was snoring heavily. His blond hair covered his eyes, and his unshaven chin moved rhythmically as he ground his teeth in time to an anxiety dream. Danny walked stealthily over to the Italian gigolo's bed. He moved the metal frame away from the wall and found the young man's backpack, which smelt strongly of aftershave. He thrust in his hand and rooted through tapes, T-shirts, underpants, jumpers, before he found the passport. An elastic band kept it, and various documents, bound together. He brought it out, and sat on the bed, holding his breath. As he expected, among the documents there was a wad of Italian lire, the same bundle he'd watched the young stud hunt through each night before going out. He removed all of it, every last note, regardless of denomination, and thrust it into his pocket. Next, he went to the German's bed. He was fairly sure where this man kept his money, so he untucked the sheets and looked for the rip in the wafer-thin mattress. It was well hidden, but Danny's fingers were tenacious and he soon found what he was looking for, a thinner wad of money. Then, he visited the bunks belonging to the two Danish boys, then the silent English guy's, the tall mystery albino, and, finally, the sleeping South African. He kept all his belongings in a small bedside table and his unconscious head lay a few centimetres from it. Danny prised open the drawer, keeping his eyes on the big man's sleeping face. His breathing had become irregular, and he had begun to fidget, as if waking was imminent. Sweat poured from Danny's hairline over his eyebrows, then into his eyes. He blinked, and saw four of everything. The drawer squeaked and he was forced to open it slower. He stopped when he could see inside: a passport, a Walkman, a yellowing John Grisham, several envelopes with the guesthouse's address on it and, underneath a small, pristine copy of a Gideon's Bible, a stack of money. With fingers like spider's legs, Danny pulled out the cash from under the Good Book, while he kept watch on the sleeping hulk. Then the Bible fell with a gentle thud to the back of the drawer, and the South African's eyes popped open, the rims pink.

Danny froze.

The South African groaned. 'What?'

Danny removed his hand from the drawer, the money with it, pushed it shut, and feigned tying his shoelaces while slipping the cash into a sock. He attempted to keep calm. 'Morning, mate,' he said, optimistically.

'What time is it?'

'Noon.'

The South African sat up, raising head and shoulders from the sweat-stained pillow. The strain, however, was too much, and he slumped down again. Danny wondered if the man could hear his heartbeat, which seemed to echo in his own ears.

The South African rubbed his eyes with the heel of his large right hand. His teeth were yellow, his tongue bright pink, and the stench that came from within his cave-like mouth made Danny want to retch. 'Fuck off and let me sleep,' he said, groggily.

'Righto,' said Danny, with false cheer.

The South African rolled over heavily. Wasting no time, Danny packed his and Flox's bags, his knees knocking. He checked his watch. Time to go.

Meanwhile, Flox had gone to visit the guesthouse staff in the mess room. They were watching dubbed soap operas, but welcomed the relative stranger without question when they saw he was bearing herbal gifts. Soon, they and Flox were all sitting on a low sofa, their knees at eye level, smoking a pungent spliff each and staring at the hyperactivity on the television screen. One of the staff, a young man with Brillo-pad hair, one caterpillar-like eyebrow, and a nose wide enough to run a train through, snorted, brought up all manner of molten mucus, and spat it into a half-full mug of tea. Another got hiccups and started to laugh. Then the others followed suit. Nervously, Flox joined in. Save for his own virgin spliff, which consisted only of tobacco, this was powerful skunk they were smoking and, cut with little nicotine, made them incredibly high. Within minutes, one was crawling around the floor making cattle noises. Another bleated then collapsed in a heap. For a horrified second, Flox thought he had died, until snoring told him otherwise. Ten minutes later, the other two were also fast asleep, at which point Flox went to work.

He muted the television, stubbed out his cigarette and began to search for as much money as he could find. He yanked open every drawer, every cupboard, sifting through empty bill books, stationery, packets of cigarettes, condoms, rotting fruit, girlie magazines, elastic bands, rubbish. Nothing of any value whatsoever. Eventually he came to a locked drawer. Shit! But if it was locked, its contents must be valuable. All he needed was the key... which he would find – where, exactly? He spun round and looked over the sleeping men on the floor. Each had a full key ring attached to his belt. He took a set, then went through the torturous process of thrusting each key towards the lock. None seemed to fit, whichever way he tried. Behind him, a man groaned. Flox turned to check on him, but he was still asleep. Key after key after key proved hopeless, but then, miraculously, success. A small copper key slid into the lock with ease. He turned it. A quiet click; overwhelming relief. Behind him came another groan. He pulled open the drawer. A cash tray. Three empty compartments, four filled with crumpled notes. Flox snatched them up and rammed them into his pockets. He heard another groan. He slammed the drawer and a voice said, 'Hey!'

Flox turned to see one of the men clambering to his feet with all the grace of a felled bull. The look of confusion on his face turned to gradual comprehension, then anger.

'Hey!'

Flox's panic swelled. He looked around and saw a baseball bat under the counter – the guesthouse's sole security device. He picked it up and swung it at the man, making contact with his neck, just below the right ear. He went down again, expelling an *oof!*. The sound woke the others.

'Hey!'

Flox swung the baseball bat wildly.

Behind him, another voice. A familiar one. 'Flox! Quick! Let's get out of here!'

Flox turned round and saw Danny, a backpack on either shoulder, heading for the stairs at the end of the narrow corridor. Behind him, in the doorway of their dorm, the South African appeared, his face the picture of sleepy disgruntlement. Flox threw the baseball bat at one of the other staff, hitting him on the chest, then ran out of the room in pursuit of Danny. The South African tore down the hall after them. The three staff members, their brains still fried but their legs in working order, scrambled after him. Danny and Flox flew down the stairs, three at a time, and out into the quiet street. Danny threw Flox the car keys, Flox got in, started the engine, slipped it into gear, opened Danny's door, then pulled down hard on the steering-wheel and lurched out into the road just as it filled with three heavily stoned guesthouse staff, one wielding the baseball bat, and the South African. He sounded the horn, increased speed, and each man dived for cover.

At the end of the road, he pulled out into oncoming traffic, applied pressure to the accelerator and shot off. In the rear-view mirror, he saw the staff and the South African come into view, but they meant nothing now. He hollered joyously. 'Did you find much?' he asked Danny.

Danny patted his pockets.

'Nice one!'

Flox slowed down, and drove for another ten minutes, observing the Highway Code studiously. Presently, they saw a bank and Flox pulled over and parked. Both men got out, hearts still racing, and entered through the automatic doors. They found a quiet corner and, as discreetly as possible, removed the money from their pockets. They made separate piles of lire, Deutschmarks, pounds, francs, kronas, and pesetas. When they had counted and recounted it, they queued, subdued, in the line for the *bureau de change*.

'As soon as we get it changed into francs, we're solvent,' said Flox, with cautious optimism.

When their turn came, they handed over all the money, smiling to the bespectacled woman behind the bullet-proof screen, and waited while she went to work with a calculator. Her fingers made light work of the large rubber buttons. She switched equipment, replacing the ordinary calculator for one which, when activated, would whir, buzz, and deposit a receipt. She pulled open a drawer with her right hand, and removed a large wad of francs. Flox held his breath as she counted, licking the index finger of her left hand intermittently as she counted off the notes at speed. She tore off a receipt, placed it on top of the money, and passed it under the glass. Flox snatched it, forgot to thank her, and beat a quick retreat.

'How much?' asked Danny.

Flox looked at the receipt that bore the total in emphatic black and white. 'More than enough for now,' he said. 'Let's get out of here.'

As they reached the car, Flox spotted a small man in uniform, with a neat moustache and an expression of purpose on his face, crouching at the rear wheel, a deep green clamp in his hands. Flox shouted at him in English, and ordered Danny to start the car. The little man looked up at Flox, snarled something in French, but continued with the job. Flox pushed him out of the way. The little man screamed for assistance from his colleague who was listening to music in the van. Flox picked up the clamp, which was far heavier than its small size suggested, and hurled it on to the kerb. The little man, now furious, lunged at Flox, but Flox was ready for him. He punched him, once, on the nose, and the man went down. Flox jumped into the car, screaming at Danny to drive, drive – *drive*!

Rubber burned beneath them as they screeched out on to the road, and raced away. Adrenaline was reverberating around the Pallas like an echo: Flox hollering, Danny screaming, both jumping up and down in their seats. The steering-wheel veered wildly left and right. Neither of them saw the pram—

It came into contact sharply and cleanly with the tip of the bonnet. It flew high up into the air and time stopped still. Flox's jaw fell open, and Danny slammed his right foot on the brakes. Pedestrians watched in shock. Cars stopped, windows opened, drivers leaned out. Flox and Danny swivelled in their seats, looked out of the back window and waited, all eyes searching out the mother, a flying baby, but they could see only an old woman shaking a skeletal fist at them. Time passed in dreadful slow motion.

Clunk, smash, clatter. The sound of mangled wire, of two small wheels spinning violently, and the thud-thud-thud of – of . . .

They fell out of the sky like hailstones, different shapes, many sizes. Flox looked at Danny quizzically, his face a mask of confusion. Danny let out a whimper. A gigantic burst of laughter exploded within Flox. The sky was raining vegetables: onions, courgettes, carrots, a string of garlic, aubergines, mushrooms. The old woman to whom the pram belonged had fallen to her knees to gather up her morning's shopping. The pram lay dead beside her, but the vegetables were just a little bruised. Life resumed its normal pace. Danny experienced a terrific need to urinate, but his relief was as palpable as mainlining class A drugs.

But then, hurtling up the avenue, came two sights to eradicate relief, and reinstate panic: an unmarked white van which, even from this distance, clearly contained the apoplectic traffic warden; and, beside it, a police van, its siren blaring angry blue neon.

Flox turned round to face the front, punched Danny's arm, and issued one directive: 'DRIVE!'

Danny considered this for the briefest of nanoseconds. He drove.

First gear, second, third, fourth, foot down fast.

Malory awoke with a hangover, her first for some time, the pillow still clutched to her chest. It was her only source of comfort. She rolled over and winced, screwing up her face, and attempting to unstick the hair from her cheek. Her head was pounding. She felt like her tongue needed a shave, and she staggered into the bathroom. She did two things: brushed her teeth, then reached for the red wine and drank deep. Intermittent memories, like the flash of a camera, came back to her in fits and starts. Memories of last night. Had she really—? She didn't actually—? Did she? Oh, boy, oh, God, oh – fuck. She waded back across the room and lowered herself on to the bed, groaning. She crawled over to the bedside table and slowly, nervously, opened the small drawer. Inside she saw a diamond bracelet, a diamond ring, a gold brooch. Glinting, gleaming, dazzling, expensive. And stolen. A low whine slid out of the corner of her mouth.

She slept another quarter-hour, got up, showered, dressed, drank a full bottle of wine, and left the room, paranoia descending on her like rainfall.

What now?

The previous day, Malory had come to a decision. She was going to be wanton. Fuck it, she had thought, yesterday afternoon, why bother with discipline any longer? She had fallen off the wagon and into the red wine, which she had had delivered to her by room service. She had drunk and drunk. And then she had gone out. Taken insane risks. Did stuff. Dot, dot, dot.

And now it was the morning after the night before. The lift to the lobby descended at an angle, then sideways. It delivered her on the ground floor practically upside-down. She giggled, righted herself and walked unsteadily to the revolving doors. She burst out into daytime Paris, breathed in the warm spring air, and giggled again. Her desperation had receded into yesterday, into tomorrow. Today she would laugh, she would be gay, she would be frivolous. She hailed a taxi, unsuccessfully, and watched as it drove on oblivious to her. Fine, she thought, I'll walk. Where, though?

The pavement beneath her was slippery, uneven, dangerous. The act of placing one foot in front of the other was confusing, a strange, cryptic game, the rules of which were temporarily alien to her. She giggled some more, saw double of everything. The trees were lush and green, fragrant and new. The cars – blue, red, black, brown, yellow, green, metallic, two-door, four-door, dented, pristine – passed her by in a blur of colour and action, movement and speed. A gentle pre-summer breeze coiled around her smooth, bare legs, under the hem of her delicate silk dress, around her midriff, across her chest, and fanned her neck and face. She felt delicious – young, vulnerable and carefree. She hadn't been this drunk in ages and right now it felt exquisite, the lightness between her eyes unusual but certainly not unwelcome. Where would she go today? Why, anywhere, of course. The day was empty, and so was she. She could go anywhere she damn well pleased.

Bar.

Good idea, she thought, and silently congratulated herself. She would get herself another drink, maybe buy one for somebody else too. Hell, she'd buy a round for everyone in the joint. Why not?

Malory squinted, and peered across the road. She saw an awning the colour of plums and, through windows that reflected her and the passing traffic, she saw people bringing cups and glasses to their mouths. Bar, she thought. Found one.

She stopped, and stood still, bringing both hands up to her head, which had begun to spin. She tried to find the nearest set of traffic lights. Which way – left or right? Impatiently, she staggered towards the kerb, then put a dainty, Agnès b-clad foot on to the road as cars roared by. I'm famous, Malory thought. I shall stop the traffic, part the waves.

And she walked out into the oncoming throng of speeding metal.

Her eyes focused on nothing, but her ears were at least partly aware of the terrible squeal of tyres on Tarmac. Ouch, she thought, turn the goddamn sound down! She stopped, tensed, and screwed her eyes shut. A car, to her left, approached her at considerable speed, but skidded to a stop just in time, its long bonnet inches from her thigh. Close call, though Malory remained unaware of just how close to mortality she had come. She opened her eyes, and saw a long green car – an old Citroën, or something – and behind the dashboard two young men with expressions of disbelief, and fear, on their faces. One looked as if he was about to burst into tears. And the other? He seemed distantly familiar to her, and looked as if he had just clapped eyes on a ghost.

Twenty

The seat was long, wide and comfortable. Every time the car turned a corner, Malory slid to the far end, occasionally bumping her head on the window. Hiccups continued to pop out of her smiling lips. Her hair fell over her eyes, and she was aware that she couldn't see clearly, but she liked the sensation: suddenly, her life was speeding recklessly. Anything could happen. A shiver chased itself up her spine.

Sitting behind the driver, she attempted, intermittently, to focus. This wasn't easy, as she was very drunk. Parisian streets came and went — avenues, boulevards, the occasional cul-de-sac. She saw blurred shops, explosions of colour, rumours of shopping, early-afternoon activity, bars and cafés. The Eiffel Tower thrust before her, then disappeared. She thought of Sunset Boulevard, La Cienega, the fulsome curves of Laurel Canyon, smog, humidity, silicon — and felt comforted that she was still so far away from it. She saw the Arc de Triomphe, and endless rows of traffic lights, red, amber, green. She was enjoying the journey: movement was good, the car was comfortable, and this man—

A sudden moment of lucidity: where was she? Who was this man – or men, in fact? She counted two of them. Neither looked round at her, or spoke. She had thought initially that this was a cab; that's why she had clambered in. Now she wasn't so sure. She looked at the back of the two men's heads. One had short brown hair, the other an unkempt mane scraped back into a scruffy ponytail. *Déjà vu* came and went, as it does. She looked at his neck, his T-shirt, and saw – or thought she saw – a slice of blue-green ink. A tattoo? Another wave of *déjà vu*. A name on the tip of her tongue.

But then—

The blaring honk of horn. The screech of brakes.

Malory was thrown forward, her knees hitting the driver's seat. He lurched forward into his seatbelt. Simultaneously, they apologised to one another, their eyes meeting briefly in the rear-view mirror. Blue irises, she noted. Pretty. Silence resumed as quickly as it had been broken, and the car drove on, slowly, through the busy streets.

Gradually, Malory thought she could sense tension inside the car. Or perhaps this was merely a figment of her drunken imagination?

She hiccuped again.

Upfront, Danny drove and Flox stared ahead. He, like their passenger in the back, watched aspects of Paris in the spring unfolding before his 20–20 vision. If Flox looked relatively calm, he was obviously still in command of some of his old acting skills, because he felt anything but. Inside, his mind was going crazy. Not only because he'd had one hell of a morning, but that — unless he was gravely mistaken, *delusional* — the inebriated American woman they'd almost knocked over and who was now rolling around the back seat, was . . . *Malory. What? Why? How?* The questions spun in his head at terrific speed. It was the first time he'd seen her in — what? — a decade? The first time he'd thought of her in at least a week. And now here she was. This was truly surreal. He wanted to turn round and look at her, talk to her, tell her everything he'd stored up over the past ten years. And, of course, to berate her for abandoning him. But no . . . not now, not yet. Pace yourself, he told himself. Just wait a while longer. Let it all distil, dilute, and begin to make some kind of sense.

And it will all make sense, eventually.

Won't it?

Danny gripped the steering-wheel so tightly that his knuckles turned white. Excuse me, he thought internally, but what the hell is going on here? Until — well, until this morning, life had been its dull, depressing, monotonous self. And now? Now, suddenly, all *this*. As if the lunatic events of the morning hadn't been enough, Danny, a man to whom nothing out of the ordinary had ever happened, was currently driving a stolen car around the city streets of Paris with a superstar in the back seat. She was — and he knew that this defied belief, but she really, *really* was — Malory Cinnamon, the famous actress. *Central Park Six*, *The Girl Who Dreamed*, the girl he lusted after with his eyes tight shut and the lights out.

He stole a quick look at Flox, who stared implacably forward, the strangest expression on his noticeably pale face.

Things had turned strange.

They would turn stranger still.

What now? thought Flox. Think. *Think*.

Bingo: change of venue.

He cleared his throat. 'Where are you staying?' he asked tentatively, without turning his head round.

Malory brought two fingers to each eye and rubbed hard. Her inebriation was subsiding. 'Le Parc,' she replied, then gave the address. Silently, her lips and tongue formed his name – *Flox* – but she made no sound.

Flox nodded to Danny, who turned the car round and drove back towards the hotel. Danny glanced into the rear-view mirror, and saw the woman smile quizzically to herself. She looked at him, and Danny averted his gaze. Then she looked at Flox, and slowly took in his profile, once so familiar to her. She took a deep breath, and swallowed. 'So, Flox,' she said, 'how've you been?'

At which point, Danny went into spasm and the car swerved so violently it almost hit a tree.

'Drive carefully, will you?' Flox chided him.

They arrived at the hotel, and were greeted by an attendant who took the keys and parked the car for them. Then Malory led them, still slightly unsteady, up to her penthouse suite. 'Come in,' she encouraged, at the door.

Once inside, Flox asked if he could use the toilet, from which he did not immediately return.

Suddenly, Danny was alone with her. He looked around the room, amazed by its opulence. His stomach felt tight and dry. He felt completely out of his depth. The famous Hollywood actress, standing no more than fifteen feet away, looked at him and smiled a smile that contained more electricity than any lightbulb he had ever seen. He felt dazzled, and petrified. Her eyes were as blue as a new-born baby's.

'Hello,' he said, his voice several octaves higher than usual. Hello? Why had he said that? They'd already met, after a fashion, back in the car. Idiot, fool . . .

'Would you like a drink?' she asked him, moving over to the drinks cabinet. 'Gin and tonic, wine, champagne, Evian?'

'No, thank you,' he replied. But, God, he was thirsty. 'I mean, yes. Yes, please. Thank you.'

'Which one?'

'I beg your pardon?'

'*I beg your pardon*,' she repeated. 'I just love your accent, and the way you talk. So English. I beg your pardon! Wonderful!' She laughed brightly. 'I meant, which drink would you like?'

Danny flushed. 'Oh. Oh, right. Water. Evian, please. That would be lovely.' He smiled awkwardly at her, then looked towards the bathroom door, willing Flox to return.

The actress fetched him a drink; their fingers touched as she handed him the tall glass. 'Thank you,' he said, again.

'You're very welcome,' she said, between delicate sips from her glass. 'I think I need to sober up some.'

Danny felt an overwhelming desire to fill the ensuing silence. Say something, he said to himself. Be natural. Mentally, he began to take baby steps towards his first conversation with her. 'So,' he began, his voice still unnaturally high, 'you and Flox ... you know Flox somehow?'

'Flox?' Malory said, sitting down on the bed, her dress riding up her thighs, a flash of electric white cotton between her legs. 'Oh, sure, we go way back.'

When Danny said, 'Really?' it came out as a squeak.

From behind the bathroom door came the sound of a lavatory flushing. Then Flox joined them. He sat down in a large armchair, crossing one leg over the other. He glanced over the carpet and at the walls.

Malory made the first move. 'Well,' she said, smiling, showing teeth, 'this is some coincidence, huh? I guess we have some catching up to do.'

Flox nodded, and Malory approached Danny, her hand outstretched. 'Malory Cinnamon,' she said. 'Charmed.'

Next, she approached Flox. He got out of his chair, but remained unable to make eye-contact. Malory kissed his cheek, and smiled. 'Hello again,' she said. Flox looked up, over her shoulder, and caught Danny's astonished gaze. He blushed deeply, and cleared his throat.

'Um ...' began Danny, uncomfortably. He pointed towards the double doors. 'I think I'll ... I think I'll go out on to the balcony and, you know, take some air ... allow you two to ... to catch up.'

Malory smiled — assent and thanks — and Danny closed the doors behind him. Outside it was hot and humid. He looked down at the traffic below, the cars like crazed ants fleeing every which way. Inside his skull, his brain did similar.

Almost two hours later, he was invited back in. He noted awkwardness in the atmosphere but said nothing. Flox had his hands in his pockets, and was perched on the edge of a coffee table. Danny looked at him and saw a stranger. Malory struck up conversation and they talked about the lure of the open road, their shared desire for new experiences, and came to a mutual decision. Malory packed her bags and checked out, signing her famous name with its attendant loops and teardrop-topped i's without, Danny noted, bothering to check the astronomical total printed on the receipt. The three left the hotel and climbed into the car, intent on leaving the city and heading south, towards different scenery, different adventures, the future.

Several hours out of Paris, the Pallas was heading south towards a lemon sunset. With every mile that sprang up between them and the capital, Danny felt a little calmer, as if the likelihood of being stopped by *gendarmes* on the lookout for a classic Citroën had diminished. Malory, he saw, was sleeping demurely on the back seat, her hair fanned out around her shoulders, while his flatmate was staring intently out of the open passenger window, clearly sorting out all manner of recently reinstated personal demons. There was plenty that Danny wanted to talk to him about, but he knew that now was neither the time nor the place.

They stopped just once, for petrol and refreshments. By now it was dark, the motorway emptying, getting emptier. The Pallas's yellow headlights sought out an indeterminate path for them. At the driving wheel, Danny felt euphoric, and kept playing recent events in his mind over and over again, constantly bewitched.

Excerpts from a notepad (in lieu of a diary, which is currently stuffed deep inside a suitcase in the car's trunk)

Guess what? I'm writing this in the back of a stolen speeding car in the dead of night, somewhere in France, the middle I think. After weeks and months of having the most boring time of my life in Paris, suddenly everything has changed — and I'm in a chase movie made real. Surreal!

Yesterday, I did a rilly bad thing — I'll explain later — and this morning I almost got killed when I walked out (drunk, I admit) into traffic. But this, it turned out, was fate. I wasn't going to get killed at all, I was merely going to meet my past, and have it catch up with me. This morning I met an old flame, Flox, someone I had gotten together with when I first arrived in LA, an Englishman. He represents a time in my life when I was still young and innocent and blissfully naive, not corrupted by the movie industry. And he, I now realize, will help me find myself — by revisiting who and what I used to be. I think it's incredible how fate works! I feel so strong now, so full of purpose.

He arrived back in my life at just the right time, too. Because I think, just between you and me, Diary, that I was beginning to go seriously off the rails. Weeks of doing

Spin Cycle

nothing back in Paris didn't suit me. Depression was turning me crazy. I got so bored, so frustrated at doing nothing that ... I did something crazy. I don't know what came over me! Desperation, maybe? (Alcohol?!!) Anyway, after a light lunch yesterday afternoon, which I washed down with wine, I wandered down the Champs-Elysees until I found a jewelry shop — and I went in. The wine was on a fairground ride inside my head, and I couldn't stop smiling. The assistant — this old hag with soft & loose skin around her neck, and eyes which, hello, had sooo obviously been pinned back by a surgeon — was all over me like a rash, obviously smelling my money and wanting it bad. I didn't even have to ask — she insisted I try on all these beautiful rings and brooches, earrings and necklaces. Admittedly, I did look fantastic in some of them — I just wish I had the right occasion to wear them (shame). Well, I thought, she's making this real easy for me. I must have spent almost an hour with her trying on stuff and I eventually settled on a diamond bracelet, a diamond ring (the kind of engagement-style ring no one has ever bought me), and this cute gold brooch. I took out my Gucci leather wallet and flashed a few credit cards in her direction just to show my intent, but before I handed one over, I got this wild idea. I asked her if I could take one more look at that stunning necklace she had shown me earlier, which must have cost something like $40,000. With this oily smile on her face, she went back out to the window display to fetch it and I simply walked out of the shop still wearing my intended purchases! I swear to God it was as easy as that! I walked to the door, opened it (no alarm went off), and up to the window where my shop assistant was carefully lifting the heavy pendant from a soft velvet cushion. She looked up at me, and I smiled, pointing at it. She smiled back, collected it up in her wrinkled hands, and motioned for me to walk back into the shop, me nodding like one of those dogs you find in the back of cars – bounce-bounce-bounce. Then, as soon as she was out of sight, I walked into the street, hailed a cab, jumped in and drove off! I couldn't believe I had done it, and I couldn't believe it had all been so easy! Hell, the assistant practically gave me the stuff!

But then, if I'm honest, that's when I started worrying. I looked up at the taxi driver, who was looking at me in his little mirror, and I burst into tears. I'm not entirely sure why?? Then my heart beat real fast and I started panicking. They must have had CCTV in the shop? What if they recognized me? What if the police were after me now? I'd be arrested and thrown into a foreign jail where they only eat rice and frogs' legs. I'd never live down the shame. It would kill Mom and Dad.

I couldn't think straight – so I just went back to the hotel, and ordered up bottles & bottles of wine. Anything to blot out all the paranoia.

Dear Diary: how did I get myself into such a mess???

Which was where fate came in to play its hand: me meeting Flox (and his sweet friend Danny), and all of us quitting the city together! Perfect! (Note to Diary: Is there a movie script in all this?) Anyway, they came back to my hotel and we got to talking – apparently, they'd gotten themselves into a bit of bother as well. Surprisingly, they offered up all the the details readily, *and didn't hold back — typical Flox, I guess, he never could keep his mouth shut, but it is so nice to see him again (and a bit weird, also, to be honest — I guess we still have 'issues'). I decided not to tell them about my jewelry theft, because even thinking about it had me in a cold sweat. Instead, I kept quiet, and the three 'items' are right now wrapped up inside a pair of stockings at the bottom of my bag, and they'll stay there until I know what to do with them, or how to get rid of them — whichever. We shall see, we shall see. All I have told them is that I'm here on a little vacation, having gotten a little fried back at home — temporarily, of course. When I said that I'd also just come out of a painful break-up with an ex, I saw Flox visibly wince — which is a good sign, I think.*

So now we are just driving south, on some kind of freeform vacation, our only solid destination being sunshine, sea and sand, and a little fun!

I can't wait!!

Living at last!

Shortly after three a.m., they hung a right off the *autoroute* and found themselves in a small town. A roadside motel flashed its lame neon sign — low wattage, few stars — and drew them hypnotically in. It was painted prison grey, and the carpet in the hall that led to the small reception desk was a psychedelic black and white. Weary, and exhausted from their journey, they checked themselves into three separate rooms, bade each other a mumbled goodnight, fell on to their respective beds and slept heavily.

Twenty-one

'Can I drive?' Malory asked, in the early afternoon of the following day. The fugitive trio had wrestled heads from pillows, breakfasted, paid and checked out – courtesy, incidentally, of the actress and her considerable funds.

It was by far the largest car Malory had ever driven, and taming it proved difficult. The only car she'd previously owned was the tiny bug almost a decade earlier. Post-TV and movie success, she was simply too famous to drive herself anywhere – if there wasn't a chauffeur on hand, then it was Cab City for Malory Cinnamon.

This, however, was fun and she threw herself into the task in the same way she would a meaty role, driving too fast and steering a little too enthusiastically. Her two passengers belted up discreetly.

They passed a road sign: 'Lyon, 46 km'.

The police car sat on the grassy verge ahead. The two policemen inside it were discussing football. Smoke spiralled from two burning Gitanes and settled about their heads and shoulders. They were bored to distraction, and longed for incident.

They heard the squeal of the engine before they saw it. It sounded high-pitched, as if straining at the leash. Then, seconds later, they saw a car wobble by. A large green Citroën, one of the old models, passed in a blur, proceeding at a speed far in excess of the legal limit. Also, it appeared to be weaving across the road. But what clinched it for them was what both policemen saw, in a flash, at precisely the same moment: blonde hair at the steering wheel, dancing in the wind.

Female.

They gave chase.

Malory was in her element. That it was an element she had never until now known existed was immaterial. Right now, she was at one with her machine. The needle was pushing a hundred and twenty k.p.h., the windows were down, and Flox had found her a radio station that played the Eagles and REO Speedwagon back to back, and she felt alive, connected. The scenery was breathtaking: rolling hills, winding lanes, blooming flowers, blue skies above.

The wailing siren intruded so loudly that 'Hotel California' was all but drowned. Blue neon flashed, bouncing off windows. Danny looked out of the back, saw the police car, and swore. It was still a way from them, but instinctively he ducked down in the seat, slid to the floor, and hid. In front, the previously liberated Malory launched herself into all-out panic. Flox tried to calm her. 'Don't worry,' he assured her, 'we were speeding, that's all.'

'In a stolen car,' added Danny, still crouching on the floor. 'In a *registered* stolen car.'

Tears sprang from Malory's eyes. The words *jewel thief* hovered in her throat.

'It'll be fine,' said a falsely confident Flox. 'Pull over.' He looked over his shoulder, down towards Danny. 'What are *you* doing?'

'Hiding.'

'Why?'

'Just in case.'

Flox turned his attention back to the driver. 'Malory, *pull over*!'

For the first time in at least an hour, Malory's right foot unstuck itself from the gas pedal, and applied pressure on the brake. Gently, she steered in towards the verge. She had stopped crying as quickly as she had begun. All the self-help books she had ever read came back to her, affirmations tumbling over directives over assurances and confidence boosts. She told herself that she was an actress, that she was placed on earth to act. She would be fine: they wouldn't search her baggage, wouldn't find what she was trying to hide. Deep breaths, calm yourself, prepare, improvise, smile – *project*. Cameras rolling . . . and *action*.

She stopped the car smoothly, and watched as the police overtook them and parked a few metres ahead. She checked herself in the rear-view mirror, smoothed down her eyebrows and puckered her lips. She ran both hands down her body, over breasts, stomach, thighs. She got out of the car, the ghost of Jessica Rabbit draped around her.

Flox watched on in wonder, awe.

She closed the car door and walked along the length of the vehicle, before perching herself on the bonnet. Today she was wearing a cut-off T-shirt that finished an inch above her stomach, and a stylish print skirt that revealed long golden thighs. She looked dazzlingly gorgeous. It was a warm, sultry day. She brought her right hand up to her face and waved her fingers to create a little breeze. As the two police officers approached, and Malory breathed in the smell of nicotine coming off them, she thought, I'll use it. *Preparation.* She blinked, slowly, and in the movie unfolding beneath her eyelids, Martin Scorsese nodded at her, and gave her the thumbs-up.

From behind the seat, Danny spoke. 'What's happening?'

Flox described what he saw between taut lips, but admitted that he had no idea what she might be saying. If there was a language barrier, it wasn't evident from where he was sitting. The policemen were smiling at her, clearly flirting. They offered her a cigarette, which she accepted. Only one, the larger of the two, bothered to look over at Flox, and it wasn't a particularly friendly look. After a few more moments of almost animated . . . not conversation but *banter*, Malory walked with them to the police car, trailing wisps of smoke. Flox narrated for the benefit of the unseeing Danny.

'Where are they now?' he whispered urgently.

'Still there,' came the reply.

With painstaking attention, Danny quietly applied pressure to the door handle, and squeezed. It popped open with a gentle click, and he opened it a crack, then further still until the gap was wide enough for him to squeeze out.

Flox turned around. 'What the fuck are you doing, Danny?'

Danny didn't reply. Noiselessly, he crawled on to the kerb and pushed the door to. Keeping his body pressed low to the ground, he inched along to the front of the car, Flox watching from the passenger seat in bewilderment. Malory continued to talk to the two policeman. One had a notepad in his hand, a ballpoint pen poised. Danny, on his knees and elbows, saw his chance and made crab-like scuttling movements between the yawning gap of either car, reaching the other's back wheel and collapsed in relief, safely hidden. The policemen and Malory walked back to the Pallas, ordered Flox out, and started to nose around half-heartedly. Flox didn't dare to check on Danny's progress.

Malory couldn't understand what had happened to Danny. Where was he? She looked at Flox, but he wouldn't meet her eyes. The police, in pidgin English, asked for the boot to be opened. Malory's flirting intensified in the aim of preventing them from searching her bags, but when she couldn't produce any documents confirming that this was indeed her car – as they had presumed – they grew terse with her, impatient. She wondered how many years car and jewellery theft would net her.

Beside the police car, Danny crawled to the still open driver's door, and relieved the ignition of the keys, then retraced his crab steps. When he reached the back wheel again, he crouched and waited.

One of the policemen told Malory and Flox to wait in

the car while they went back to their own to radio for information on the number-plate. Danny saw his chance and scurried back to the Pallas, jumped into the back seat, and instructed Malory to get the hell out of there.

She looked at him, stunned, her eyes wide.

'I've got their keys! Now come on! *Drive!*'

Malory started the engine, thrust it into gear, and screeched out on to the road. The police officers panicked – one jumped into their path and waved manically at them to stop, the other tried to locate the missing keys to start their car and give chase. Laughing hysterically, Malory sounded the horn and in the back Danny rolled down his window and threw out the car keys, watching them dance in the air before they disappeared from view.

Much later, as the sun dipped out of sight, replaced by the blanket of a starry night, Flox steered the great, thirsty car down a succession of small winding roads towards a tiny village. Ten minutes earlier, he'd seen a sign that read: 'Lamarque 7 km; Italie 90 km'. He was tired, Malory was fast asleep on his shoulder, dribbling saliva on to his shirt sleeve, and Danny's head was lolling after the drama of the day. He stopped at a petrol station, filled up the car and posed a one-word question to the man behind the counter: 'Hotel?'

The small man nodded, and pointed.

Without even trying, they had stumbled upon a nirvana of sorts.

Lamarque was tiny, a micro-village situated somewhere between the towns of Seyne and Digne, and so small it wasn't on any map. It consisted of farms, orchards, and a handful of shops. But it also had an illustrious guesthouse that catered solely for wealthy Europeans looking for a little countryside solace. Danny and Flox were overjoyed, and Malory was happy to oblige, financially speaking. They took two rooms, the men in a twin, Malory in a large double so steeped in majesty she felt she'd stepped into *Dangerous Liaisons* territory. There were sixteen rooms, and all but two were occupied. Most of the guests were elderly, dignified men and elegant women, all dressed in a manner that screamed personal fortune, and they liked nothing better during the day than to potter about the lush green grounds playing *boules*, drinking brandy, and shooting the breeze. They welcomed the three veritable youngsters – foreigners, at that – warmly, and whenever they strayed into the bar, sought to engage them in conversation. Flox thought this highly amusing: in the city, these people would have gone to great pains to avoid someone like him; here in unfamiliar surroundings, where everyone was more relaxed, they treated him like an object of amusement, a good way to pass the time between one four-course meal and the next.

The pace of life here was slow and languid, and the week passed leisurely. They would wake mid-morning, take their time over breakfast, which would effortlessly segue into a rich lunch, then head back to their rooms for a siesta. Later, carrying bottles of wine in a shoulder-bag, they took long, meandering walks through the grounds, barefoot in deep grass, looking for the perfect place to lie back and laze. They'd walk down sleepy paths to small spots of sunsoaked land surrounded by apple trees and a small stream which, a few hundred yards into the distance, became wide and deep enough to swim in. Here, they sunbathed, paddled, came out to dry, dozed and drank, Malory reacquainting herself with her former beau and getting to know Danny. She told them Hollywood stories, about the ups and downs of her career, and tried to explain to Flox just why she had felt she had to sever links. In response, Flox claimed that he'd never forgotten or forgiven her, but that his life since had been a bed of roses, his career progressing in leaps and bounds. When she told him how glad she was that life had been kind, he looked away and squashed ants under his thumb. Together, they regaled Danny with stories about their heady times together pre-*Central Park Six*, and the air around them grew thick with laughter.

And when Danny spoke about himself, Malory listened intently, taking both his hands in hers and holding tight. If only Amy could see me now, he thought. When he spoke about the death of his mother, Malory threw both arms around him and drew him close, weeping on to his shoulder and pulling him between two distinct emotions: loss and new love.

On their last night in this haven of tranquillity, they decided to take dessert and several bottles of wine up to Malory's room, and play parlour games. Malory suggested Charades first, and proceeded to mime a succession of American films, books and TV shows that neither Flox nor Danny had ever heard of.

Predictably, Flox grew bored and, under the considerable influence of drink, suggested Spin the Bottle.

'Whoever the bottle stops on,' he explained, while emptying the dregs of another down his throat, 'has to . . .' He paused to think, then brightened. '. . . has to talk sexual partners. How many, where, when, how often. All right?'

The others nodded. Flox placed the bottle on the carpet and they sat around it, cross-legged. The bottle spun and stopped between Danny and Malory. They spun again. This time, it pointed to Flox. 'Shit,' he said. 'Me first.'

Flox had become a man, as he put it, a few days after his fourteenth birthday. She had been sixteen, and a Scorpio, which apparently counted for plenty. It was during half-term, in her bedroom, pictures of John Taylor staring from every wall. She had done all the leading, and Flox had followed eagerly. It was over before it had really begun, but those thirty seconds were among the most cataclysmic of Flox's young life. After her, he had to wait another year before getting it on with Hilary, a girl in his class with a name that suggested everything she wasn't. They discovered sex properly, together, and continued to do so for another delirious year, until she left him for someone older and in possession of a full driving licence. By seventeen, the one-night stands began in earnest. In his early twenties, when he travelled America, there were so many he lost count – although he did remember a certain Alicia Feldstein. His first serious adult relationship took hold a year later, back in London, and for the following thirteen months, they had talked of marriage and children. But disillusion had set in, and Flox was soon single and sexually voracious once more. His final tally? Well, a conservative estimate suggested thirty, maybe thirty-five, forty – or was it even more than that? Who knew? Not Flox. Flox had been too busy to keep count.

When his confessional came to a wheezy conclusion, Danny and Malory spontaneously burst into a round of applause.

'You really should have stayed on in Hollywood, you know,' said Malory. 'They love exaggeration there, too.'

'Piss off, both of you. Every word is fact, the absolute truth.'

They spun again – the bottle pointed at Flox once more. Malory groaned, and before he had a chance to launch into another lurid memory, spun once more. This time it settled on her.

She talked sketchily about early boyfriends, the loss of her cherry at fifteen to the local hunk and school baseball star, and about her first love, Chip, son of long-distance truck driver Chad Travis. Chip was a confused young man, regularly beaten by his drunken father, and forever mourning the loss of his mother to leukaemia. Malory and Chip were so in love by their seventeenth birthday that marriage was the logical next step. Chip proposed at the local rib shack in a nearby shopping mall over two glasses of complimentary champagne, and presented her with a ring he'd bought from a catalogue. After the meal, they went back to announce the news to both parents, his first. Chad Travis flew into an immediate rage, batting his son clean off his feet with a single swipe of his meaty arm. He grabbed Malory by the scruff of the neck and pushed her up against the wall. 'This fuck got you pregnant, did he?' he asked. Malory screamed. Chip, his nose bloody, jumped on his father's shoulders, and a terrible fight ensued.

Flox, fidgeting ceaselessly, interrupted. 'Sorry to cut in,

Mal, but aren't these supposed to be sweet, sexy stories, not tales of *Twin Peaks* lunacy?'

'Oh, right, sorry,' she said, suddenly checking herself. 'Okay. Anyway, then I met John – John Colby, wannabe rock star.'

'Hold on,' said Danny. 'What happened to Chip?'

'We split up a week later.'

'But I thought you were in love, about to be married?'

'We were. But then I met John.'

'Oh.'

'Hey, I was young, I was confused. What can I tell you?'

John lasted another seven months, by which time she was itching to leave for California. After Flox, Malory dated a veritable conveyor belt of men in New York, many of whom were already famous or were about to be. At Flox's insistence, she mentioned a few household names, with their often dubious sexual proclivities. The last few months, she admitted, had been somewhat lean. In fact, she'd been virtually celibate, if you didn't count an almost excessive use of her vibrator.

Flox didn't.

Bizarrely, the bottle seemed intent on ignoring Danny, no matter how many times they spun. Malory urged him to confess all anyway.

Reluctantly, Danny told them about his first girlfriend Maria and he told them about Amy, the details scant, unelaborate.

And then Flox suggested another change of game, this time cards – his ultimate ploy to be revealed in good time. Bridge lasted less than a quarter of an hour, all three conceding that they barely knew the rules. Snap scaled new peaks of boredom, as did pontoon. 'What next?' Malory asked.

Flox saw his moment, grabbed it, and suggested poker – *strip* poker. Malory looked at Danny, and giggled.

'Well, I'm game if he is,' she said, pointing a finger in the approximate direction of Danny, who gulped audibly.

The game began, and Danny sobered up quickly. A glimpse of Malory's white bra-strap tight across her tanned shoulder was enough to bring him back to all senses immediately. And when, later, she removed at least one item of underwear, he'd never felt more alert in his life.

Initially, Danny had several decent hands in succession. So far, he'd lost only his socks, while Flox had had to shed those almost immediately, quickly followed by his T-shirt, and he was now clearly sucking in his stomach in attempt to hide the onset of British beer belly. Politely, Malory looked the other way as he disrobed. She had forfeited both shoes and her skirt. Danny was all eyes. Unless he kept his mouth tight shut his teeth chattered. Danny looked at Flox, who had his mental swagger back. He was drinking room-service red wine from the neck of the bottle in great gulps. He was loud and funny and gregarious and happy. Malory, too, looked cheerful – seemingly unaware of the sexual frisson she was causing. As far as Danny could surmise, she felt she was with friends, having a blast. There was no innuendo, no lead-me-into-temptation: this, for her, appeared to be purely chaste fun.

Flox was dealing a new hand, his fingers moving nimbly over the cards, betraying that he'd done this kind of thing before, although usually for money and fully clothed. His attempts to impress Malory were working: her laughter was almost continuous. Candles flickered, shadows stalked one another about the room, and empty wine bottles lay discarded everywhere. Moments later, they were fanning their new hands, weighing up their chances, sneaking sly glances. Malory couldn't help but grin, while Danny shuffled his cards nervously. For Flox, though, this was a serious challenge, and one that he intended to win. There was a certain flamboyance to his pose: as he examined his cards, he didn't blink. He'd even bummed a fat cigar from one of the old chaps downstairs and had it clamped between his teeth now, unlit as Malory refused to allow it to stench out her room. His brow furrowed, and from his mouth came many mmms and hmms. He shuffled cards, glanced up occasionally at the opposition, the enemy, and scowled. Danny took his turn, Malory after him, Flox last. Round and around the floor it went, but this time, Flox emerged the victor, his flatmate the loser. Danny reluctantly removed his shirt, revealing a thousand goosebumps and two lonely nipples. He saw Malory take all this in, and felt himself shrink under examination.

'Where's the wine?' he asked, before finding a half-full bottle and up-ending it down his throat, droplets splashing down his chin.

Another hand later, and one long, feminine groan alerted the two men to the joyous realisation that Malory had lost this time. Blinking rapidly, smiling awkwardly, she slipped dainty buttons through sheer silk eyelets and let her blouse fall casually to the floor to reveal a pair of perfect breasts that sat inside an ornate white balconette bra. She was now down to her underwear, and nothing else. She, a famous Hollywood actress. The sound of teeth chattering swamped the room – Danny's.

Instinctively, all three helped themselves to more alcohol. Sexual frisson was now part of the equation.

Three tentative hands later, and Danny and Flox had joined Malory in her state of near total undress: only a pair of boxer shorts and Calvin Kleins, respectively, saved their blushes.

'Shall we stop here?' Danny wondered, attempting to make it sound like an affirmative statement, although it came out more like a timid question. 'We may as well call it a night, yes?'

'It's not over till it's over, Dan,' said Flox, snapping the cards together in preparation for another round. And they played on, but the mood had noticeably changed. There was an air of threat in the room now, of danger, and a wariness that the drink did little to disguise. Between Flox and Malory, it was doubly awkward: what once he had known so well – the smooth planes and curves of her body – he now had no claim over. Theirs was an old history that was only now creeping up towards a present, but some things remained strictly out of bounds – at least until Malory beckoned him forward, which she had yet to do. Danny's presence also made it difficult – why couldn't he just piss off and let them, well, *get down to it*? Did Malory share similar intentions? Would she ever let him know? Didn't she realise how strongly he still yearned?

Danny, on the other hand, was simply worried about the potential for humiliation.

And Malory? Malory wasn't sure how she felt.

Spin Cycle

The only sounds around the floor were of cards snapping and measured breathing. They played on.

Danny lost the first hand but refused point-blank to remove his boxer shorts. Malory lost the next, but she, too, declined to disrobe further. Increasingly frustrated, Flox played to lose. If anyone here was to take the bull by the horns, then it was to be him. Cards were placed on the floor, fingers were crossed. Flox scrunched his face up in what he thought passed for the agony of defeat, threw his own cards into the air and watched as they scattered all over the thick, plush maroon carpet.

'Shit! I lose!' He stole furtive glances at them both, and noticed them looking at each other, not at him. And so he got to his feet.

'Rules are rules,' he said, in mock resignation. Malory and Danny exchanged drunken stares, smiles like upturned horseshoes, and watched as, with considerable ceremony, Flox placed two thumbs under the waistband of his Calvin Klein's. Then, with a clearing of the throat that acted as drumroll, he bent at the waist and whisked them off.

'Ta-da!'

Flox was now naked. He assumed a crucifixion pose, eyes tight shut. Across his face spread a mad, intoxicated smile. Danny had never previously had the luxury of viewing Flox's bare genitalia, which impressed him little. Malory, meanwhile, was rolling about on the floor in laughter, a reaction Flox had not anticipated. Suddenly embarrassed, he cupped his manhood in his hands, and ran out of the room howling.

Malory, recovering from her fit of laughter, now sat

up straight, wiped tears from her eyes, and attempted to compose herself.

'Oops,' she said, covering her mouth with a hand. 'Do you think I offended him?'

Danny beamed. 'No.' He grinned. 'I'm sure he'll recover.'

They were alone now in her room. Outside, the dark sky was lightening, and birdsong was gearing up at the approaching dawn. They sat there looking at one another across the pile of cards. Malory, swaying slightly, put both hands behind her back. She shed her bra, and now sat quite topless.

'I would have done it eventually, you know,' she said, smiling at Danny.

The following morning, Danny and Flox took breakfast in the garden. It was a bright day, the sun golden and heating up fast. The hotel's other guests bade them *bonjour* as they took their seats, and a waiter brought coffee, orange juice, and croissants. A French newspaper sat on the empty chair beside Danny. He picked it up and browsed through it, focusing mainly on the photographs. On the front page, there was a large black-and-white shot of Cate Blanchett smiling enigmatically. She was wearing a dress the colour of diamonds and was standing on what was probably a stretch of red carpet. Behind her was shimmering sea, and beside her a European director of whom Danny had never heard. He could make out several more famous faces, too, all wearing the same rictus smile. From the caption below, he ascertained that this had been taken at the Cannes Film Festival which – he checked the date –

had been launched a few days earlier with a screening of Blanchett's latest film.

He heard footsteps approach, glanced up, and saw Malory coming towards them. Flashes of the night before came to him, fizzled, then faded away. She looked transcendental, wearing a near see-through white dress and no shoes. Her bright blue eyes were hidden behind sunglasses. Flox, his back to her, was picking apart a croissant, placing the occasional morsel into his mouth, and scattering the rest across the plate. He appeared to be sulking, but refused to tell Danny why. They had yet to speak about last night; nor did it seem likely that they were going to. Behind him, Malory smiled at Danny, pulled her sunglasses down the bridge of her nose a little, made complicitous eye-contact, and brought a slender index finger to her pursed lips. He understood, and, no matter how inevitable this had been, he felt his heart bruise like a peach.

'What are you reading?' she asked, as she sat down beside Flox.

Danny held out the newspaper and pointed to the photograph of Cate Blanchett. 'Cannes Film Festival,' he said.

Malory tossed her sunglasses on to the table and grabbed the paper from Danny's hand. 'What? Film Festival? *When?*' Excitement rippled through her voice, like cold water over pebbles.

'Now,' said Danny. 'It started the other day, and carries on for the next week or so, I think.'

Malory took in the information slowly. She felt a huge rush to the head. This was, this was . . .

Epiphany (i-pif-ani) *adj.* any moment of great or sudden revelation.

A waiter came to take her order, but she failed to notice him, and he slipped away, mildly offended. Suddenly she was as focused as a Leica. The word *destiny* had imprinted itself in her mind.

'How far is Cannes from here?' she asked.

Danny and Flox looked at each other, and shrugged. 'An hour? An hour and a half?'

She shivered. Destiny, destiny, *destiny*. 'Can we go?'

'Why not?' Flox said. 'When?'

'Now. This very minute. *Now*.'

'What's the rush? Do you have friends there?'

'Probably not,' she said, breaking out into a mischievous giggle. 'But I will have.'

Twenty-two

Why Cannes? Why a foreign film festival when the world of movies was what Malory Cinnamon had fled to France to escape? Did she really want to go back into such shark-infested waters? Had she even belonged there in the first place? These and other questions swam around her head as they drove south, Italy lying to an indeterminate left, the magisterial allure of Cannes on their right. Should she just cut her losses, face facts, and tell her driver to head towards Venice, where perhaps a *vino* and gondola romance awaited her? She wound down the window and stared out into the unremarkable landscape that hugged either side of the *autoroute*. Doubt assailed her, but so did a saying Flox had taught her years earlier when they opted for ketamine instead of a new, relatively unknown narcotic called Phorse: 'Better the devil you know.'

If Malory had learned anything during her sojourn in Paris, it was that her occupational skills were few, her professional options limited. She couldn't type, could barely compute, she had never understood law, had little ability to teach, was too old to model, and sufficiently bad with financial matters to ensure that she'd never be able to grasp how to produce movies. All the self-help books in the world wouldn't – *couldn't* – direct her on to a more fruitful path in a million years. She'd long since stopped being Alicia Feldstein, anyway; she was Malory Cinnamon, *actress*. That was what she did – what she *was*. And the more she thought about it, the more she convinced herself that fate had steered her, every step of the way, towards what was probably the only destiny she could ever lay claim to. Another saying, this one from a girl she had known in New York: 'You don't fuck with fate.'

Perhaps Cannes would allow her a second chance, a rebirth? Where else in the world could she meet so many of the industry's movers and shakers in one place, at one time? Hollywood? Give me a break. Hollywood was a town of closed doors unless you had the right key, and Malory had lost it a long time ago. Cannes, however, would be different – or, at least, *could* be different. Malory had been off the scene for a while now, enough to make her recent whereabouts an item of interest, of potential gossip. Were she to breeze in unannounced, uninvited, looking delectable in Dior, to a succession of parties, then, you never know, Malory Cinnamon might become the talk of the town all over again. Sounds unlikely? Hey, happens in movies all the time.

She closed her eyes to the wind and thought private thoughts.

The Pallas nosedived towards the coast. Cannes was careening towards them, and with every passing kilometre, collective expectation rose.

* * *

Cannes was full. You couldn't move for people, couldn't drive for traffic. It was chaotic. They inched along the approach road, making staggeringly slow progress, until Flox began to lose it – slow-motion road-rage – and attempted a three-point turn, which he completed in seven complicated moves, intent on taking another route. Eventually, they saw a sign for Nice, a good hour up the coast from Cannes, but their only option.

'We can drive in from there,' he said, and the others agreed.

Eventually, they arrived. The weather was beautiful: although it was still only May, the temperature was more appropriate to mid-August. The sun suited Nice, bathing it in a beautiful electric yellow, making everything – the bars, the people, the beach, the sea – crisper and more delectable.

In the back seat, Malory was beside herself with joy. Like Beverly Hills, the streets here were lined with palm trees that arced up gracefully into the lagoon blue sky, and the pavements were peppered with Beautiful People, many of whom hadn't necessarily been born that way. The ambience was casual. Things moved at a leisurely pace: it was not where you were going that was important but the style in which you arrived. Malory was convinced that she had found her spiritual home: Los Angeles with fresher air, a better view, more handsome men, and an atmosphere of intrinsic romance. As they drove, she made eye-contact with several people, all smiling regally while their toy poodles trotted on tiptoe beside them, noses in the air, tails erect. Beyond them, the sea lapped against golden sand, deep blue with white foam, lush ripple after lush ripple. The only thing missing was a giant pink bow to tie the whole package together.

They drove slowly through the town centre, past countless hotels bearing the FULL sign in their windows, and towards the outskirts, up a hill to the last hotel in town, a magnificently rustic establishment that boasted spectacular rooms with spectacular views at spectacular prices. Fate had dealt them another winning hand here because there were just two rooms left.

The rooms were large and old-fashioned, but discreetly littered with all the latest mod cons. The television was cable, the phone had a fax, and the laptop on the oak desk encouraged e-mail. The beds were big and solid, and the aquamarine marble bathrooms had sunken tubs and powerful showers. In the bedrooms, wooden doors opened out on to sunbaked balconies that overlooked another side of town, away from the sea, where small ancient farmhouses dotted the deep green hills and chimney-stacks smoked languorously into the sky.

Malory was in heaven. She dumped her bags on the floor and padded out on to the balcony, the soles of her feet burning on the hot tiles. On the balcony to her left, Flox and Danny had already settled themselves on wooden chairs, feet up, heads back, eyes closed, smiles spreading across sunkissed cheeks.

Danny opened his eyes, squinting, and brought a hand up to his forehead as a shield. He could just make out Malory's hazy form against the bright daylight. 'Thank you for this,' he said, bashfully. 'You're being very kind to us by paying for it all.'

Malory beamed at him.

'Yes, cheers,' added Flox. 'Very decent of you.' He squinted at her, and saw the dubious look she was giving him. 'No, really. I mean it.'

'Tonight,' she said, in a tone that disguised the extent of her eagerness, 'we hit the Croisette, okay? But before that we take you two into town to get you something to wear. I'm not having you embarrassing me. Understood?' Her tone was maternal.

'Sure, whatever you say,' said Flox, while his flatmate murmured as sleep enveloped him.

In the end, it took them ninety minutes to reach Cannes. Flox blamed Malory – her backseat driving had made him miss the turning. They parked the car on the edge of town when they realised that it was impossible to drive any further. Around them hundreds of people were headed in the same direction so they merged with the flow, each appropriately attired.

It had taken Malory almost two hours to dress for the occasion. In the end, she had opted for a sheer silk Donna Karan, cream-coloured, low back, fine straps, which the early-evening sun lit perfectly. Her long hair was tied up in a bun, with several strands falling across her face like shadows. Aviator sunglasses sat high upon her head. Her shoes were also cream, flat, and simple – but even a fledgling fashion expert would have been able to assess their price. On her left wrist was a small gold watch, on her right the stolen gold bracelet, which felt both appropriate for the occasion and exquisite against her skin. When it caught the sun, it threw up a kaleidoscope of rainbow colours.

On the third finger of her right hand she wore the stolen diamond ring, which she was sure would set tongues wagging. Her neck was bare, her tan was deep. She looked breathtaking, she looked famous, she looked a million dollars. And she was flanked on either side by two surprisingly elegant men. Earlier in the day, she had taken them both to a select boutique and instructed them to keep quiet while she and an obsequious assistant dressed them. Both wore linen suits; Danny's was a shade darker than Malory's dress, Flox's a light grey. Their shirts were silk and they had on soft leather moccasins. Flox had shaved and pulled back his unruly hair into a ponytail, and looked like a young Hollywood player. They felt like new men, as though they were playing a role in Malory's latest project. It unnerved and thrilled them.

'Check out the action,' said Flox.

Alongside them were streams of self-aggrandising media types, the majority of whom had red ears screwed into tiny mobile telephones, dictating copy with unnecessary volume. Almost all wore suits – khaki-coloured high-street copies of bespoke originals – and from each neck hung a laminated card with their colour image smiling out. Photographers and camera crews were everywhere: MTV, BBC, CNN. The hustle and bustle were electric, expectation almost palpable. Danny felt intimidated, Flox considered everyone a flash wanker, and Malory? Malory had pure adrenaline coursing through her veins. She was *home*. Until this moment, she had had no idea just how much she'd missed the industry, the buzz, the constant level of anticipation. Here, she was someone. She mattered. And she was *recognised* – ah, the sweet bliss of recognition!

Spin Cycle

People waved and acknowledged her. Someone from the MTV crew, a short woman with bobbed hair, tortoiseshell glasses, and lip implants, honed in on her, ushering her team to follow. Within seconds, Malory was surrounded by a camera, a soundman and a director. While she was still walking, she was asked an avalanche of questions by the woman whose oversized microphone bounced between them like a tennis ball. Instinctively, Malory brought the sunglasses down from her forehead, pushed them up the bridge of her nose, and curled back her lips into a smile that showed off her perfect teeth. On top of the camera, a red light burst into life.

'Okay, we're rolling,' said the cameraman.

'Okay, we're here, live, at the Cannes Film Festival, and we've just run into Malory Cinnamon from TV's *Central Park Six* and movies like *The Girl Who Dreamed*.' Pause, smile to camera, faltering steps forward. 'Malory, hi. Great to see you. Why are you here at the Festival? Do you have a movie in competition? We haven't seen you around for a while.' Pause for breath, smile at star, try not to trip over feet.

Malory smiled back. On screen, Flox pressed up closer to one side, while Danny slunk out of focus. 'Oh, no, nothing like that,' she said. 'I'm just here on vacation. I've been in Paris for a while, reading literature like Sartre and *Captain Corelli* and things like that. You know, rediscovering literature as *art*, if you like.' She looked directly into the camera. 'All movies start from the printed word, and that's what I've been getting back into recently.'

'Fabulous, fabulous,' said the interviewer blankly. 'So

you're, like, just here to hang out and catch up with people?'

'Oh, absolutely,' said Malory, her smile increasing in width and breadth. She brushed a loose strand of hair from her face to behind her ear. It fell down again, as it was meant to. 'I just thought I'd take this opportunity to meet up with old friends, say hello to all the old gang.'

'*Fab-u-lous*,' said the interviewer, stretching the three syllables to infinity. 'Who have you met so far? Which movies have you seen? Madonna's in town apparently. Can you confirm that?'

Malory laughed gaily. 'Honey,' she said, 'I've only just this minute arrived! You're the first face I've seen. And by the way, I love your glasses. They are just *sooo* you.'

The woman blushed. 'Why, thank you. And I just love your dress!' She caught sight of the finger candy. 'Hey! Is that an engagement ring?'

Malory blushed perfectly.

'Tell us!'

'This old thing?' she said, bringing it up to the light and watching it glint and sparkle. She contorted her face into an expression of covert mischievousness. 'This is just . . . No, I'm sorry, I can't say for now. My lips are sealed – I'm on a promise. But, hey, watch this space. That's all I'll say!'

'Ooh, you tease! Okay, anyway, how about you tell us about you? What have you got coming up? It's been some time since your last feature. We've missed you, girl!'

'Oh, you're too nice! Well, I can't divulge too much at the moment, or the director will kill me! Let's just say that I have a few things in the pipeline.'

'Well, whatever it is, we look forward to it, Malory Cinnamon. Have yourself a wonderful Cannes.'

'Thank you,' said Malory.

'Cheers,' said Flox.

They walked on, rejoining the throng. Danny was starstruck: the Malory he had grown so close to this past week had transformed herself back into the Hollywood actress. Reality became unreality once more; he needed a drink. Flox, meanwhile, was her agent, boyfriend, co-star, minder – whatever role was required, he instantly fulfilled it. As they approached the promenade where all the action was, he became more and more excited. And so, simultaneously, did the female lead by his side.

They were outside a pavilion where hundreds of press had gathered. Velvet ropes sectioned off various large tents. Beyond lay the sea and, before it, a long stretch of sand upon which several women with unnaturally large, occasionally bare breasts were being snapped by a phalanx of men juggling expensive cameras. Opposite, yet more members of the world's press were pouring out of a cinema, commenting on the film they'd just seen. Danny looked across the sea of faces and noted with satisfaction that the frowns outnumbered the smiles. Many walked directly in front of the trio, who had now stopped to take everything in, and formed a long queue outside one particular pavilion. Hastily erected film posters flapped in the breeze from mini flagpoles around its circumference. At the entrance stood two thick-set bouncers, necks squeezed into starched white shirts, huge arms behind backs. Malory scanned the list of credits on the posters and watched the guests – the media, and occasional lesser-known stars –

pour in. Her heartbeat quickened, and she could feel her pulse everywhere. Momentarily, she wished she had a pill or a few lines. But no, that was the old Malory Cinnamon. The new model doesn't do that. She's clean, sober, naturally *confident*. She breathed deeply, levelling herself out, and told her friends to follow.

They joined the rapidly diminishing queue, and waited patiently. An elegant woman in her mid-forties dressed in a long black number stood at the entrance, flanked by the bouncers. In one hand, she held a clipboard, in the other, a fountain pen. Her fingernails were painted electric red. On her heavily made-up face was a bizarre smile that looked like it used to belong to Batman's nemesis, the Joker. In a matter of minutes, they'd reached the front of the queue. Malory swallowed.

'Hi,' she said breezily. 'I'm Malory Cinnamon.'

The woman looked up from her clipboard and, as she placed her, flashed teeth.

'Why, Ms Cinnamon, hel*lo*.' Nervously, she scanned her guestlist, but found no mention of Cinnamon, M. 'Um, we weren't expecting you?' She made it sound like a question, her voice full of doubt.

Malory changed gear instinctively. As the woman double-double-checked the guestlist, she glanced up again at the movie poster, and cleared her throat. Her voice took on an authority that she had only ever used before on a pilot TV show about two female detectives that had never been commissioned.

'Well, Marty called me in Paris the other day, and told me to come on down.' She smiled, curtly, in a downward fashion, as if to say: Challenge that. 'And here I am.

These,' she added, motioning to Flox and Danny, 'are my guests.' As she turned to point them out, she noticed the MTV crew hovering eagerly behind. The interviewer waved enthusiastically. Malory winked back. 'And MTV are here filming a documentary about me. In Cannes. At all the parties.'

The woman forced her painted red lips into a thin smile. She blushed crimson. 'Marty's not here yet,' she began, 'but you are, of course, welcome. All of you.'

They trooped in, followed by MTV.

The champagne, served in crystal glasses, wasted little time in racing directly towards Danny's head and making his brain swim. It was hot in here, and the sweat was pouring off him. All around him were dizzyingly famous faces: actors, actresses, pregnant supermodels and nonentities with slicked-back hair who Danny didn't recognise but who, he noticed, dressed in a manner that suggested he should. Within minutes of their arrival, and two gulped-down glasses of fizzy stuff, Malory had left their side to work the room in earnest. Flox, heading in the other direction, did similar. Now Danny stood alone in a corner and watched carefully. The bigger the actor, the colder the shoulder Malory received. He watched as her chest heaved at each new knockback, on the brink of tears, but she helped herself to more champagne, composed herself, and moved on to actors lower down on the scale of power. She ended up chatting animatedly to two young actresses Danny recognised vaguely from recent films, but couldn't place. Nevertheless, as he saw them air-kiss and embrace, he felt a flood of relief. She looked happy, and that for him was enough.

And Flox? Danny's eyes scanned the crammed room for the ponytail. Eventually he spotted it, practically in the centre of the pavilion, talking loudly, with one hand on the broad shoulder of Michael Douglas, who looked a little bewildered at this unannounced vocal assault, but gave the impression that he was most interested in whatever Flox was babbling about. He nodded continually with a studied, actorly interest. On Douglas's other arm was his young wife, who could barely conceal a frown. Danny downed another drink, laughed to himself, and sought out a waiter for replenishment. Later, he somehow got himself introduced to a female British film journalist, Paula Nicholls, and spent the rest of the evening in her company. The buzz in the room was practically kinetic.

For Flox, the evening was truly magical. He made his way methodically around the large tent introducing himself to actors and actresses he'd long admired and, in some cases, had masturbated over when still a teenager. He interrupted the hyperbolic conversations of short fat hairy agents with voices as loud as cannonfire and pitched to them a succession of stories, plots and movie ideas, some of which he'd harboured from the old days back in LA. By three in the morning, he'd pocketed seventeen business cards from industry people, most of whom were located in Hollywood. He had got drunk with three gatecrashing pop stars, had kissed the cheeks of half a dozen supermodels and shaken hands with their actor boyfriends. It was hard, hot work, and to keep him calm and level in the absence of drugs, he'd quaffed as much free champagne as he was offered.

At some stage during the long, murky night, he and several others had transferred from one party to another further along the Croisette, this one purportedly thrown by Elton. By now, he was firm friends with Gaz and Dok, singer and guitarist from Manchester's latest rock sensation, Sluice, and between them, *en route* to Elton's, they'd managed to score some skunk and had smoked so much that their brains felt like lead and their eyes oozed pus. A swig of champagne afterwards tasted practically medicinal.

Gaz had misplaced his girlfriend, a model with aspirations to act and possessed of a lethal temper, while the steadfastly single Dok was five foot six of determined testosterone, and made a play for any female who came into his immediate radius by glowering at them from beneath his bushy mono-eyebrow. Elton's was rammed. Here, dazzling strobe lights melted into pounding rhythms that blared relentlessly from gigantic speakers. The bold and the beautiful all dived on to the dance-floor where peculiar gyrations merged with loose limbs and light heads. For twenty-five seconds – he counted – Flox had danced side by side with last year's nineteen-year-old Oscar nominee for Best Supporting Actress. Elsewhere, he frugged with an endless procession of luminescent young French waifs, wannabes all. Gaz and Dok danced centre stage, hands thrust deep into the pockets of their zipped-up parkas, a gaggle of girls surrounding them. Rumour had it that Gerard Depardieu was also careening somewhere on the dance-floor, a bull in a china shop that played house music, but Flox didn't see him. He did catch sight of Juliette Binoche, however, moving gracefully all by herself. He sidled up to her, winked, then moved on to more attainable prospects. Flox was in his element, incandescent, the happiest he'd been in ages. He wanted tonight never to end. The DJ then put on a Bee Gees medley, and the place erupted.

Erupted.

'No, no, I've been resting, is all. Actually, I was getting tired of the business – just temporarily, of course. I hadn't had many good breaks recently, and I just felt I needed to get away, you know?'

They knew – oh, yes, they *all* knew all right. For sure.

'What about the – you know, the rumours?' said one, cautiously.

Thank God Malory was a little drunk. Otherwise the fear and paranoia would have truly set in after such a direct question. But it had not been malicious, she was sure. These actresses were in the same boat as her. They truly wanted to know.

'Which rumours, exactly?' she asked hesitantly.

'Oh, like, you know, the drugs and stuff.'

She drank from her champagne glass, and tried to decide just how much to give away and whether a frank confession would come back one day to haunt her. 'All that was, like, *sooo* exaggerated,' she said. 'Okay, if I'm completely honest about it, then, all right, yeah, I did, like, experiment a little. I guess I was depressed. Hey, it happens. But it was always prescribed stuff, never, like, off the streets or anything. Prozac, mostly. Maybe a little Valium, some Xanax. What can I tell you? I was low, the roles were drying up and Gwyneth was landing everything.' She shrugged theatrically, and sighed, waving a loose hand in the smoky air.

'Tell me about it,' said the other three actresses in unison.

'It's getting so difficult out there these days,' said one. 'And so cliquey. If it's not Gwyneth then it's Claire, and if it's not Claire, it's Angelina or Jennifer or Neve or one of those younger girls with double-barrel surnames and cleavages that cost them ten thousand bucks.' Everyone laughed. 'You know, I'm seriously considering returning to TV. I've had enough of taking minor roles in someone else's star vehicle. I can only be Screaming Girl On Campus for so many movies before it starts to get a little, you know, *limiting*.' She downed her champagne, then reached for more from a passing waiter.

'You don't mean . . . ?' another said warily.

'Uh-huh, you got it. Soaps, daytime.'

The others breathed in sharply.

'Well, look at it this way,' she reasoned. 'It's regular work, and the money's good, which is all I care about now, to be honest. And, look, the way I'm going, I'll be lucky if I don't have to resort to porn. The only reason I'm here in Cannes at all is because I bribed my agent – because, like, I've got something on him.' She dropped her voice to whisper. *'I got him by the balls!'* The others laughed and toasted themselves. 'Hey,' she continued, 'maybe that's what we should all do – go back to TV. And then, when we've all made enough money, we should bail out and open a restaurant in the Valley, call it the B-List? What do you think?'

They all cheered, though no one committed herself. The actress reached inside her pocket book, casting sly glances over each slender shoulder, and retrieved a tiny metal tin. With a manicured index finger, she popped it open to reveal four pills, each with the tiny imprint of a unicorn on them. She looked up at Malory, and grinned knowingly. 'Shall we, ladies?'

Four sets of eyes peered into the tin, then up again.

'Waiter,' called the pill girl, 'more champagne, please!'

Four mouths opened wide. Pop, swig, swallow. And then, gradually but beautifully, four pretty little heads floated up into the clouds.

'Let's dance,' said one.

Michael Douglas was barged aside rudely as they fought for space.

Marty, who had arrived with a large entourage, grabbed the pale hand of his wife, and followed the girls' lead.

The dancing began.

Hours crawled by, very drunkenly. Despite the lateness – it must have been the middle of the night – the Croisette was teeming with inebriated life. But the time had taken its toll, for ties had been loosened, and shirts had come untucked. Some minor celebrities had trouble walking upright, while others lay in gutters sleeping it off. As the genuinely famous Hollywood and European glitterati left their parties to retire for the night, the attendant media felt able to relax and enjoy even more voluminous drinking. Discarded beer glasses were everywhere, cocktail umbrellas littered the streets, crushed underfoot. Vomit Jackson Pollocked the pavements.

'Dear God, this is disgusting!' said Paula, the journalist who had decided to attach herself to Danny for the rest of the night. 'Let's get out of here, shall we? Fancy a drink back at my hotel?'

Without her, Danny would have spent a lonely evening among a bunch of famous strangers and weasel-like press folk. He was considerably grateful to her for rescuing him. She might not have been ideal company, but she was company, so he accepted her invitation. 'I've not got much money, though,' he said.

'Don't worry about that, love. I'm on expenses here, anyway. Or at least I will be. So come, my treat.'

With some difficulty – which Paula remedied by standing in the middle of the road with a hand outstretched – they flagged down a cab which, for an extortionate amount of money, took them twenty minutes out of town to Paula's sorry-looking hotel. They made their way through Reception and settled in the bar, with the journalistic dregs from other spent parties propped up in chairs around them.

They ordered French lager with whisky chasers. Across the small table, through his red-rimmed eyes, Danny was able to study Paula. She was his height, but wider, heavier, and probably a few years older. Her plain features were haloed with strawberry blonde hair which, on closer inspection, would have benefited from a good wash with some dandruff shampoo. The lights were out in her dull brown eyes and her makeup had smudged, faded and coagulated in tiny lumps. She was here, it transpired, not on commission but on a whim and a hope. Any sliver of gossip she heard, she scribbled down, added colour and exaggeration, then placed a call to one of her showbiz editor contacts back in London in exchange for a week's rent money. If she saw two famous people in proximity to each other – shaking hands, hugging, air-kissing, or merely passing at a party and waving – then in her notebook, in a shorthand all of her own, they would quickly become a couple, an item, to headline the tabloids the next day. Occasionally she attempted to elicit a quote, but she found eavesdropping on private conversations far more fruitful. When she did wish to speak to them, she explained to Danny, her best form of approach was attack.

'I'm telling you,' she told him, 'if you want that all-important killer quote, then provoke them,' she said. 'Mark my words. You'd be amazed at what comes out of the mouths of stars when they're pushed.'

Danny looked sceptical.

'No, really. Anyway, they live such cosseted lives, these people, they deserve a little roughing up every now and then. Keeps them grounded. Look at it that way, and I'm doing them a valuable service.'

Danny nodded listlessly, and began to think that Paula had served her purpose for the night. She was becoming insufferable. When he failed to respond to what she'd been saying, she called him dull and hardly worth the price of the drinks she was plying him with. But as she said this, she placed a pudgy hand on his knee and squeezed. He panicked. She wanted sex. To steer the conversation in other directions, he mentioned the name of Malory Cinnamon and that he kind of, sort of, knew her. He didn't, of course, go into detail – she was a journalist, after all – just told her that they were acquainted, and that she was in town. Big mistake. Like a leopard on a scent, she sat up and started sniffing, no longer interested in the possible pleasures his body might bring her, but hungry for another all-important *story*. Questions tumbled out of her large mouth.

Danny cowered in the face of them, wishing he could turn back the clock, or at least change the subject. But he couldn't. She was ravenous.

'Which hotel is she staying at? What was she wearing? Who was she with? Which film is she in? How do you know her?'

Danny held up both hands to shield himself from her rapid-fire questions. 'Look, I misled you. I don't know her well, I just bumped into her.'

'How? When?' Her eyes were wide, her tongue visible between her lips.

Danny flailed. 'Um, yesterday in the hotel.'

'Which hotel? *Which hotel?* Here in Cannes?'

'No – I mean, yes. I don't know which one, though. Sorry.'

'When are you seeing her again?'

'Oh, I don't know.' He was tired, drunk. He wanted to get out of there, away from her.

'Well, you can introduce us,' she continued, unthwarted. 'I'll do an interview, bring her back into the public eye. Because, let's face it, the haggard old mare – no offence, of course – could do with the exposure. *Central Park Six* was years ago, and all those films she's done are a right pile of crap. She wasn't on drugs when you saw her, was she?

Because there's rumours, you know. And plastic surgery. I've heard she's had her tits inflated. Has she bumped into any of her old boyfriends here? I'm sure she has — she's been out with most of heterosexual male Hollywood, as I understand it. This is fantastic! Great stuff! Another beer?' She got to her feet. 'Is she bulimic? Anorexic? Feed me info here, Danny, and I'll treat you like a king for the rest of the week. Anyway, I'll get the beers in, while you think hard and see what you can come up with.' She winked. 'Be right back.'

Seizing his chance for freedom, Danny tiptoed through the bar and out to Reception as Paula attempted to attract the attention of the barman. He tumbled out into what was left of the humid French night, and breathed an almighty sigh of relief. He wandered towards the main road and stuck out a thumb resignedly, hoping that someone would give him a lift back to the hotel.

The next day. In three different locations, at different times of the late morning and early afternoon, three people reached for their toothbrushes and forced them into the kind of mouth that nothing should ever be obliged to visit.

Danny introduced his far too early, feeling groggy, dehydrated and alone. His companions had yet to return, and to pass time he worked the brush around his mouth for over three minutes, desperate to annihilate the taste of last night.

Flox borrowed somebody else's shortly after midday in a room he didn't recognise, his mouth a vulture's crotch, while flashes of last night's drug-fuelled excess assaulted him like a mental mugging.

When Malory had finished cleaning her teeth with a new brush she found sitting in a glass in an unfamiliar hotel bathroom, it was used then to awaken the mouths of the three other hungover actresses, before it ended up, discarded, in the sanitary bin next to the toilet.

Outside, Cannes blazed.

Twenty-three

What do you do with your life when you don't know what to do with it?

Danny sucked cold lemonade through a straw, and thought hard. But he couldn't come up with any satisfactory answers. This in itself wasn't surprising. He'd never come up with a satisfactory answer for anything in his life, so why would he start now?

Nice was basking in glorious late-afternoon sunshine. The view Danny saw was of endless rolling hills, smoking chimney-stacks, blue sky, wisps of white cloud. It was a beautiful part of the world, he had to concede, a glorious sunspot. And, yes, he was happy to be here. He breathed in air unsullied by chemicals or pollution, and as his morning headache receded, his appetite made itself known. He ordered scrambled eggs on toast, the typical Englishman abroad.

As he ate alone, waiting for Malory and Flox, sadness settled in him. Life had stalled in neutral, after almost a decade of 2CVing along in unspectacular second gear.

The marriage and family to which he had been seemingly headed with Amy had vanished. His mother was dead, and he didn't want to go home to London – who would, in his position? Yet he knew that return was inevitable. As delightful as the South of France was, he didn't belong here. Cannes was a playground for the rich and famous, for the likes of Malory Cinnamon, not ordinary Danny Fallon.

His friends joined him, one by one. Flox ordered himself a hair-of-the-dog beer, and closed his eyes against the headache that pounded his skull. Malory ordered a Bloody Mary, and sipped it delicately, her face tilted towards the sun. A half-smile played on her lips, and her eyes were hidden behind her sunglasses. Even from as unambiguous a pose as this, Danny could detect in her a sense of renewed ambition. From what she'd told them so far, the previous night had been productive. She'd lived it up at a succession of parties with three other actresses, and her face had been seen in all the right places. Tonight, tomorrow, and as many other evenings as it would take, she would return to the Croisette and put herself about, press flesh, exchange pleasantries and extend feelers. Despite the inevitability of this, Danny was taken aback by her determination, and felt somehow spurned. What about us? he wanted to ask.

'What about everything you said?' he began. 'I thought you hated the business. I thought you'd finished with it. You've done nothing but complain about it since we met.'

An awkward silence followed, which even Flox detected.

'I still do,' said Malory. 'But, let's face it, it's all I know. If I don't return, what will I do for the rest of my life?'

If Danny had an answer to that he kept it to himself.

Imperceptibly, the glue that had bound them together was weakening. With Malory's new-found purpose, Danny and Flox's roles had diminished, and they were now merely supporting actors, extras even. She no longer needed them, and the vacation was coming to an end. With her imminently out of the picture, what fate lay in store for them? They couldn't drive a stolen pea-green Citroën DS Pallas around Europe for ever, could they? Danny's sadness returned.

Flox chuckled. 'Christ. It's all slowly coming back to me. Last night. Danny, did I tell you I met Sluice? Great lads. I met Michael Douglas too, I think, and a whole bunch of agents.' He checked his empty pockets. 'I've still got their cards somewhere. Some of them even told me to give them a call. Do you think they're genuinely interested, Mal?'

Malory shrugged. 'Yes, sure, maybe. Give it a go — what have you got to lose?'

Flox turned to look at the view, wishing he hadn't left his sunglasses in his room.

'You never know,' he said to Malory, a little later, 'I might be joining you in Hollywood yet.'

'And me?' Danny said, inadvertently speaking private thoughts.

An answer didn't come, the question presumed rhetorical.

That night, after another couple of hours' meticulous preparation in front of the bathroom mirror, Malory was again accompanied down the Croisette by the MTV crew, who were only too happy to tail her from party to party. Malory loved the company of the camera. It made her feel relevant again. Also MTV's presence alerted other press to the fact that she was worth following, so they did, all hoping to snag a quick interview, a cute soundbite – at least, until someone more famous came along. By the time they'd reached a large pavilion in the centre of the Croisette, outside which had convened a thick human traffic jam hoping to squeeze itself into a party that Malory was gearing up to gatecrash, she was surrounded by a veritable throng of media folk, all asking where she'd been recently, what she had coming up, and to whom exactly she was betrothed. One journalist was particularly forceful, an overweight Plain Jane waving a tape-recorder. She introduced herself as Paula Nicholls, the *Daily* something-or-other.

'Tell me, Ms Cinnamon,' she said, her voice far louder than the others', 'are the anorexia problems behind you now? I would've thought a boob job on such a skinny upper body would have made you rather top heavy, no?'

The other journalists swivelled round to look at her, fancying that this was a spoof for an alternative-comedy TV show. But no punchline was forthcoming. Malory's smile faltered, and she strode towards the front of the queue, praying for immediate access, with MTV in tow. Plain Jane wasn't giving up easily, though, and she pushed past her, turned, and faced her again, causing Malory to stop suddenly. Behind her, the camera crews all bumped into one another in a mini pile-up. This time, the journalist was asking for Malory's confirmation of certain rumours. Her questions were crude, blunt, forceful. Malory was annoyed, not least because she realised that the rest of the press were loving this, that they enjoyed watching a star squirm under the spotlight. Then Paula Nicholls asked if she was washed up, yesterday's news, a drug addict, and if rumours of her recent engagement were false. Anticipating verbal abuse, Paula stuck her tape-recorder so close to Malory's mouth that she could have kissed it. A throng of media people surrounded them, all watching, listening, waiting; wolves preparing for the kill.

And then something flashed behind the actress's eyes, a bright white light. Goosebumps, caused not by excitement but by distress, shot down the length of her back. She opened her eyes wide and the Plain Jane's horrible face appeared to distort. She saw bug eyes, a hideous smile, stained teeth, a bleached moustache, lumpy makeup. Hatred filled her and, like mercury in a thermometer, her anger turned silver and shot up towards her head. Plain Jane, convinced she was about to land a fantastic story of superstar strife, continued to fire rude questions, keenly aware that it was only a matter of time before Malory Cinnamon could hold her tongue no longer and would unleash a highly quotable stream of expletive-laden verbiage.

And then it happened, in an extraordinary instant. Malory curled her right hand up into a tight fist. She drew back her arm, then let fly. The MTV camera was rolling, as was the BBC's, Channel 4's, CNN's, Rai Uno's. Malory's fist knocked the tape-recorder out of the journalist's hand, and it clattered on to the ground, breaking into six pieces. Then the fist landed right in the middle of Plain Jane's blank face. Her nose cracked and caved in, accompanied by the flash of countless cameras. A cry of pain burst out of her. Time slowed, and everything seemed to stop. Blood poured from her nostrils on to her white blouse. Camera flashes turned the sky white. Then, commotion. Whooping, cheering. Another cry of pain. A sharp intake of breath. A round of applause. Plain Jane's face was smeared with makeup, blackened tears, and ribbons of blood.

Malory's fist was on fire, but she ignored the pain. Her face was implacably calm. Coolly, she turned to face the still-rolling MTV camera. She looked directly into its lens, then brought down her sunglasses from the top of her head and slid them into position.

'Sometimes,' she said to viewers, who would watch this clip again and again throughout the world over the coming days, 'enough is enough and you have to take matters into your own hands. My private life is private. Anyone who interferes,' here, the camera panned to the bludgeoned journalist who was doubled over, face in her hands, before panning back to Malory, 'will live to regret it.'

A huge cheer rose from the swelling crowd into the early-evening sky, no one's voice louder than that of the MTV presenter, who now babbled superlatives to camera, her wide face framed in close-up. The crowd grew and grew, elbows, microphones, cameras, cramming into every available space, all focusing on just one person.

And that was how Malory Cinnamon became famous all over again.

About an hour later, on the other side of town, Flox found himself sprawled across a large double bed in an enormous suite, with half of Sluice prostrate around him and several mysterious, scantily clad young European women. He had just lived out one of his most cherished, if clichéd, ambitions: snorting pure white cocaine from a mirror with a rock 'n' roll band and beautiful women. The high, when it came (and it came in a rush, a rollercoaster of speed breaking free of the rails and hurtling towards outer space), rendered him a gibbering buffoon capable of nothing but grinning expansively and making strange, non-verbal sounds from his nostrils. Beside him, Gaz was in the process of creating another song – 'Ain't nothing more inspirational than being off your face,' he slurred. Disjointed words flowed from his mouth, not rhyming but somehow fitting perfectly, and his brother Dok picked out accompanying guitar chords on his unplugged electric. Gaz's model girlfriend, Tiki, watched him adoringly. This went on for another ten minutes, until boredom set in. Dok complained of a raging thirst. One of the girls reached over the side of the bed, pulled up a bottle of Perrier and offered it to him.

'Nah, love, none of that fizzy shite for me. I want some Highland Spring.'

Gaz groaned. 'That's fucking typical of you, that is,' he said. 'We're in France, home to some of the most famous mineral water in the world, and you want Scottish stuff.'

'And you have a problem with that, do you?'

'Yeah, I do.' He threw a pillow at him. 'Twat.'

Dok leapfrogged one of the girls and jumped on his brother, smacking him sharply in the face. A careless fight ensued, a couple of six-year-olds attempting to assert dominance. A duvet was destroyed, an ashtray fell to the floor and the telephone fell off its hook.

Flox staggered to his feet, and took the hand of one of the nubile young women.

'What's your name?' he asked.

'Emmanuelle,' she replied, in a delicate French whisper.

'My favourite film,' he said.

They disappeared into the adjoining bedroom, and closed the door behind them.

Several hours later, Flox, Sluice and attendant groupies were barefoot on the beach, watching the moon throw shadows across the liquorice sea. They collapsed on the sand, watching the waves lap gently towards them, licking their toes with foam. Tiki rose, and started to dance, leaving wet footprints on the shore, watching them disappear as the water came in, then making her mark all over again. Gaz felt moved to write a future B-side about the sky at night when you're far from home, rhyming 'sea' with 'we', and 'believe' with 'dream'. They passed around a bottle of Jack Daniel's.

Gaz nudged Flox. 'Come with us,' he said, his breath laced with alcohol.

Flox regarded him with incomprehension, vision blurred. 'What?'

'Come with us.'

'Where?'

'Anywhere. On tour. From what you've been telling us, you're doing fuck-all with your life, and we can always make another space on the bus. Come on, it'll be a laugh. You can be our vibes master. We'll put you on a wage.'

Flox's swimming vision did a backflip, and he grinned. He had already lost the business cards of the agents he'd met the previous evening, and he knew deep down that nothing would have come from them anyway. His destiny was not Hollywood, not now, not ever. His association with Malory, he realised, was as close as he'd ever get to it, and that in itself was transitory. When she moved on, as of course she would, what would he do? Go home? Back to the listings magazine? No way. He'd sooner take a blade to his wrists than return to yesterday when tomorrow was infinitely more alluring. He might never achieve his ultimate ambition of personal fame, but he could plump for second best. Gaz's offer was more than a little tempting. It was electrifying. There was only one answer. 'Fuck, yes!' he said.

'Nice one,' said Gaz, grinning. Tiki gave him a kiss on the cheek and squeezed his arm. Gaz woke his brother, and they spat on their palms, then shook hands firmly. 'Deal.'

Flox had to fight back tears. He looked out to the horizon where, if he squinted, he could just make out a rumour of light. New dawn. 'Did I tell you I used to write songs?' he said. 'No? Well, I've got thousands of them up here.' He tapped his head. 'I play a mean lead guitar, too.'

The ensuing laughter confused him, but didn't dampen his spirits.

That night Danny didn't hit the Croisette. His hangover, and other things besides, had come back in the early evening with a vengeance, impersonating the symptoms of flu. He stayed in his room and channel-surfed, eventually settling on MTV. Between naps, he could have sworn he saw Malory on television punching that awful woman he'd met the night before – Paula the journalist. Later, he dreamed he had a premonition: that tomorrow everything would change, and he, Flox and Malory would move on.

Separately.

Twenty-four

Malory

The following day, once again, the three friends didn't meet up again until late afternoon. Danny had spent the morning mooching around the hotel, sunning himself by the pool, trying not to think about the inevitable. He was dozing, assisted in that direction by a couple of potent cocktails, when Flox arrived, loud voice booming Danny's name. Danny shielded his eyes with his hand and saw his friend standing before him, a silhouette against bright light.

'There you are, mate,' Flox said. 'I've been looking for you.' He sat down beside him. 'Listen, let's go and get a drink at the bar. I've got something to tell you.'

Here we go, thought Danny. He got to his feet, and followed his friend. Two ice-cold beers were ordered, and they sat at a table that afforded them a stunning view.

'What did you get up to yesterday, then?' Flox asked him.

'Oh, not much, really. I wasn't feeling too well so I just hung around here.'

'Are you ill?'

'No, no. I'm fine. I just needed to rest, that's all.'

'Right, right. Good.' He leaned forward in his chair. 'I met up again with Sluice last night, and had an incredible time. Man, I wish you could have been there.'

Danny's concentration was interrupted, because Malory appeared at the french windows and walked over to their table. Did she appear cautiously excited, or was he imagining it? As ever, she looked beautiful.

'Morning, boys,' she said, then checked her watch. 'Afternoon, I should say.'

A waiter came to take her order, and she asked for mineral water with a slice of lime. No alcohol today. Today was important, and she was going to remain clear-headed. She wanted to savour every second.

The previous night had been a stellar success. She couldn't have scripted it any better because she really was the talk of the town. Word of her flamboyant right hook had spread like wildfire, and everyone had seen it, either on the television screens inside every pavilion or on the tiny video-cameras that almost everyone owned. Her little fracas had made her the belle of the ball, and no one thought she'd acted unjustly. Indeed, in this climate of privacy for the rich and famous, everyone had decided that she'd behaved admirably. She was applauded and courted by everyone. Actors and actresses way above her level – those who had ignored her just the night before – came to shake hands and kiss cheeks. Directors and producers seemed desperate to engage her in conversation and, most vitally of all, agents hovered around her like so many flies on shit. And the absent Helena Finklestein? Helena *Schminkelstein* – old news, darling. Malory was hot once more – tsss, red hot – and had her pick of the top agents. All night long platitudes came her way, and she blinked, smiled, bowed and curtsied to a conga line of admirers. The friends she'd made the night before now only got as close as her periphery; they were no longer important to her, no longer necessary for her eventual goal. Cruel, yes, but this was business. And everyone knew, and played by, the rules.

By two in the morning, she'd confirmed a dozen meetings with agents based in LA over the next seven days. They had all said the same thing: Malory Cinnamon was the name on everyone's lips, and she had to strike now, while the iron was hot. One particular agent, Josh Katzenberger, a small man with a blazing shine on his bald head where lacquered hair had once been, and who represented many of Hollywood's most important talent, was so insistent that she fly home – with him – the following evening that he booked two tickets on his cellphone there and then. Of course, she accepted graciously. By the time she'd arrived back at the hotel, tired but wide awake on the buzz of hype, she was tingling with excitement all over, feeling as if every nook and cranny of her body was experiencing its own individual orgasm. In less than a day, she'd be home, and France would recede into the background. She would never forget it, though, and would always view it as the perfect holiday, the perfect rebirth. Her mid-career crisis was now officially in regression: Malory Cinnamon was back on the trajectory once more. She closed her eyes as she lay down on her bed and saw stars and stripes, the familiar creases of every A-list actor up close, the vacant chair immediately to the right of Letterman, next year's Oscar ceremony. She sucked air through her teeth and tasted the hundred and one possibilities as they danced on the tip of her pointed tongue.

And so to sleep.

But before she could get airborne today, she had to face her two friends and tell them her news. Unexpectedly, this made her feel both nervous and sad. She loved these two guys, and she'd surely miss them.

Her mineral water arrived, and she took a small sip. 'Listen, guys,' she began, 'we need to talk.'

In her mind's eye, the camera panned down and closed in on two increasingly apprehensive faces. The imaginary soundtrack swelled, a mixture of strings and heavy bass. Danny looked at her warily.

'It, um, looks like I'll be going home soon.'

The news hit them both hard, even Flox. Deserted once more, he thought.

Danny spoke first. 'Home? When?'

'Well, tonight, actually.'

'Tonight?' Flox repeated, rather too loudly. People at nearby tables looked round.

'Where?' Danny asked. 'To your parents?'

Malory blushed slightly. 'No. No, I'm going to . . . to LA.' She allowed herself a proud smile. 'Looks like I'm going to be an actress. Again.'

'Oh.'

'Oh, right.'

'Tonight, you say?'

'Uh-huh.'

'Why so soon?'

'Well, as weird as this may sound, it seems like I'm hot again, so everyone is saying I should strike now.'

Danny had a flashback of his dream: Malory punching that Paula woman. He decided not to mention it.

'I'm really sorry it's so sudden,' she continued, 'but all these opportunities are coming my way. I'm wanted! If I don't grab them, I'll never forgive myself. I have to give it one more go. Perhaps it's my destiny.'

Regardless of his own plans, Flox spoke up. 'And what about us?' he asked, sounding hurt.

Malory didn't know what to say. She just smiled sheepishly, and laid a hand on his, squeezing slightly.

'This is Los Angeles all over again, isn't it?' he asked, referring to the events of ten years ago.

Malory was offended. 'No! Absolutely not! This time I'm not abandoning you, and I swear I will keep in touch. I swear!' She put her other hand on Danny's. 'Both of you. You've got to believe me.'

Tears flooded her eyes — and Danny's.

'I'm really sorry, you guys, but I hope you understand just how important this is to me. I have to go.'

They gave her a weak smile of encouragement.

'What will you do now?' she asked.

Danny shrugged, and looked at Flox, who did similar.

'Don't worry about us, we'll be fine,' said Flox curtly. 'You just go off and become famous all over again.' Then he apologised, learned towards her, and they fell into each other's arms. The people at the other tables were watching now with interest. Danny stared back at them blankly until he, too, was gathered into Malory's arms in a hug he defied himself ever to forget.

* * *

The taxi was waiting outside the hotel a little before six. Malory, surrounded by bags, stood beside it. She looked resplendent in a white A-line dress. A silk scarf was tied loosely round her slender neck, and her hair was pinned up in a bun. Her beauty, thought Danny, standing beside her, was almost ethereal. A porter began the complicated task of trying to squeeze all her bags into the boot of the car.

'Listen,' she said emotionally, fiddling about in her handbag, 'I've got no use for this any more, so please take it.' Having already paid the hotel bill for both rooms until the end of the week, she thrust a bundle of high-denomination francs into Danny's hand and nodded at him in a way that suggested she wouldn't take no for an answer — and, worse, she'd be offended if he tried. 'And here's a number you'll be able to reach me on in LA. Just leave a message and it'll eventually get to me, I promise. Once I'm settled, you must come out and visit. I'll treat you both to the vacation of your life.'

There were more tears.

'I love you both,' she said, planting red lips on white cheeks. 'And I'll never forget all this, our special time together.'

She hugged them both one last time and then, in a flurry of actressy movements, got into the taxi, which sped away. From the back window, Malory Cinnamon waved her famous hand until the cab turned a corner, and she was gone.

Flox

Later that evening, at the same time as awards were being handed out to gushing recipients at the Festival, the two former flatmates sat in a bar, drinking in earnest. They were reliving their last few weeks, from the botched kidnapping onwards, all recent events having taken on a distinctly unreal aspect. It felt as if everything had happened only in their imaginations. Between them, on a three-legged, uneven table, there were upwards of eight empty bottles. Flox ordered a couple more.

'What were you going to say earlier?' Danny said. 'You said you had something to tell me.'

'When?' Flox said, knowing exactly what he was referring to, but needing another few deep breaths and some fresh beer down his throat before he broached the subject.

'Just before Malory came down from her room.'

'Oh, yes. That.'

Two more beers arrived, and Flox attacked his first.

'Well?'

'I told you about meeting Sluice, didn't I?'

Danny nodded, and Flox became the second person that day to tell him about receiving an offer too good to refuse. As his friend spoke, he allowed a benevolent smile to spread across his face. When Flox had finished, Danny congratulated him. 'Well done,' he said. 'I'm really pleased for you.'

'Are you sure? I can't help but feel I'm abandoning you.'

'Don't worry about me, I'll be fine. Honestly.'

Flox had an idea. 'I know! How about I ask if you can come too? I'm sure they wouldn't mind. It's a big bus.'

Even before Flox had finished talking, Danny was shaking his head. 'No, really, I'll be fine. I never liked Sluice anyway. You go. You'll have a fabulous time. When do you leave?'

Flox cleared his throat awkwardly, nervously. 'Well, later on tonight, actually. Round about two or three in the morning.'

So soon? thought Danny. 'Right, right.' He attempted to ignore the wave of sadness that revisited him. Over the last few months, almost everything in their respective lives had packed up and abandoned them, in one way or another. For Danny and Flox now to go their separate ways too was almost poetic. Nevertheless, he felt empty, isolated.

'What will you do now?' Flox asked. 'Will you go home?'

'Maybe. Maybe not.' He really had no idea.

'Why don't you drive around Europe? You've got the car. As long as you leave France, you should be safe. And the money Malory left us should see you pretty well for a while.'

The money. Danny felt embarrassed – it was still stuffed in his pocket. He went to retrieve it, to split it equally with Flox, but Flox waved a hand. 'No, no. I don't need it. Keep it. Please.'

'Are you sure?'

'Sure.' He changed the subject. 'Listen, we'll have to meet up when I get back to London, okay?' Although neither had broached the subject, they didn't need to:

neither of them would be returning to the house in Shepherd's Bush, not after all that had happened to alter the course of their lives. Things change, people move on. 'If you don't go back to the flat,' said Flox, 'just let Sanjay know where you've gone and I'll track you down.'

'Fine, I'll do that.' Danny watched Flox run a hand through his unkempt hair, and pull at the neck of his T-shirt, familiar habits. He wondered whether he'd ever see him again, the friend he'd known since childhood.

'And then we'll go over to Hollywood and see Malory, yeah?'

'Yeah. Definitely.'

'A toast,' said Flox. 'To you, to me, to Malory. And to Paris. Because whatever happens, we'll always have Paris.'

Their bottles met across the table, and clinked melodiously.

The tour bus didn't pull out of the hotel until well past four o'clock in the morning. The band had been slow to get ready, and Tiki was even slower. It made its hulking way through the sleeping town's narrow streets in low gear, the burly driver content to inch along gradually until he was on the *autoroute* before putting foot to floor. On board, the band, littered across various armchairs and couches, were blissfully drunk. MTV was blaring in a corner.

'What time will we be in Rome?' Flox wondered aloud.

Gaz shrugged, a large spliff alight between his lips. 'Some time tomorrow, the day after? Whenever, really. It don't matter. The first show isn't until Monday anyway, so we've got plenty of time before the tour kicks in proper.'

He handed Flox a beer, and told him to drink up. 'We're going to be on the road for at least three months, so here's a tip for you, mate: never worry about arriving, just try to enjoy the journey. Relax.' He passed him the spliff.

On television MTV was reviewing the Cannes Film Festival, which had wrapped up a few hours earlier. Amid the prizes and the endless star-spotting scenes, the occupants of the bus watched, with considerable hilarity, footage of television and film actress Malory Cinnamon throwing a punch into the face of a large female journalist. As her nose exploded with a waterfall of claret, the band whooped and cheered.

'Fucking unbelievable right hook!' cried Gaz jubilantly. 'Good for her! Media scum!'

Beside him, the band's new vibes master, Flox, dissolved into giggles, realising now why his old flame was suddenly so hot once more. Pride filled him like sunshine.

Some hours later, just as morning was breaking across the border in Italy, the bus pulled into a service station for an early breakfast. The band ambled off, heading directly for the café, all desperate for a fry-up, a little taste of home. Inside, around a small table littered with endless bottles of luminescent relish and ashtrays overflowing with spent and still-smoking butts, the mood was jovial and celebratory. Over cans of beer that they had smuggled in, they toasted Flox's arrival, and everyone said how happy they were to have him aboard and along for the ride.

'Fucking nice one,' said the drummer, opening his mouth for the first time in Flox's company, before falling silent again, as drummers do.

The smile wouldn't leave Flox's face. It was surgically

attached to him, glued, permanent. He felt incandescent. Him and Sluice! It defied belief – it described the most fantastical dream. The open road lay before him, with endless possibilities. He'd woken up in Fantasy Land, sitting between Dok and Tiki, grinning inanely, drinking ice-cold beer.

Half an hour later, the band made their way back to the bus.

'Flox,' said Gaz in the car park.

'Yes?'

Gaz took him to one side, a paternal hand draped over his shoulder. 'We've got a little job for you,' he said. 'All the band think you're great, and Tiki loves you. Me an' all. Which is why we trust you enough to ask you what I'm about to ask you.'

Anticipation burst inside Flox's chest. Excitement mixed with fear and intrigue. Gaz led him on to the bus and into the back lounge area, pulling across the small curtain for privacy. He fell to his knees and began rooting around under a chair. With an outstretched arm and a look of determination, he began to pull at the fabric. The sound of ripping Velcro filled the small lounge, and slowly he pulled out one, two, three clear plastic bags full of white powder. He laid them out carefully on the table. 'Ever been to Colombia?' he asked.

Flox, eyeing what looked like a small mountain of cocaine, shook his head.

'Well, one snort of this and you'll be there like that,' he said, clicking his fingers. 'You've already had some back at the hotel the other day. Remember?'

How could he forget?

Gaz continued. He spoke slowly, as if to a small child. 'Obviously, a band like us can't cross borders in a tour bus this size without attracting a very particular kind of curiosity from certain people.' He opened one of the bags, licked a finger, introduced it into the powder, then placed the digit on his tongue and around his gums. He offered the bag to Flox to do likewise, which Flox did. 'Now, we normally get our accountant to transport this for us, but he's currently in a bit of a jam back home. Possession, actually, but that's by the by.' He rubbed his hands together. Cold? Excited? Both? 'Which is where you come in.'

Flox swallowed hard.

'Across the other side of the car park, there is a car,' he continued, 'a brand-new Mercedes, English number-plates.' Gaz went to a closet and opened the door to reveal a selection of tailor-made suits. He looked Flox up and down. 'You and me are roughly the same size. The idea is, we'll get you up in one of these,' he pointed to the suits, 'and wrap you up in sunglasses, so you'll look the business, and stick you behind the wheel. Because of the Festival, it's going to be even easier than usual. You'll look like some young buck film producer, and you'll sail right through.'

Flox gulped again. 'Where?'

'The border. But don't worry, you're a mate, and I'd never put you in any kind of danger – honest.' A look of sober seriousness descended on Gaz's features. 'And don't forget I'm trusting you here with a lot of stuff that cost me personally a lot of fucking money. I wouldn't jeopardise that for anything.' He sat down on the couch beside the table, and encouraged Flox to join him. 'Here's what'll happen.' He talked him through it slowly. 'We'll drive up to the Italian border together, you first, us right behind.'

Flox had a question. 'How did the Mercedes get here?'

Gaz tapped his nose with his finger. 'Contacts,' was all he said. Then he continued. 'So we'll drive up to the border together, you first. As soon as they clap eyes on the bus, they'll wave you through and pull us over. Happens every time, believe me. Your passage through couldn't be easier. Just in case, though, we'll strap these,' he leaned over to pat the bags of cocaine, 'to your thighs. Even if they do decide to give the car a once-over, they won't do a strip-search on you. We'll be detained for anything from five minutes to five hours, but the bus will be clean, so we should be out of there within thirty minutes, max. Meantime, you'll carry on driving until you get to the first service station on your right. Right, not left. Meet us there.' He smiled widely, and clapped Flox on the back. 'So, up for it? There'll be a hefty bonus in it for you too.' He winked.

Flox considered it carefully, and came up with countless logical reasons why he should say no, why he should walk away now, while he still could, a free man. Instead, he looked into the open face of Sluice's Gaz, and nodded.

'Fantastic! Nice one, Flox!'

The bags of coke were sellotaped to his thighs, which were then doused in air freshener ('Just in case,' said Gaz. Then, in purported explanation, 'Sniffer dogs.'), and he was dressed in an Ozwald Boateng, the colour of mahogany, stitched to perfection. The ponytail was tied back, and the Ray-bans afforded him the look of either complete ponce or a million dollars. The full-length mirror suggested, he felt, the latter. Flox wanted a photograph for posterity. And got one.

When he pulled back the curtain, the band and Tiki gave him a round of applause.

'See you on the other side,' they chimed in unison.

As he walked across the early-morning car park, all he could hear was the sound his new shoes made on the Tarmac, giant steps into tomorrow.

The car started first time, and purred like a tiger. Flox felt excited in a way he'd never experienced before. He slid the car into reverse, then nosed out in front of the bus, pulling out on to the *autoroute* gradually, careful to adhere to the speed limit. It drove like a dream.

Within a quarter of an hour, the border was in sight. His heartbeat increased slightly, but he was conscious of no nerves, merely adrenaline. Every fibre of him felt alive, alert, intoxicated with the thrill of danger. He checked in the rear-view mirror. The tour bus was right behind him, and behind that lay a grey stretch of south-east France. In front of him, past the barriers and the uniformed guards, was unknown Italy and beyond.

Flox adjusted the loose linen of his trousers, checked his reflection in the side mirror, and drove onwards, grinning.

Danny

Cannes was empty now. The movie industry had packed up and moved back to its small corner of Beverly Hills. The town had become a quiet seaside resort once more, teeming only with local life, but the lull was temporary. May was now almost June. Summer was fast approaching, and with it thousands of holidaymakers. But that was yet to come. Right now, in the crystal clear presence of today, Danny had a nice stretch of golden sand to himself. This little spot, just metres from the sea, had become familiar to him these past few days. He had come here every morning since his friends had left, to sunbathe alone. The sadness that had enveloped him in the days prior to their departure had now evaporated. Danny had decided to give in to fate as Malory had recommended. Large stretches of the day would pass without a single thought making itself known inside his head. He just lay back and enjoyed the simple pleasures of doing and thinking nothing.

Aside from the hotel suite, courtesy of Malory, Danny had lived frugally since they'd left. Breakfast was a brioche, lunch a filled baguette, he'd have maybe a mid-afternoon sorbet, and dinner, more often than not, passed by without his notice. His lack of daytime activity somehow prompted in him an incipient tiredness that took firm hold by sundown. After dragging himself off the beach, returning to his room, luxuriating under the shower, and collapsing on to the bed with a vague intention of channel-surfing, sleep was pulling him under for the night. He would always wake the following morning fully rested.

There were occasions when he felt an urge to make contact with someone, anyone, just to remind himself that he was still alive, that still, in some way, he counted. But he never knew to whom he should turn. Calling home, his childhood home, was no longer an option, and the few times he had tried to get in touch with Sanjay, he had never found him in. That left who, exactly? He could hardly call Amy.

But such moments of self-doubt, of self-pity, were fleeting. Instead, he concentrated on the here and now. The weather was gorgeous, and a suntan suited him. He would remain on the beach until the sun began to dip, and he'd gaze at the sea, which was clear and sharp, shockingly cold, and went on for ever. All that was missing was a girl. But, given that this is a work of fiction, she wasn't missing at all. In fact, they came into almost daily contact.

Yes, there was a girl.

She worked as a waitress in the café Danny visited every afternoon, where he had, first, a coffee, and later a sorbet – always ordered separately, thereby allowing him to speak to her twice. She was of medium height, slim build. Her eyes were hazel, her skin clear and milky white. She had a small beauty spot on her left cheek, just below the bone. Her hair was shoulder-length, so dark it was almost black, and for work she tied it back in a ponytail with an elastic band. Beneath her white blouse and black skirt, her body looked tight and perfectly proportioned, her breasts alert and firm beneath white cotton. A pencil sat behind her right ear. She rarely made eye-contact with Danny but then, he reassured himself, she would rarely make eye-contact with anyone. Everything about her seemed cautious, but he was convinced that her shyness would melt upon deeper acquaintance. And indeed, by the fourth day, Danny's arrival prompted a flicker of recognition in her face, which he took as a major breakthrough. So far, he had yet to say anything to her save for *café, sorbet, s'il vous plaît* and *merci*. Lack of proficiency in the local language and pronounced timidity around beautiful women prevented him entertaining the idea of striking up conversation, but he yearned to with a ferocity that made his heart ache and his blood pump faster.

There was just one day to go until he left Cannes, probably for ever. That morning, he'd given the Pallas a spin to check that everything was working as it should, had filled the tank with petrol and topped up the oil. She was dusty, but, as far as Danny could tell, raring to go in whichever direction he pointed. After checking out tomorrow morning, he planned just to drive, not considering left or right until he got to each junction. One thing was certain: he would leave France, but from there, the world might prove to be his oyster, at least until the money had run out. If his basic knowledge of geography was anything to go by, he was vaguely aware that Switzerland lay somewhere off to his left, with countries like Italy and Slovenia straight ahead, while down to the right, there was Greece and its infinite islands. Perhaps there was the possibility of work down there? Every location sounded alluring to him, not for any specific reason but rather for the mystery. Danny was not particularly well travelled, but he had every intention of correcting this.

He left the beach at three o'clock that afternoon, his body sizzling. He shook sand out of his hair, pulled on a T-shirt and shorts, his Birkenstocks, and headed over to his usual café to offer a silent goodbye to the beautiful girl of his dreams. When he arrived, she was making sandwiches behind the glass counter, looking exquisitely flustered. At the sound of the door, she looked up, saw him, and smiled. A lock of lustrous brown hair fell across her eyes and kissed the tip of her nose. Danny sat at his usual table, and pulled a book from his back pocket, *Chronicle of a Death Foretold*, by Gabriel Garcia Marquez, which he'd bought from the hotel bookshop a day earlier specifically to read in her presence. His aim? To suggest to her that here sat no ordinary lad, but a literate, potentially intellectual young man well worth knowing. It was worth a try.

The café was busy, and an indeterminate amount of time passed. Eventually, the waitress – who, he would later find out, was called Sandrine, was twenty-four, and single – approached his table, holding a pad and pen in her hand although she knew full well that she wouldn't need them, that he ordered the same thing every day, this Englishman, with his sweet predictability and his nice eyes. Danny looked up from his book, and in that instant his world was filled with her face, her delicately featured hazel-eyed face. She looked down at him semi-expectantly. Her lips were full, a natural pink, and her teeth were orderly and white. Before he had a chance to open his mouth and slowly form the word *café*, she offered him another smile, which filled Danny with a sense of something he hadn't felt in a long time. It was as if everything inside him had become weightless, floating dreamily. He felt . . . he felt *hope*. She continued to smile, holding it for several seconds, and then she spoke her first word to him. 'Hello,' she said.

Hello.

Postscript

Report in the *Sun*'s Bizarre Column, 21 July 2001

Sluice Sack Guitarist!

Just a week before Sluice begin a three-night residency at Wembley Stadium, frontman Gaz Scott has sensationally sacked his brother Dok from the lineup. 'And this time it's for good,' he said, on the telephone from his Hampstead home last night. 'He is a f***wit, basically, and he's doing more harm than good in my band. It's not like we didn't give him no chances. Two days after we arrived in America, he pissed off to f*** knows where and didn't turn up again until we reached Chicago, four days later. That says to me that he's not taking the band seriously, and that his heart isn't in it. Well, it's my band, so he can f*** off!' Scott then immediately announced his brother's replacement as Quentin Flox, who has spent the past year as the band's 'vibes master'. 'Flox is f***ing great. He can't wait to get out on the road and play with us. He knows our songs better than what we do, so when we hit Wembley, we're going to be premium f***ing Sluice, no question!' The singer's wife, model Tiki Stixx, also joins the band's live setup on tambourine. Dok Scott was unavailable for comment.

News report in the *Daily Express*, 7 August, 2001

Hollywood Sweet On Malory Cinnamon

Former *Central Park Six* actress Malory Cinnamon last night announced her engagement to Josh Katzenburger, one of Hollywood's most powerful agents, at the premiere of her latest film, *Daze Like These*. The film, a true story about a woman suffering from amnesia after a near-fatal car crash and having to learn to love her husband and children all over again, is already being hotly tipped as a major contender at next year's Oscars, with Ms Cinnamon up for Best Actress. 'It's a bit premature to talk about the Oscars just yet,' said the actress, 'but I do think it's my best performance yet, so we'll see.' On her impending marriage, she said, 'Josh is an absolute darling. My life has changed dramatically over the past year, I can't even begin to tell you. I've had some tough times, but now that I'm back on my feet, his proposal was like a dream come true, the icing on the cake.' Elsewhere, earlier reports that the actress was wanted in connection with theft from a jewellery shop in Paris last year have proved unfounded. A lookalike living on the outskirts of the city has since been arrested. *Daze Like These* opens here next month, and the actress's diaries, *Me, Myself & I*, published by Hodder & Stoughton, £16.99, is out now.

A Post-it note on the fridge, this morning

Daniel,
Salut, mon coeur. I didn't want to wake you — you looked so peaceful! I will meet you on the beach after work — four o'clock. I cannot wait! Je t'aime.
  Sandrine
  xxx